THE
GARDEN

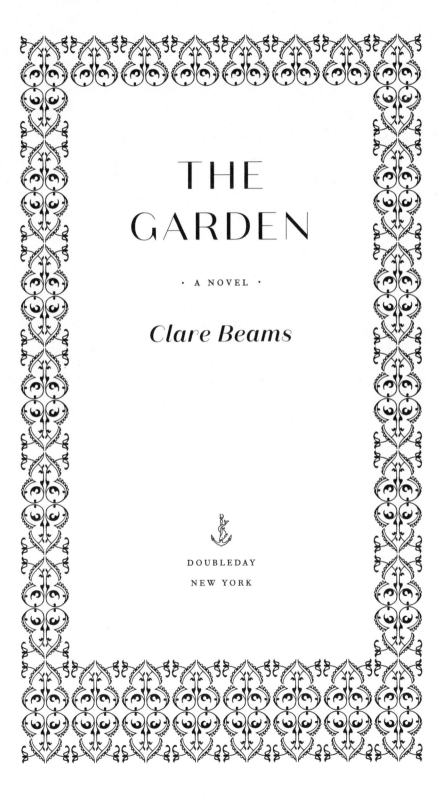

THE
GARDEN

· A NOVEL ·

Clare Beams

DOUBLEDAY

NEW YORK

Copyright © 2024 by Clare Beams

All rights reserved. Published in the United States by Doubleday, a division of Penguin Random House LLC, New York, and distributed in Canada by Penguin Random House Canada Limited, Toronto.

www.doubleday.com

DOUBLEDAY and the portrayal of an anchor with a dolphin are registered trademarks of Penguin Random House LLC.

Front-of-jacket photograph: *Uterus 21* © Catharina Suleiman
Jacket design by Emily Mahon

LIBRARY OF CONGRESS CATALOGING-IN-PUBLICATION DATA
Names: Beams, Clare, author.
Title: The garden : a novel / Clare Beams.
Description: First Edition. | New York : Doubleday, [2024]
Identifiers: LCCN 2023009601 (print) | LCCN 2023009602 (ebook) |
ISBN 9780385548182 (hardcover) | ISBN 9780385548199 (ebook)
Subjects: LCSH: Women—Fiction. | Pregnancy—Fiction. | LCGFT: Novels.
Classification: LCC PS3602.E2455 G37 2024 (print) |
LCC PS3602.E2455 (ebook) | DDC 813/.6—dc23/eng/20230228
LC record available at https://lccn.loc.gov/2023009601
LC ebook record available at https://lccn.loc.gov/2023009602

MANUFACTURED IN THE UNITED STATES OF AMERICA
1 3 5 7 9 10 8 6 4 2
First Edition

For all haunted women

What we observe is not nature in itself but nature exposed to our method of questioning.

—WERNER HEISENBERG, *PHYSICS AND PHILOSOPHY*

Everybody in the house is asleep—everybody but us. We are wide awake.

—FRANCES HODGSON BURNETT, *THE SECRET GARDEN*

The

Berkshires

*

1948

WEIGHT

1

The house held still, and behind it the garden rested, brown turning green.

*

Doctor and doctor, Mr. and Mrs., came out onto the steps to watch the approach. They did this when they could. Welcome made a difference.

Without turning to him she said, "Remember not to talk too much."

As if he ever did or could or wanted to when she was there.

*

George and Irene drove toward the house that held their future and saw the doctor and doctor standing at the top of the main stair, right in the maw of the gaping door. That was the way things looked to Irene: the steps the tongue, the portico the brow, the facade the wide marble face.

George slowed the car, just enough, Irene feared, to be noticed. "Jesus," he said. "What is this place? Why are they watching us like that?"

"Speed up. They'll think we're afraid of them."

"Reny, we are."

Fear wasn't the feeling Irene had been aware of before this moment. But as the car neared and Irene kept an eye on the doctors, waiting for them to move, she understood that all along she'd been imagining a hospital, like the one where they'd met these doctors the first time. Instead it seemed she had to face the mammoth, patient creature of this house, which was stationary, yes, but stationary like a living thing holding still on purpose only until it could take her inside. Look, even its arms were extended— two long wings, angled in, ready to close.

And she had to face these complementary doctors too, fixed as the statues that flank entries. If it were Irene standing there with the woman doctor, the match would be nearer. "You look alike, a little, did you notice?" George had said to her after their first appointment. Irene had noticed only that feeling of hard-to-place familiarity that makes a person ask, *Do I know you from somewhere?*

The doctors' eyes weighed, and Irene wondered how clearly they could see her and George through the windshield and if the doctors could read lips. "You're really going to leave me here?" she said to George, trying not to move her mouth much.

She meant it to sound playful, but to be here they had both peddled themselves. George's forehead gathered.

"No, it's all right," Irene said.

They were close enough now to see smiles rising to the doctors' faces.

George stopped the car and came around to Irene's door with the rollicking gait she loved. She put her hand in his so he could help her out. Every time he stewarded her lately, he seemed to be rubbing her face in his stupid hope, when she had enough of her own. She climbed forth. She touched the slippery rose-colored fabric of her new maternity suit. This was the color she'd wanted right away from the catalog's many choices, warm and bloomy.

"Good morning!" the woman doctor called, and descended the stairs to press George and Irene's joined hands.

George broke his grip then to reach up the stairs and greet the man doctor, still a few steps up, as if sealing some bargain.

"How was the drive?" asked the woman doctor.

"I tried to take the corners slow. For her stomach," said George.

"What a good *sign*," the woman doctor said.

Irene peered into her face. Not a perfect mirror, no: something similar about their chins and the hard set of their mouths, the lift of their eyebrows, but this woman's eyes were blue where Irene's were wheat-colored, and Irene's hair was darker. And, of course, the doctor was older too. How old? Older than Irene's own age, twenty-eight, but much younger, she thought, than her mother. In that middle territory, what happened to a childless woman? Irene had begun finding out for herself. Kitchens and bedrooms and living rooms full of screaming quiet. Sun on carpets, rain on doorsteps. Quiet so loud she could hear nothing else. But she wondered if for this woman doctor it might be different.

"Very promising," said the man doctor. He had charm, but there wasn't much to wonder about him.

The doctors led the Willards up. Stairs brought out the sluggish drag of the weight at Irene's center, and even here she didn't like this awareness, which had never led anywhere good before. Her body had over and over proven itself a liar. She'd started to suspect this might just be a new uncovering of a trait it had always had.

As they fed themselves in, one by one, Irene had time to notice that up close the marble of the house was in fact veined like skin.

Twin mahogany desks stood within the doctors' study, a line in two segments whose edges did not quite meet. The doctors bulwarked behind and left George and Irene to chairs in front, as if they were disobedient students. Only Irene had been such a student. She and George had been in school together, and though she knew he loved her already, he'd never understood why she had to say just one word too much, why she had to twist her mouth, raise her eyebrow, poison the milk of someone else's dumb joy. *It makes me feel delicious,* she'd said to him, back when she could say to him anything she wanted. She'd faced many people across many desks and each time thought, *Well? Talk, talk, talk, talk. What can you do to me? You can't touch me.*

Except the doctors could—she'd begged them to. The only

other time they'd all met, when Irene had been a robed patient on their examination table, he and she had lifted her arms at the same moment to take her pulse, neither of them noticing the duplication because each was talking to George. *In these cases* . . . Her body at that moment occupied the physical space of the doctors' marriage. As an omen, how could that be bad? She'd felt suddenly able to meet George's eyes with ease: here she was, winning fallow ground, so ready, once they chose her and set about solving whatever her trouble was, to produce every baby he'd come back from overseas wanting. These doctors had solved this trouble with other women. They were the only ones solving it. All she had to do was make them choose her.

Then they'd tipped her back on the table and put a cold, slick metal instrument inside her and peered with a light at some sore region deep within, and she'd felt the ache like a name that she'd been trying to remember. *Oh, there it is.*

In spite of herself, though, Irene was starting to feel less sure now. No person she'd faced across a desk had ever in the end succeeded in shaping her in any corrective fashion. George reached across the space between their chairs to take her hand again, and she let him—poor, sweet, wondrous George, who had also failed in so many ways.

"Are there any questions Dr. Bishop and I can answer before your examination?" the man doctor asked softly, considerately, as if they were fragile, or maybe his voice was just soft. Irene watched George noticing. George still had ideas about men left over from football. She hoped the man doctor's handshake had been firm.

"Aren't you married?" Irene said. "Aren't you both Dr. Hall, then?"

The woman doctor spoke. "Technically, but it got confusing for everyone. So here, I use my maiden name. We find it's easier for the patients."

Irene wondered if this woman had wanted the feeling of having created herself out of the soil of her own life only, of having let nothing stick to her since.

"How many other patients do you have here?" George asked.

"Eighteen, at the moment," said Dr. Hall.

"They're all . . . ?" Irene said.

"They all have much your history."

Irene didn't like the word's turning of her into a set of occurrences. She hadn't considered the other patients much. "They're all just like me? All at the same point?"

Dr. Bishop gave a bright laugh. "That would be a real miracle of timing, wouldn't it? No, they're at various stages now, but everyone joins us right around where you are now, Mrs. Willard, just about fourteen weeks."

"Is there something special about that time?"

"All the times are special."

Irene smiled. She'd only ever made it this far.

"But it's the optimal time for beginning our treatment, yes. A time when the healthy fetus is growing rapidly and we can intervene to the best effect. You're entering the stage when you'll even begin to feel movements. You haven't felt any movements yet, have you, Mrs. Willard?"

Irene sat up straighter. Instantly she seemed to grow a new sense there at her middle, waiting for—what? "Should I have?"

"No, no, not necessarily. It would be quite early."

So again, already, there was a bar Irene was failing to clear, and now they would ask and check until her failure was unmissable. Irene wasn't sure she could bear this after all, being here, herding herself with these like-circumstanced women, making those circumstances the only part of her that counted for anything. Giving up her whole life to steep here in failures, comparisons, and other women's sounds and smells.

Panic rose and she stood—the panic climbing her throat, the weight, that central weight, pulling, stretching her between. "George—" she said.

Right away he stood too. He would take her from this room if that was what she wanted, and they could go home and wait to see what happened this sixth time, wait for what she knew was coming. A disaster, but at least a familiar one.

Dr. Bishop's eyes were on her again. Irene could see that this woman knew what Irene was remembering; she felt the doctor's gaze on all of it. The fourth time and the blood on her mother's couch, a stain the shape of a bell, ringing iron all through her. Her trembling hands, her mother's mouth drooping at the corners, and the sound her mother made then, low, urgent, indecent, Irene had thought distantly—this wasn't happening to her mother, who did her mother think she was? The first time, when Irene had thought maybe this was only some part of the process no one spoke of— her family doctor hadn't spoken much at all when she'd gone to her appointment the week before, had just beamed at her as if she'd turned out to be very pleasing when Irene had never been pleasing in all her life—so it might be normal, this small smear of red brown on her underclothes marking where the crease of her had been. A decorous sign of itself sent forth by the thing growing inside. The third time as slight to begin with, the blood more red than brown but no more of it, but by then she'd known better than to read decorousness there. She'd run her finger down and down that sticky red line, that awful error, trying to wick it away. The second time, the worst. Late enough that her outlines had begun to yield to a firm paunch she'd patted before her mirror in the evenings, so hard under palms—as if her inner self, hard, always, was being revealed, and this was what people meant by *showing*. Then sudden waking to blood, blood, blood in a pool in the bed, George screaming, and in the washroom a hot ripping wave and beneath her the sound of something wet dropping, and she knew, she knew before she looked what she would see, but still she looked: the lump of skin and two small dots—were they eyes? *Why is such a terrible thing allowed to happen?* she'd thought, with no clear idea of what should have intervened on her behalf.

She'd had a senseless fear of touching the thing in case touching might hurt it.

That wasn't true, though—that the second was the worst. The fifth was the worst, though it had been another so early she'd passed only a little more blood than it was usual for her to pass every month, with only one big clot, half-dollar-sized, that she could pretend was just more blood. The fifth was the worst because the most recent always was. This one, then, would be worst of all.

Irene watched Dr. Bishop see this with her. She couldn't do a thing to prevent Dr. Bishop from seeing.

When Dr. Bishop spoke, leaning forward with her elbows in lovely angles on the desk, it was straight to Irene. "Mrs. Willard, of course you can leave if you wish." She paused and let the pause linger.

Dr. Hall filled it. "But really, you should understand that this is your best option."

"Yes," Dr. Bishop said. "That's what I was going to say. Our results are quite something. Of the women who've gone through the program so far—"

"How many is that? You haven't said," George interrupted.

"Forty have completed their time with us. Thirty-four have had healthy babies."

"So six . . ."

"Six is a lot, isn't it?" Irene said. "One or two, you might think it was a fluke—they had worse problems than the rest, or they did something wrong. But six, doesn't six mean you aren't fixing something?"

"Remember, these are patients who, like you, Mrs. Willard, have experienced *repeated* fetal loss. For inclusion in our program, at least three losses prior to the current pregnancy. So having produced from their ranks so many healthy babies—it's a real success."

George looked at her. "Irene?" As ever, he would do anything she wanted.

Dr. Bishop waited patiently. This woman knew Irene would never choose the familiar thing if there was any other option, no matter what the other option was; would never go home by choice to wait for the wave, the streak, the clot, the pool, the groan, the clench, the seep, the first slight cramp, each moment a terrible balance of hoping and dreading, listening and trying not to listen, feeling and trying not to feel. The waiting, Irene had come to think, was worse than what had come eventually every time.

No, that was a lie too.

Irene took in a breath. In breathing at all, she was feeding the weight, her body making that choice again and again. She couldn't get away if she wanted to.

"Yes, all right," she said.

So the doctors led them to the second floor, up a wide, curving staircase made of a pale white stone that looked as if it would feel soft if Irene touched it. These steps were so shallow that going up them hardly jostled the weight at all—they'd been measured out for taking time and turning the climber or descender into a spectacle for people below. No one below now, though Irene could hear other people, these other women with their *histories,* moving around in unseen rooms.

The examination room itself also owned its purpose only halfway. The sheeted table and the gown Irene would wear were white, but the rest had been left jewel-toned: the deep blue drapes covering the high arched windows and the rich, thick carpet, which was patterned like stained glass. A beautiful room, she tried to notice that it was a very beautiful room, even if its beauty was of a kind that suggested enchanted sleeps.

Irene hesitated on the threshold. "This isn't much like most hospitals," she said.

"It used to be my family home," said Dr. Bishop. She didn't mean a present-tense family, Irene understood, but one that stretched back in time like a line of cemetery stones. Feet upon feet upon these same floors. Neither Irene nor George had any such family, just middle-class parents bluntly proud of what they'd made.

Dr. Bishop took Irene by the elbow to get her moving again, steered her into a corner, and pulled a curtain shut between them. She produced a light chatter while Irene took off her clothes and put on the starchy white gown. "We only spent the odd weekend here before this all began, but it turns out to be the perfect place. Fortuitous!" Fortuitous, yes, the inheriting of ancestral estates. Irene could see the tips of Dr. Bishop's fingers, wrapping around the cloth and shifting as she held it shut: she was so close. The curtain didn't do much to relieve the strangeness of taking off clothes in a room that held these other people, and Irene sat to be sure she wouldn't fall and embarrass herself while removing her boots. The gown pulled and scratched against her breasts, which, as happened every time, had become foreign to her, so large and so tender that a stray bump could bring her to tears. She watched George's feet beneath the curtain, moving. Dancing, if she'd been judging by ankles.

She closed the gown and shifted the curtain aside, pulling it from Dr. Bishop's grasp. Without looking at any of them, she hefted herself onto the table and put her heels in the chill metal stirrups, like mounting a horse, maybe, a thing she'd never done. Dr. Bishop must have. Already the gown was parting enough that it might as well not have been there.

They flanked her again, the doctors; they seemed to settle naturally into the flanking of things. They paused, and she saw that they were coming to a decision about who would take the lead: a glance, something (what?) exchanged, then Dr. Hall stepped to the center. "Slide forward, please," he said. Maybe they wanted to communicate that while this was Dr. Bishop's house, while she had mostly talked to them today, there was a man here too in charge of all of it, a doctor as she and George were used to seeing a doctor.

Irene slid her bottom to the base of the table, so far she seemed about to fall off, though surely he'd tell her? No one could want that. To herself, looking down, she appeared to be covered by the gown that spanned her knees, but she could feel small drafts below. She was two pictures that didn't belong together: a chimera of a naked woman and a clothed one, joined at the middle. The weight lived somewhere right at that seam.

If it still lived.

"Hmm, yes," Dr. Hall said pleasantly, with his hand deep inside her. There was a stiff, slightly painful resistance in its stretching. "Nice heavy uterus. That's promising."

"Mine, you mean?" Irene said, because it bothered her that he hadn't said so. Then: "Heavier than when you checked last time?" She wished she could get her voice to sound less plaintive.

"Yes, I'd say there's been continued growth."

He pushed down on her abdomen from above, pinning something within her between that hand and the hand inside, finding that something's perimeter the way he might have prodded the outlines of an object buried in a thick blanket. He withdrew. She hollowed.

"Good," he said. Dr. Bishop gave a surprising relieved sigh. Irene felt its echo in her chest, but she had to look away from George's face and its unbearable joy.

They sat her up then. Irene stuck moistly to the examination table, as if she'd been turned inside out. Dr. Hall tied a tourniquet around her arm and drew blood—a quick sting. She turned her head so she wouldn't feel swimmy. *My, how will you ever bear labor?* the gleeful vicious nurse at the family doctor had asked in her very first pregnancy, when Irene had done the same thing. That nurse never said it again, not with any of the others, though Irene turned her head each time.

Dr. Hall finished and taped her arm up, and Irene saw the vials in his hands. They'd be warm there, against his palm. Hers and not hers; his and not his.

"What do you test it for?" she asked.

"Primarily the levels of hormones," Dr. Bishop said. "That's where our therapy takes aim: at stabilizing those levels, evening out the excess variability you've shown."

Irene had been too preoccupied with the question of whether she'd be one of the handful selected to pay much attention to anything the doctors had said during their first meeting. She considered now. *Stabilizing, excess variability.* "That's what's wrong with me? That's why this keeps happening, because things are unstable?"

George's eyes flicked to hers.

"That's the thinking," said Dr. Hall.

"So how do you stabilize me?"

"Our approach is two-pronged," Dr. Bishop said. She held up a young-looking finger—Irene noticed that her hands were much larger and thicker than her own. "First, we supplement and manage hormone levels through chemical means. Before fetal demise, hormone levels tend to swing, often quite dramatically. If we can monitor for and regulate these swings, the crisis seems in many cases to be preventable."

Crisis. That was a good word, active and chaotic; better than *loss,* which had always made Irene think of demure weeping.

"What chemical means?" George asked.

"We use a drug, a new drug from Europe, that we saw could simulate the particular combination of hormones that support optimal pregnancy. It's been our breakthrough." Dr. Bishop said this without a hint of modesty. "A simple injection."

"That's it? That will do it? Just some shots, that's all I need?"

Dr. Bishop gave her graceful laugh again. "Not quite." She held up a second finger and turned her eyes, blue like a wrong note, on Irene alone. "The second prong of our approach aims to rectify the maternal environment in a more overarching way. In these repeated cases, our theory is that the general state of the mother may be implicated."

Irene felt herself go very still.

"So we try to address that too. We conduct our treatments here, in this secluded environment, to reduce stress. And we provide you a full program of support. The correct kinds of healthful food. Activities, both mental and physical, of the right degree and kind. Plenty of rest. And regular talk sessions with me, to help you understand and then let go of your more unhelpful feelings."

"The talking on couches?"

"Our own version of that."

"Dr. Bishop's version, anyway—it's her specialty, not mine," Dr. Hall said fondly.

"But what can talking do?" said George.

"The body and mind," Dr. Bishop said, "are intertwined. In the gravid patient these connections are particularly muscular, particularly effectual. We use them here to move things in the right direction."

Within herself Irene pictured a web made of fleshy pinkish strands, pulling one thing toward another thing.

"The women often find it's an important outlet. And it lets me just keep tabs on how everyone is doing."

"I had a girlfriend at school called Tabs," Irene said. "Tabitha, really, but that's what we all called her. I haven't thought of her in years." Ruddy-cheeked Tabs would have babies upon babies by now.

Dr. Bishop kept talking as if she hadn't heard. "And then, of course, when the time comes, you deliver."

"Here?"

"We've made ourselves into quite a state-of-the-art hospital, with additional support staff we bring in when the occasion calls for it. We have everything you might need."

"How often can I come see her?" George asked.

"We have our visiting days every couple of months or so."

"That's not much," George said. Since they were fifteen, the only time they'd been apart for more than a few days was when he was deployed. The prospect of all those hours and days and weeks without George in them made it hard for Irene to breathe.

"We're trying to give our patients a break from their real lives, that's all; a time of undisturbed quiet," Dr. Bishop said. "It's difficult, I know, but keep reminding yourselves what we're trying to accomplish. Hold that in your mind, like a prize."

Dr. Bishop's mind, Dr. Bishop's prize—Irene would have liked to see them.

Still, she did try holding her own in her mind while she dressed, while she kissed George goodbye on the front stairs. Wasn't that prize worth everything? And wasn't this the first place that had offered her steps, actual steps, to get it, keep it, give it to George?

"There's a lot I would say, if you didn't already know," George told her, her chin cupped in his palms.

"I know."

Irene watched him get into their car and drive it away. She bore it by imagining their home, just as it was, but with a further person inside. A small face that was a blur of light.

*

George drove slowly down the driveway, then very fast after he knew he'd passed her sight line. He wasn't sure why. It didn't seem a good moral sign, this fleeing from his dearly loved Reny and what she contained, as if all of it were a mess he had made.

It was a beautiful spring morning, and he drove and drove into it.

2

Dr. Hall appeared after George's car had vanished—he waited until then, considerately—and took Irene's elbow to show her back up the stairs. Instead of turning left, toward the examination rooms, they turned right this time, onto a mirror-image hallway. "The bedrooms are this way," Dr. Hall said. He had her suitcase in his hand. She'd lost track of it at some point.

"Where's your wife gone?" Irene said.

"Oh, she'll be working away somewhere."

"Why's it so quiet? Where are all the others?"

"In between group activities and mealtimes we encourage rest. You're expending enormous amounts of energy all the time."

But the sensation of the weight at Irene's center felt like the opposite of using energy, like the heaviest quiet. It dulled her.

The hallway extended, long and straight, windows to one side and doors to the other. The drapes were all closed here too, disorientingly—Irene couldn't keep hold of the angles in her mind to know what part of the grounds she'd be seeing if she could see anything.

Dr. Hall opened one of the doors in the line of other doors and waved Irene in. So this was where she'd be doing all her resting and waiting. A bed with high, proud posts, a desk, a chair, a bureau, all of the kind of dark, visibly dense wood that marked them as a separate species entirely from Irene and George's light and flimsy bedroom set from Macy's. Thick, deep-colored blankets and carpet. Curtains, closed again, and a clean but unoccupied smell in the air. On the bedstand, a jarringly modern alarm clock and lamp, like stowaways. Irene imagined other identical rooms stretching to either side of this one in the trick of multiplication you can get when you point mirrors' reflections into each other.

The doctor came into the room after her and set her suitcase down on a luggage stand beside the bureau. "Now, no lifting this. You can take the clothes out from right there. Do you have everything you need to get settled?"

"Sure. I've never been anywhere so fancy. *Old* fancy. I mean, not shabby or anything, just everything seems like it's been here forever."

"This kind of America is the closest thing we have to Europe, that's what I've always thought." Dr. Hall laughed. So he could joke about the house—it wasn't his.

"George and I used to talk about taking a European trip someday. I wonder if he'll ever want to now."

Dr. Hall pressed his lips together sadly, as people did when they were women, or too old, or for any other reason hadn't been in the war. "Well, we hope you'll be comfortable here, Mrs. Willard."

"I think I'm too afraid for that."

He fixed her with a serious look. "Try your best not to be afraid."

"Why, does it know?"

"The fetus is quite resilient. Unlikely a passing worry will affect it."

"But?"

She could tell he hadn't expected that.

"It's true that part of what we're doing here is treating your mind like a powerful instrument that can work for your baby's health or against it. We'll try to help you understand how to direct it productively, while also taking medical steps to safeguard the uterine environment."

"That's me, the uterine environment?"

"You could say so."

"Glad to hear I'll be safeguarded."

Here was Dr. Bishop, at the door. "I see you've found your room, Mrs. Willard."

"Hi there, Lou," Dr. Hall said. "She's just getting settled."

Dr. Bishop came to stand with Dr. Hall and laid a hand on his arm. Even this invulnerable doctor hadn't wanted to leave her husband alone with a woman who looked a little like her but younger, maybe. Their white coats were touching. Irene wondered if they got them from the same supplier.

"I wanted to tell you that dinner begins at six o'clock, in the dining room," Dr. Bishop said. "You can meet the others then."

What a treat, Irene almost said but stopped herself from saying. George was her good influence; without him, she would have to try harder. "Thanks."

She stepped to the window, hoping this would show these doctors they could go away, and began shifting aside the curtains, so thick and multifolded, covered in their purple fleurs-de-lis, that they reminded her of a medieval queen's dress. She couldn't seem to find the part.

"What are you doing, Mrs. Willard?" Dr. Bishop said.

"Letting in some sun."

"How about lying down for a while instead? You'll feel more peaceful without all that strong light."

Irene dropped the curtains.

Dr. Bishop nodded, and the lamplight shifted around on top of her hair, which had found all the shine there was in this dim. "Then we'll see you at dinner."

Irene made herself leave the curtains alone after the doctors had gone. They knew many things she didn't, that was why she was here.

A while later, maybe twenty minutes, maybe an hour—she'd dozed off on top of her new bed's thick, soft quilt and couldn't be sure—Irene heard women's voices in the hall outside her bedroom. She suspected them of having stopped right by her door on purpose, knowing she was newly inside. She rose and went out so she could get meeting them over with.

The two women standing there didn't in fact seem startled when she opened the door. "The new girl!" said one, offering a hand. "I'm Margaret."

Too old is her problem, Irene thought. Very clear, even though Margaret's cheeks were plumply rosy, shiny as ripe apples, and the belly-rounding she rested her other hand on looked firm. She put Irene in mind of a happy mother in a storybook, but a happy mother who should be well into having her children. A few of them should be scampering leggily around her by now, according to the clock of her life, which had left its marks in a telltale slackness around her eyes and neck and mouth, not the kind of thing that could be hidden.

"And I'm Pearl," said the other, who stood in a hunch to hide her considerable height and keep it from offending, with her hands still clasped. Her name suited her in a way that did not flatter, for she *was* pearly pale and delicately twitchy, with light gray eyes that jumped at and then away from Irene's face. *Too nervous,* Irene thought.

"Irene. Nice to meet you," she said.

How would they each be diagnosing her? But the doctors must have deemed all their limitations surmountable.

"We're both just that way," Margaret said, nodding farther down the hall.

"How long have you two been here?"

"Over a month now," said Pearl. "Margaret and I got here about the same time."

"So that makes you . . ."

"Just about eighteen weeks, and Pearl's nineteen," Margaret said. Irene could see it was a feature of this place, having the weeks burned into your brain that way, an identification as crucial as your name. Margaret's proud hand circled her stomach as if she were rubbing a lucky stone. "You?"

"Fourteen," said Irene, feeling remedial. Stupid: they all were.

"I remember week fourteen. That was *right* around when I really, finally started to feel like I could stand to eat again," Margaret said.

"Do you both have . . . other children?"

They shook their heads. "I don't think they let you come here if you do, do they? I just meant this time," Margaret said.

"This is the furthest I've ever gotten," said Pearl.

"You're further than I ever have."

Margaret leaned toward her. "How many for you, before this?"

Irene tensed, and the skin between her shoulder blades tightened as if Margaret had breathed on it. "I don't have to tell you that."

"Of course not, I just thought—"

"Excuse me," Irene said, and turned back into her room.

Why be nice? She wasn't required to make friends here. That wasn't part of the rules as they'd been explained to her. She laid herself down again in coffin-position on her bed to wait for the women to go away. What did it matter if her inner self was like these other women's somehow—the corridors or caverns all their babies occupied, or even their minds? No one could make her own that self, whose contours were only visible in what it had killed, as her true one. She was here, yes, incidentally, and she would do everything that it was necessary for her to do here, but she wouldn't do a thing more.

Once the hall outside was quiet, Irene rose. She didn't want to see another person today. She would skip dinner—who needed dinner? Not her. If the weight did, well, it could take what it needed from other places inside her, help itself—that was what her family doctor had told her when she couldn't stop throwing up.

She took her coat and started down the stairs, unseen and free as a ghost.

Outside, though, instead of freer, she felt pinned by the low-ceilinged afternoon. The clouds were thick and pewtery and hung without moving in the air, near enough they appeared touchable with a leap were she not so heavy. Patchy snow here and there on the hills still, well into March. The only tells of the season were the earth's slight ripeness beneath Irene's feet and a hint of green visible only in the periphery, as a sort of haze around the branches of the trees, hovering like a trick of light above the grass.

Irene wandered up the drive a ways, then turned to look the house full in its face. It seemed ready to spring forward at any moment and set all the bulk of its balustrades, columns, porticoes, and grand monarchical porches moving. Everything was a little too crisp-edged to be authentically ancestral. Why hadn't she seen right away? It wasn't really a very old house. It was only pretending to be one.

Was Irene allowed to be out here? No one had said she wasn't.

Facing the house like this, she could just see crumbling lower walls she hadn't noticed on the drive in, jutting out from behind it, like the ruins of a previous structure. These were brick, not marble.

Irene wound her way toward the mystery while the glossy windows of the house watched. Clouds, all those clouds, reflected themselves at her. There was relief in turning the corner to be unseen again. In back everything seemed abandoned, though the grounds in front—a large lawn running from the circular drive all the way to the woods at the sides—were freshly mown. Why had these rear shambles been permitted? Because this part wasn't seen most of the time, maybe; because someone, everyone, had lost interest.

And here were the crumbling brick walls, bordering something. A wrought-iron gate stood crookedly ajar. Dead brown ivy hung in the way, and Irene pushed it aside to enter. It brushed closed again behind her with a windy sound.

Inside, she found a traditional kind of walled garden, now become a plotted world overrun. Trees at the four corners, meant to produce ornamental fruit at human height, had outgrown their stations and were higher than the surrounding walls. Shrubs had crept and snarled together, bristling. Roses upon roses upon roses upon roses had spread shaggily and tumbled over the paths, with all the wet brown paper of last season's blooms snagged in the bramble. Beneath Irene's feet, snow-flattened thickets of grass, unmown years' worth.

Irene forded the wreckage to the garden's midpoint, where there was a dry fountain, a cherub at its center with a stain in a dark, troubling river running over-chin. A tiny strawberry of a penis peeked from between his chubby legs. The tip had broken off, and two of his fingers. She sat on the rim and peered over. She had the feeling she was looking into the center of the center of this place.

Within she saw black muck, old leaves, sticks, stones, all the things bones break from, and there, amongst the leaves, yes, something broken: a small dead field mouse. As if only sleeping, as they say—as Irene herself had said, but it wasn't true, the eyes had never looked enough like eyes to be closed. It wasn't true for this mouse either, with blood on its fur, with one eye open. Nothing had ever slept like that, or like her babies. The field mouse must have fallen into the fountain's bowl, trying to reach water that wasn't, and been unable to climb back up those steep sides, and then something had taken advantage of its exposure and killed it and perhaps left it here for later. It was browner than the mice the doctors would have used for the tests they must have conducted on their way to their *breakthrough*.

A sob welled in her and escaped in a desperate gulping note that was like the sound her mother had made for the bell of blood, and it startled Irene in the same way: *But this isn't yours.*

She couldn't seem to stand leaving the mouse trapped in there like that, though, even if of course it didn't matter now. She took up a stick and poked it—wet, with more heft and resistance than expected, trailing its long skin-colored tail—and pinned it against the side of the fountain bowl. Carefully she slid the stick beneath, balanced the mouse on the end, and lifted, then placed it gently on the fountain's brim. She steered the tail into a curl against its side. Then she found an old brown leaf and covered it up, like tucking it in.

Maybe her tragic feeling for this small dead thing meant something hopeful. She'd lain down in the dark like she was supposed to for a while; maybe she was already getting better at the task she'd come here to complete. Irene tipped her face up to the sky, so that she knew those clouds were reflected in her eyes, on her wet cheeks. As if she were painting herself with this place, a new coating over all the old facts of her.

On the way back in, she met Dr. Bishop, of course, coming down the stairs. "Where have you been?" the doctor asked. The question seemed meant for a child. Even as a child Irene had never liked it when other people tried to decide where she should be.

This was the trouble, really: Irene didn't like this doctor, she was deciding, and she knew from long experience that the decision couldn't be helped once it was made.

"I'm not allowed to walk?"

"We do take walks as a group, and spend time outside, as a group. During your free time, though, we encourage you to consider your energy. Think of it like budgeting."

And that was something you'd say to some kitchen-table housewife who delighted in receipts. None of the roles this doctor wanted to assign Irene fit. "What a good analogy, thank you."

Dr. Bishop had stopped close to Irene, very close, eye to eye.

"It's strange, isn't it?" Irene said.

"Pardon?"

"We look a bit similar. Don't you think?"

"Do you think so?"

"George noticed too," Irene said defensively. She could feel her cheeks warming.

"Well," Dr. Bishop said in a humoring way. "Why don't you go rest again for a while now."

"I was just resting before."

"Good! But more is even better. Go ahead and rest until this evening. We have a little concert planned for tonight after dinner."

"Concert?" Irene echoed, picturing the pregnant patients resting violins atop their stomachs.

"Some local musicians."

"I thought I might skip dinner, actually," Irene said.

"Oh, we can't have that."

*

When the dinner hour came, Irene thought of George and resolved again to be better, as much better as she was capable of being. She went downstairs and followed the sounds of talking, the muted clinks of silverware on the edges of plates, down a broad hallway to the dining room's double doors. It was a vast, dark space, like a cathedral or a high-ceilinged cave. You put a room this size in your house to declare you could summon enough people to fill it. Irene supposed Dr. Bishop had: three round tables covered in white tablecloths had been set in a line down the center, and around them were all the women, some looking like regular women anywhere, others swollen to impossible-looking shapes. Their modern clothes in bright factory-made colors again gave Irene the sense of two time periods laid on top of each other. Everyday housewives at an ancient banquet. Some of their clothes were fancier than others'—now that she was here, Irene understood that Dr. Bishop's family money must really be funding this place, and the fee they were all being charged was only nominal— and some were older than others. But they were all equally out of place in this room.

The women chatted, crossed and uncrossed their legs, and moved their hands through the air. The doctors made a slow circuit and surveyed their plates. Dr. Bishop noticed Irene and gave her an approving nod that made her want to turn right back around.

But of course where could she go, really?

There was an empty chair near Margaret and Pearl at the far table, so Irene slipped into it. Better the enemy you know, et cetera—at least she'd already told these two her name and how far along she was and wouldn't have to go through all of it again. She tried looking mostly at her plate and its piece of pale, glistening chicken, its carrots more yellow than orange, to signal that nobody needed to talk to her.

But Margaret sniffed and said, "I didn't mean to get off on the wrong foot, earlier." Margaret must be the kind of person who could not release her grip. Her dress was red, with a childlike white Peter Pan collar, different from the dress she'd worn in the hallway. Maybe dinner was an event to these women, worth changing for.

"Let's forget it," Irene said.

Margaret shrugged and chewed.

The curtains in here were closed too, which made the room feel unanchored even in daily time. Irene knew some light remained outside, but in here they had only the tea-colored lamplight that fell from the chandeliers. Was sunlight meant to be bad for them? Were they supposed to sit still endlessly in the dark like bulging root vegetables?

At home, George would be eating a casserole left for him by one of the neighborhood ladies, Irene just knew it; they hadn't advertised Irene's absence, but everyone would have caught wind of it anyway.

Irene stood, looking for something to drink. Instantly the servingwoman was by her side. "What can I get you, ma'am?"

"I was just going to get some water." Irene pointed toward the sideboard with its pitcher and glasses.

"Why don't you let me," the woman said, not a question—she was already doing it.

Irene sat again. "They don't want us walking?"

"They want us to rest, I think," Pearl said.

"So I keep hearing. What are we supposed to do all the time?"

"Well, *rest*," Margaret said.

"There are activities and things, and our appointments. You'll see, the time goes," Pearl told her. "Sometimes I think I'm busier here than at home."

Margaret laughed. "Not really, though, Pearl? I mean, my Ladies' Auxiliary meetings alone run me ragged. They made me be president again this year somehow."

"Well, you must need the rest, then," Irene said. Her water appeared. She sipped. The tumbler had heft enough to bludgeon someone if she were so inclined. The water was cold and satisfying after the carrots, which had filmed her throat with that bitter rising warning taste the weight had made her prone to.

"I *do* wish they'd let us have salt," Margaret said. "It's so hard to get through all this without it."

"We can't have salt? Really, is this prison?"

Pearl snorted, the most genuine sound Irene had heard out of her yet. Irene resisted the urge to glance at her, lest she accidentally form some alliance, a bridge to a place she didn't want to visit. When they all left this house, she would make sure she never saw either of these women again.

"And what do you mean, *get through all this*? Surely we don't have to eat it all."

"They like us to," Margaret said. "They've weighed everything so it's the right amount."

"I've never heard of such a thing."

"It doesn't hurt to be on the safe side, I guess," Pearl said, recollecting herself, adjusting her hair.

Oh, but it all hurts, Irene thought to say, but she didn't think Pearl needed to hear it.

"The sugar's harder, I think." Pearl sighed piningly. "But then I have such a sweet tooth. You know, I used to carry a box of Good & Plenty around with me while I did the housework. Iron a shirt, get two; mop the kitchen, get three. I stopped when Joe told me I was eating so many they were turning my skin pink."

Though her pale, thin skin was pinkening even under the strain of telling this story. Irene pictured Pearl, with her anxious height, hunched over the candy pellets like a lanky, jumpy heron.

"No sugar either?" Irene said.

"You get used to it," said Margaret.

A bite of Irene's chicken slipped from her fork onto her lap, where it left a grease print on the silk of that rose-colored maternity suit, as if someone had touched her with a dirty hand. Was it possible she'd put this dress on this morning in her own bedroom? Irene dipped her napkin in the tumbler and rubbed, even though she knew better with silk.

On the far side of the room, Dr. Bishop leaned over the sideboard and its extra plates of chicken. Those spares were punishments, maybe, to be doled out if anyone misbehaved. Dr. Bishop put a fingertip to the chicken, then put the fingertip to her tongue. She caught Irene watching her and fixed her face into its professional expression.

Then she moved to the edge of the center table. "Good evening, ladies!" Dr. Bishop said. "I hope you've all had a pleasant and peaceful day. If you haven't had a chance yet, please be sure to say hello to our newest arrival, Mrs. Irene Willard."

Arrival, such a loaded word in this room full of these women. They turned toward Irene and waved. The doctor stepped back again.

"Aren't you eating, Doctor?" said Irene.

"Excuse me?"

"Doctors don't eat?"

Dr. Hall, who'd been standing sleepily off to the side, woke up a little.

"We eat later, Mrs. Willard," Dr. Bishop said.

"Can't break bread with us mere mortals?"

Pearl gasped. The other women close by were beginning to listen too. Irene felt a recklessness pulse all the way down to the bottoms of her feet, which she pressed hard to the floor.

"It's just easier if some aspects of our lives and routines are distinct. You're new, of course, Mrs. Willard, but you'll find that one of the elements of your treatment involves conversation of a different sort from what we might engage in around a dining-room table. It's better not to muddy the waters—you don't need to be talking to me in your session in the afternoon and then inquiring about my sister's health over dinner in the evening."

Irene wondered if Dr. Bishop actually had a sister.

"I guess I don't want to be analyzed while I'm eating my chicken," said Margaret.

Some of the others laughed. They lifted their forks again. Irene cut herself another bite of chicken too.

"Are you getting enough, Mrs. Crowe?" Dr. Bishop asked Margaret then.

"Me? Why? Am I not—"

"Oh no, no reason, just checking." Dr. Bishop smiled reassuringly at Margaret.

Irene felt a dizzying wave of gratitude she herself hadn't been asked this question.

"Is there any salt for the chicken?" she said.

"Let's hold off on the salt for now," Dr. Hall told her, from his station.

After the tables were cleared, they processed into the foyer. Chairs had been set up in rows in the big space between the front door and the staircase, and a group of middle-aged men sat on the landing behind music stands, dressed in suits, holding their instruments.

Dr. Bishop climbed the first few steps to stand before the group. "May I introduce the West Berkshire String Quartet," she said. "Look, this is something like a stage, isn't it? I've always thought the acoustics in here would be something. Tonight they're going to play a piece by Beethoven for us, which I understand is a new project."

A balding violinist said, "We've played it for years."

"But never *performed* it," the cellist said.

"Well, we're looking forward to it," Dr. Bishop said. She turned to her women. "Those of you who are further along— it's possible your fetuses are actually able to hear a bit of ambient sound now. Think of that, as you're listening."

The first violin took a loud breath through his nostrils to start them playing. They were pitchy, and the cellist's rhythms blurred, sped, sagged, and the high ceiling, instead of magnifying the sound, swallowed and distorted it. Irene could see the four play- ers panicking, reaching for one another by bobbing their heads and throwing significant *no, no* glances. They were probably used to practicing in their living rooms.

The women around her all sat politely. Irene ached for George to raise her eyebrows at. She imagined the string sound making its liquid, swampy way through her abdomen to the weight.

You must not like it either. How about moving, to show me?

But nothing happened.

How stupid of her, to hope that coming here would make some- thing happen.

As Irene went up to bed, she wondered about Dr. Bishop, put- ting a string quartet on this particular stair and a crowd of patients in this particular foyer to watch it. Maybe Dr. Bishop was reclaim- ing as well as experimenting in bringing them here. She wondered what that might mean, for all of them.

MOUSE

3

Irene awoke reaching for George, who for the first time in years wasn't there. The phrase *for the first time in years* was like a wail in her head, and baldly untrue: this was her third day here with these doctors, and George had been overseas, and Irene had visited her parents, and after the second time she'd needed two nights at the hospital. Her dramatic tendencies were just speaking. Maybe this was a *symptom*. Today she might learn if thoughts of this kind could be somehow killing her babies.

Irene rolled onto her back in bed and laid her hands atop the small, hard mound between her hip bones, faithful battlements. Their loyal guarding seemed tragic when the threat was already inside. She tapped softly, one-two-three, to see if she could make anything within do something she could sense. Then she waited, listening/feeling. Nothing. More of the quiet, heavy nothing that the weight had always been, this weight and all its predecessors. She left her hands there a moment, trying to communicate her apology through her fingertips for having failed so abjectly at being a mother that she'd failed to ever even become one.

Foolishness, that's what Irene's own mother would say. Had said, when Irene produced such thoughts and savagely hurled them.

She kept thoughts like these from George, though once she'd thought she could tell George anything, because it turned out there was a nakedness below nakedness. She worried, though, that George had seen anyway. After they were married, but before George had been deployed, his cousin Elizabeth had brought her three-month-old baby to visit them in their newlywed house. Irene couldn't remember the baby's name now, but it had been a boy. Sam? Tim? Something long made shorter. Elizabeth had been carrying him out in the garden, where George was making her look at some roses he'd planted—he'd suddenly become the kind of man who planted things—when she turned an ankle, made a wounded noise, and sat down on the grass.

"I'm sorry! The baby made all my joints so loose," she said.

Irene had looked at the baby with horror.

Sitting didn't seem to fix anything: the ankle ballooned exuberantly. They all eyed it and discussed while the baby rested on Elizabeth's lap like a fat, bored dog.

Eventually they decided George should drive Elizabeth to the doctor. "Thank you for watching him," Elizabeth said to Irene, and handed the baby to her, and hobbled to the car with her hand on George's shoulder.

The baby felt heavier than Irene had anticipated. She stood there smelling his milkish smell while she watched the car pull out of the driveway.

She shifted the baby on her hip and climbed their little stoop. Really he wasn't so bad when you carried him the right way. This wouldn't be so bad, she was coming to feel. But then she turned their doorknob to let herself back into the house and it wouldn't turn. George had the key.

Irene yelled the way she did in these moments—not a word, just a loud, angry sound—and the baby flinched, then started to cry.

"No, no, I'm sorry," she said. He wouldn't look at her. She petted his little leg, his dumpling-knee. "I'm sorry." But he kept crying, increasing his volume, like a siren drawing near.

All right. This was all right. Babies cried. Irene didn't really know much about them—she was the youngest child of two youngest children, and there'd been no little siblings or cousins for her to tend—but she knew this was true. She staggered with him into their backyard, getting away from the road so at least no one would see them and stare at her, wondering what she'd done. "Stop stop," she whispered as she walked. She shut the gate behind them, carried him to the back corner by the little fruit tree, and put him down in the grass, where she expected him to sit— he'd sat in Elizabeth's lap—but with nothing to lean against he flopped backward and lay there screaming, writhing, thrusting his small fists to the sky.

What did he need? Was he too hot? They were in the shade. Was he hungry? Irene couldn't feed him. She had no milk, no diapers. "Shhshh," she said, and put her hand on his stomach. He squirmed beneath it. His whole face was pursed, red, as if she'd agonized him, pricked him with something, maybe. As if she were rotting and he'd smelled it and was furious about his inability to escape from her. He was astonishingly loud—she'd never in her life heard another person of any size make so much noise for so long without stopping.

So Irene stood, moved away from him. Went to the opposite corner of the yard and sat down with her back against their brand-new oak fence.

When she revised this memory, Irene considered the possibilities for what might have happened next:

1. She breathed deep, settled, and found within herself a waiting reserve of warmth and calm ready to tap. She closed the space between them and lifted the baby, and the crook of her arm soothed him in the way it sculpted itself to the curve of his back. She rocked him. He quieted. They waited together in peace for his real mother, but really Irene was almost as good.
2. She crossed the lawn and slapped the baby right across the reddest part of his red, red cheeks.
3. She found in her pocket a teething ring, provided by the universe. She crossed the grass and slipped it between his lips, and he stopped crying and gnawed contentedly, amazed

that she had understood what he needed after all, that he'd misjudged her, and she cupped his little foot in her hand.

4. She overturned their empty garbage pail on top of the baby to catch the noise, at least.

5. She found an open window in their kitchen. She slid it up and climbed through, unlocked the door, and took the baby inside to a bed that could hold them both, where they slept for days.

All these possibilities seemed about equally likely.

What happened, though: George and Elizabeth made it to the stoplight three streets over before realizing they'd forgotten Elizabeth's pocketbook, so they turned back for it. When they pulled into the driveway, George heard the noise and came around the corner of the house to find Irene sitting as far as she could get from the baby, back pressed to their fence as if she hoped she might push it down.

But of course their child, Irene and George's, would be different. It would be theirs, which meant that Irene would love it beyond all reason. She would do anything for it, and she would know right away what the right things were: that was what being its mother would mean. She was here, now, to make that baby come to them. So it didn't matter how much she hated this place, how much pre-weighed and tasteless chicken she had to eat, how many hours she had to spend sitting in the dark, because making this baby come, to her and to George, was worth anything.

Irene rolled over in the bed, trying to get comfortable—maybe she would sleep more, why not.

And then she saw the mouse.

It scurried in her peripheral vision. It was cutting the hypotenuse of the dark triangle of shadow beneath the chair, slinking, that hunch and then that low line of back and tail. Quick, quick. Her skin shivered all over. She turned her head to look directly at it, but there was nothing there. The mouse was gone.

Not *the* mouse, no. Not the one from the fountain. Only *a* mouse. Foolishness again. That was the thing about all this lying down in a dark and quiet room—these long stretches with nothing to feel or see or hear except the absence of movement, sound, sensation. You could start needing something to sense so badly that you supplied it for yourself, in the end, and attached more meaning to it than you should. Irene might so desperately want movement that her mind had made it for her, in the wrong place.

Anyway, high time, Irene's mother would say, to get up and get on with things.

Irene pulled the blankets of her bed up. Some maid she'd yet to spy came in while they were eating breakfast to do this over again, better, leaving everything crisply invaded, with the bedspread tucked around the pillows in a neat crease Irene had never achieved in her life. Downstairs, she sat once more with Margaret and Pearl. They were served some sort of dry oatcake with the right crumbly texture but the taste of sawdust, exactly half a cup of coffee with cream if they wanted but no sugar, and a tall glass of water.

"Remember, finish it all if you can," said the servingwoman, who walked by at the wrong moment and saw Irene smashing some cake to powder with her fork's tines.

As she left the dining room after, walking behind Margaret and Pearl, Irene found herself having to stop short so she wouldn't collide with them. She peered up ahead. There was a buzzing of some sort in the foyer, where a knot of their fellow patients moved toward the front door.

"They're already in the car," somebody said.

"*They. They,* not *her,* just like that."

Their voices had a different emphasis and pitch than Irene had yet heard in this house. "What?" she said.

Nobody heard her. She and Margaret and Pearl were borne outside by the swirl of other women. At the top of the house's front stairs they all waited in the cold no one was dressed for.

"What are we doing?" she said.

The doctors stood at the foot of the stairs, nodding to people inside a stopped car.

"Ellie Giller's leaving with her baby. Can you imagine? How she must feel," said Pearl.

Irene could not. She could tell from the faces of the women around her that none of them could—that was why they'd come out here, to get as close to the feeling as it was possible for them to be.

"It's a girl," Pearl said.

"But when did she have it? Why didn't we hear?"

"A couple of nights ago. Delivery's up on the third floor," Margaret said.

So seismic a shift, someone actually managing to move from their desperate camp into the desired one—Irene would have thought she would know it was happening from a mere floor away. She'd have thought they'd all smell it in the air, that they wouldn't be able to eat or drink or sleep for smelling it.

"The baby . . . ?" Irene whispered. She could just see Ellie's face through the back seat window, very round and smiling at no one in particular. She could see a blanket-enfolded something in the corner of her arm too, tucked there in a way that made Irene think of fairy tales. Irene craned but couldn't make out the baby's face.

"Healthy. Ellie's taking her home." Margaret's mouth puckered around *home* as if around a sour taste, this prize that wasn't, yet, for her. She met Irene's eyes and remembered to smile.

"Goodbye, Ellie!" some woman was calling, then another: "Goodbye, goodbye!" because everyone wanted the last word of this farewell. Everyone wanted to be Ellie's dearest friend. Irene almost said it too but caught herself.

The car started down the drive. Finally they all turned to go.

"Samantha Thompson also left last night, did you hear?" Pearl said in a richly secret tone, much quieter, looking behind her as she spoke, as if she worried the doctors might hear. But the doctors were still at the bottom of the stairs, waving to Ellie's car.

"Oh *no*," Margaret said.

"Isn't it good to leave?" said Irene. "Wasn't this whole bit just now because somebody was leaving?"

Margaret shook her head. That knowing, salacious gesture had been perfected, Irene imagined, at the head of the Ladies' Auxiliary table. "Samantha must have lost it."

As if this Samantha had put her baby down someplace and forgotten where, or let it slip through a tear in a bag. Irene felt her throat tighten. "How far along?" she said.

"About twenty weeks? She was already here when we got here, wasn't she, Margaret?"

A chill descended. Which room had been Samantha Thompson's, where was it in the reflected row? The maid might put a mark on the door to remember she didn't need to clean that one anymore, until the next woman came to fill it. No one would tell that new woman anything when they let her inside for the first time.

For all Irene knew, her own room could have held, before, a woman who had left that way.

And here were Margaret and Pearl relishing their luck in not being Samantha. Didn't they see? A thing like this happening here, it made them all unlucky. It should remind them all what further unluckiness might still await.

"I guess she didn't get a send-off," Irene said. "I bet she stole off in the night, never to be heard from again."

Pearl tsked her tongue. "Irene. She could try again and come back."

"Would they let her? Has anyone ever done that?"

Pearl and Margaret shook their heads.

"I don't know why they'd want to take someone back when it hadn't worked."

"It could work the next time. They're trying to help," Pearl said.

"They're trying to prove they're right."

Pearl drew back. Margaret narrowed her eyes. For a second Irene thought one of them might slap her. "Well, they *are*," Margaret said.

Behind them, two soft claps sounded.

"Time for calisthenics, ladies," said the receptionist. She made a picture in the doorway. Every line of her was clean, especially her waist and its neat little nip that proclaimed she wasn't one of them. She was quite a young woman, years younger than Irene, though she wore a wedding ring. When had that happened, that Irene herself had been supplanted in the youngest category of the fully grown?

"Calisthenics?" Irene said.

"Mondays and Wednesdays, right after breakfast."

"I'm not dressed for it," Irene said, pulling the skirt of her pleated silk dress wide. All the others were, she saw: smock tops and loose cotton skirts, even a pair or two of slacks.

"I'm sure you'll be fine," the receptionist said blandly.

She led them down the hall, past the dining room, into a part of the house Irene hadn't seen yet. This hallway was broad and high-arched, probably so that full parties could move along it without clogging its throat.

"*You* wear many hats, don't you?" Irene said to the receptionist.

But she was up ahead and didn't hear, or had been trained not to, and Irene was stuck with only Margaret and Pearl and the embarrassment of having spoken without being answered. Pearl pretended not to notice, but Margaret smirked. Irene decided she hated Margaret.

The receptionist opened a double door into a red-walled ball-room. Gold-painted curlicues clung like growths to the ceiling and along the corners where walls and ceiling met. The polished floor was so shiny it looked wet and reflected the red right back up again: balls, Dr. Bishop's ancestors must have been thinking, were for dancing in the blood of enemies. The drapes here had actually been left open for once, and the whole space was bright enough to hurt Irene's eyes.

The crisp taps of the receptionist's heels rang with monstrous echoes as she crossed the empty floor: no furniture here but a few stiff gold formal couches that had been pushed to the walls, clearing the center of the room for a missing spectacle. Though not missing anymore, for here they all were, women of every shape and size and some range of ages (look at that one with her lined face but her shiny ponytail like a schoolgirl's—who did she think she was fooling? look at that one, she couldn't be more than twenty) in their ready-to-wear. Dr. Bishop might have had some sort of coming-out party in this very room. Irene tried to imagine her spinning through this space on somebody's arm, with her fancy mother and father watching her, but her mind kept stopping Dr. Bishop and stuffing her back into her white coat.

"Face me, please, ladies," the receptionist said. "Go ahead and give yourselves plenty of room."

They spread out, arm's lengths apart. Here on this floor meant for dancing, Irene felt leaden with their stillness. Margaret and Pearl spaced themselves out to her left.

"I'm Marian," said a woman to Irene's right.

"Dorothy," said another.

"Irene." She said it with a little discouraging cool. Both of them were so much more pregnant than she was: Dorothy was tiny and birdlike, and Marian tall and plain, but the shapes at their middles were uniform, that rounding that beckoned the touch of strangers. Even their faces had a heavy, dewy, superior sameness. They stood closer together than they were supposed to, as if they wanted to mark themselves off.

"Ellie won't be sorry she's missing this," Dorothy said. Marian laughed.

Ellie was ours, that was what they meant. They were imagining their own walks down the stairs and out the door. In their minds they were already leaving Irene and all the rest behind, because they were near enough to doing it that the time between now and then didn't matter anymore.

"And what about Samantha, will she be sorry?" Irene said.

They stopped laughing.

More echoing steps: Dr. Hall had arrived. The receptionist waved an arm at the women, indicating for him the work she had done. "Thank you, Mrs. Conrad," he said, and she *rang, rang, rang* her heels away to the front corner of the room, where a record player stood, and dropped the needle into place. A peaceful orchestral swirl of sound moved through the room like wind.

Dance class? Irene wanted to say, but none of the other women seemed surprised.

"All right, ladies. Stand up straight, arms above your head, and hold it there, one-two-three," Dr. Hall said, demonstrating. Irene waited for someone to laugh at him, this dancing doctor, but the others just did as he'd asked. Surely they could have hired an instructor for this. Irene wondered suddenly whether these doctors might be trying to limit the number and kinds of eyes on what they were doing here. She stretched as high as she could. It was a relief, in a way, to finally be allowed to move. *One-two-three.*

"Gentle!" Dr. Hall said. "Gentle and careful. Now bend your knees and hold it there, one-two-three."

One-two-three.

"Now reach to the side, one-two-three."

One-two-three.

Trying to make her body match Dr. Hall's felt like trying to reach some object on a too-high shelf. Irene's heart knocked harder about its work. She wondered if the weight could tell what she was doing from the shifts she was causing in its walls. If it chose this moment to move for the first time, she'd miss it entirely, she'd never even know it had happened.

She could hear Margaret and Pearl, to her left, puffing. To her right, Dorothy bit her lip with effort, and Marian looked done in. *Sit down,* Irene wanted to tell them. Was Dr. Hall noticing what it was doing to these women to make them exercise this way after so much resting? Was it *gentle and careful* to get so tired? He didn't look winded at all.

Over her shoulder, in the doorway—where a belle of a ball might pose herself before entering—Dr. Bishop appeared, accompanied by a small group of men in white coats, holding clipboards. She was saying something Irene couldn't hear. Two of the men were scribbling down notes. One was looking at his fingernails. One squinted at the women as if trying to figure out what on earth they could be doing.

Irene saw Dr. Hall notice their audience and straighten his shoulders, still speaking to the women, still modeling for them, but watching the men. Irene's awareness of wanting to perform well angered her: Why should she care how she measured up to a bunch of other women in a calisthenics class?

When she saw Dr. Hall's attention slacken, she knew that Dr. Bishop and the men had left, even before she checked for them.

Dr. Hall stopped doing the exercises himself soon after and told them what to do instead while he circled. "Straighter here," he said, and moved in to touch Pearl's leg, "at the knee." Irene caught a twinge of pleasure in Pearl's mouth.

"Pull in the lower back, no rounding," he told Dorothy, pressing his palm flat to her. Under the exhaustion, her face focused.

He stopped by Irene. "Try to relax." He gripped her shoulders. His hands were like a soft, warm yoke. They made her expect he was about to steer her someplace. She held still until he removed them. She wasn't interested in wondering what she felt.

Some minutes passed: Five? Twenty? Irene had begun to think maybe he'd keep them going forever, exercise them all the way through until they dropped their babies to the parquet beneath them. But finally Dr. Hall stopped and held up his hands. He nodded again to Mrs. Conrad, who came forward to turn off the music.

"Well done, ladies," Dr. Hall said. "Let's return to our rooms now. Not you, though, Mrs. Willard."

Irene stopped short. *What have I done?*

"It's time for your examination and then your talk session with Dr. Bishop."

"Don't worry, you'll get so you know when to expect things," whispered Pearl.

Dr. Hall left through a different side door from the one the women were all using to leave—it seemed it wasn't Dr. Hall's job to bring Irene where they were both going—and Mrs. Conrad stepped forward again to usher her out into the dim hallway. As they walked, Irene put out a hand to touch the wallpaper and the curtains that were drawn closed over the windows they passed, trying to slow herself down.

"Careful, Mrs. Willard," said the receptionist.

Irene stopped touching things. "So how long have you worked here?" she said.

"Oh, since the beginning."

"Which was?"

"Almost two years ago now. Time flies."

But time weighed Irene's body down. Two years ago she'd been an entirely different person, a woman who'd lost only one.

"What were those other doctors doing with Dr. Bishop just now? Here for the show?"

No laugh at that. "Those are colleagues, some of the doctors who come in sometimes to help with labor and delivery. Dr. Bishop likes to show them other aspects of the program too."

"So it *was* a show."

"They're interested in how the doctors do things here."

The examination room surprised Irene again by not being the expected white. Mrs. Conrad opened a drawer, extracted a gown.

"Are you a nurse too?"

"I can handle fetching a gown, I think."

"I could even get out my own," Irene said. She wanted so much for this woman, not Pearl or Margaret, to look at her and laugh with her. This young, young woman—this was the camp she wanted to be in.

But Mrs. Conrad gave her only the gown and a crisp, pressed smile. "The doctor will be with you shortly." She closed the door behind her.

Irene wrapped herself in the gown as fast as she could. Then she sat and pinched at the waxed paper covering the examination table, making peaks and valleys, a landscape for an imaginary race of miniature people she could crush with one hand if she felt like it, and crush their mountains too.

Dr. Hall knocked and entered in one motion. "How are we today, Mrs. Willard?"

"We just saw each other downstairs."

He laughed. "But I didn't really get a chance to speak with you." He looked newly polished, reassembled, his hair neatly brushed back and his white coat straight and even.

"I'm fine," Irene said, lying back. "A little sick-feeling sometimes still."

"That can last the whole pregnancy, in some cases."

"Oh, wonderful."

He palpated only from the outside today, then put on the cuff to take her blood pressure, which made Irene's arm feel like detached meat. She found his quietness and absent expression encouraging: her body must for now be playing along. Even though she hadn't felt anything so far, that must not matter too much yet.

"Now for your first injection." He went to the vanity to prepare it, out of a drawer where people had probably once stored their toiletries.

"The hormone stabilizing?"

"That's right." And he was on her with the needle. It bit at her. She felt a sting in an expanding circle around the place.

"So now? When will we actually know if it's working?"

"We just have to be patient."

But that was what Irene had been trying to do on her own, before she came here. She looked at Dr. Hall, this man without his wife. Despite his neatness he seemed unbolstered somehow in Dr. Bishop's absence, more like a man who might suddenly grin at her or touch her again, here in this barely disguised bedroom, less like a man who should be injecting her with things.

"How sure are you about all this, really?" Irene said.

"Oh, we try not to use words like *sure* too often here."

She waited, and let him feel her wait.

"We do feel very confident in our results, I can tell you that."

"Your women keep on having their babies, then."

"Our women keep on having their babies," he said, and patted her arm, and left her so she could get dressed.

Mrs. Conrad arrived again to bring Irene from the examination room to the talk-session room. Irene watched her tailored back move down the hall ahead. She wondered about Mr. Conrad. Did the two of them have babies? The Conrads probably weren't in a rush, probably figured they had plenty of time.

Mrs. Conrad knocked for Irene—as if, left to her own devices, Irene might never do it—and moved off down the hall.

Waiting there, Irene felt sure for a second that when the door opened it would be Samantha Thompson standing inside. Though Irene had never met Samantha, she'd know her on sight. Samantha would be pale and emptied-out-looking from her ordeal, from bleeding the ties that had connected her to her best hopes dry.

Welcome, Irene, Samantha would say. *This is the room where nothing moves, so this is the room for you, isn't it? It doesn't matter how many other rooms they take you to, how many things they have you do inside. This is the one that will always be yours.*

"Come in!" Dr. Bishop said.

4

Irene opened the door—what choice did she have?—and stepped through.

No Samantha, of course. Only Dr. Bishop sitting across the room, in a chair.

Foolishness again.

Irene's mother would have called everything about this room foolishness. She had a sister, Irene's aunt Gloria, who'd had analysis done—who'd remained unmarried longer than Irene's mother felt was prudent and had become, along the way, pretentious, self-absorbed, and silly. She'd taken several trips alone to Europe as a middle-aged woman, before the war, and it was during one of those trips that she'd gone to a psychoanalyst. For years afterward she wouldn't stop talking about everything she felt she'd uncovered, though Irene's mother had said, *But Gloria, what on earth difference can any of that make?* Aunt Gloria was puffy-faced, with thick distorting spectacles, behind which her eyes were always watery. Hearing her talk fawningly of hypnosis had grown the scorn Irene had always felt for her larger. The idea of laying oneself out for display like that, as if one couldn't be trusted with one's own thoughts. As if somebody else could know better. Irene feared susceptibility to this kind of foolishness herself, eventually, if she couldn't keep the weight where it was supposed to be.

And the idea of opening herself up to Dr. Bishop, of all people. Somehow it seemed that if she gave Dr. Bishop what she wanted, if she let her inside, she herself, Irene, would disappear. Irene felt sure that there could be room for only one of them.

Well, Dr. Bishop could make Irene come here, could make her talk, even, but she couldn't make Irene tell her anything worth knowing. That was what Irene decided, in the doorway.

Dr. Bishop regarded Irene from her upholstered chair across this room, which was the size of two of the bedrooms joined together but lower-ceilinged than the large public rooms downstairs. A strange new cavity inside this house's body.

Irene said, "Before I forget, I wanted to tell you: I saw a mouse in my bedroom this morning." She hadn't even thought to tell Dr. Hall this. It hadn't seemed like a fact that had anything to do with him.

Dr. Bishop's brow gathered. "I'll speak to the maid." She paused, peered at Irene. "It upset you in some way, this mouse?"

"Who likes mice?"

"We'll take care of it. Now, please." She gestured to a couch, floral patterned like something from a sunny sitting room—and that, Irene realized, was what this large, low room must once have been. The drawn drapes (a swirling botanical pattern here, bright flowers and green vines) had changed it, but there was a vanity against one wall and a writing desk against another, and the chair the doctor occupied was a visitor's chair. In this house's prior life, women would have sat here to spend some of their too-abundant time.

"Do I really have to lie down?" Irene said.

"It's best."

Reclining, Irene found her flesh felt ticklish and exposed. Dr. Bishop made her feel doubly watched, by the doctor and somehow by herself too. She kept imagining what she might look like through the chill blue screen of Dr. Bishop's gaze. Prostrate and defenseless—dull earth for digging in.

The doctor moved to a chair positioned behind the couch. Irene raised her eyes to the ceiling and caught the movement of

Dr. Bishop's pencil in the periphery in the same way she'd caught the mouse's movement.

"You're going to hide back there?"

"It's how we do things."

"Who is *we*?"

"Practitioners of psychoanalysis. More immediately, the two of us."

"We're in this together, then."

"Of course."

Irene rocked her body a little. "How common is it to be a doctor *and* a psychoanalyst, I wonder?"

"It's not unheard of," Dr. Bishop said. "I doubled my specialties, that's all. Though the therapy provided here isn't quite like the therapy provided elsewhere. Now, are you comfortable, Mrs. Willard?"

"Sure." Irene did consider the question of comfort: the weight and how carrying it felt, which was not comfortable; the way she felt pinned by it to the couch; her sense that she might move her limbs all she liked, but the movement would only be wheel-spinning around that fixed point. Waiting for something there, in that still place, to move, though it never had before, and why should it now? She couldn't begin to imagine what that movement would feel like, even. So every hope she had depended on something that felt impossible.

She should probably tell Dr. Bishop about these thoughts. They were likely the kind of thoughts this therapy was meant to uncover, truths that pinned the still, central point of her spinning mind, and she'd come here for this doctor to try to help her—she understood that. In theory, she did. It was just that the understanding stopped a fingertip away from her. What actually touched Irene was the knowledge that she wasn't ever, not ever, going to say these things out loud to this woman.

"Could you tell me more about the point of this part, maybe?" she said.

"Well, Mrs. Willard—Irene—a mind is a layered thing. We're trying to reach the deeper layers together so we can assess whether anything there might be causing trouble."

"Trouble for my babies?"

"Let's just say that in this room you and I are trying to make room for your motherhood to fill you."

Irene thought of George's cousin Elizabeth, loose-jointed from being so full and then so empty.

"We'll begin today with your own original family," Dr. Bishop continued. "Tell me, what is its makeup?"

"I have a mother and a father, as people do. Two brothers."

"Older or younger?"

"Older, both."

"How much?"

"Four years and two."

Dr. Bishop waited.

"Am I doing something wrong?" Irene asked.

"Our talk time will be most useful if you offer a bit more. I would love to know your brothers' names, for instance, and what they're each like."

"George and Herb. They're men, menlike. I doubt most people could tell them apart."

"You're not most people, though, are you? You're their sister."

Irene exhaled, wriggled her fingers at her sides as if she were floating on her back in a pond. (She had done that, naked. George, her George, swimming naked with her, had caught her to him and lifted her out of the cold water to press her against his skin. Strange to have that memory visit her now.) "George is oldest. He's a banker, very serious, just like my father. Really he might as well *be* my father. Herb is funnier. He runs an insurance firm in Hartford."

Dr. Bishop's pencil swished like the sweep of small, dry wings. "Interesting that your husband and your oldest brother have the same name, isn't it?" she said.

"A common name."

"We may come back to that. Tell me more about your parents."

"My father manages the town department store. I could count on one hand the number of real conversations I've ever had with him. He always left that part to my mother."

"*Why* do you think you're unable to talk to your father?"

"Why can't anybody talk to somebody else?"

"But your mother—you do find you can talk to her?"

Irene remembered the way the bell of blood had hollowed out her mother's face. "Some of the time." She shifted on the couch, feeling Dr. Bishop hovering out of sight like a god who'd never had a human problem.

"Let's try a different tack," said Dr. Bishop. "Please list for me all the words that come to mind when you think of your father."

"Words?"

"Just begin with the very first word you think of, then allow the list to continue. Don't worry at all about sense."

"Do my feelings about my father seem important to you?"

"It's just a starting point. I'm trying to determine if anything about your life might be causing stress, for you and, consequently, for the fetus."

Irene imagined a dark river snaking from her mind to her midsection and tendrilling.

"My father," she said. "Old. Boring. Dusty, irascible, inflexible, unsympathetic, jowly, sleepy, throat-clearing, coffee-drinking, fussy about egg eating, smells like shoe polish, newspaper-reading, says *the trouble is* a lot, numbers, numbers, numbers, numbers." She stopped. "How was that?" she said.

"Try to let your thinking relax. You aren't really allowing yourself irrational leaps."

"Are *you*?" Irene said.

"Irene, I'm trying to help you." Irene heard a rustle of cloth and smelled rose perfume, which meant Dr. Bishop was leaning closer. "The problems we're looking to address won't lie in the territory of your conscious thoughts, and that's what you've just given me, your conscious thoughts about your father. We're going to have to try, together, to get to a deeper place."

The weight like a black sucking hole, deepest deep.

"I have a question," Irene said. "Can I ask you a question? Or is that against the rules?"

A slight pause. "Of course."

"Do you have children, you and Dr. Hall?"

"No, I never really had a maternal bent."

"Isn't that funny?"

"The way I've always explained it is that the painter just paints the picture, he's perfectly content not to own it." Dr. Bishop laughed at her own line. "My work takes up that space in my life."

"And Dr. Hall never minded?" Irene tried to make the question sound as sharp as it was.

"He knew quite early on. It seemed important to be clear."

The idea of that: a husband knowing from the start there wouldn't be children. Irene found herself picturing George's face, enormous and sunlit, the way it looked hovering over her in their bedroom in the mornings. The sense she'd had ever since he got home from overseas was that if she looked long enough at this face she might see right through it to the pit of need beneath.

Dr. Bishop sighed. Irene heard her pencil tap once, twice. "Perhaps that's enough for our first day."

On her way back to her room, partway down the line of their bedroom doors, Irene saw the mouse again. It darted across the threshold of a door someone had left open, there and then not there. She peered closer at the place where it had been. It stayed gone.

Many mice in the world. Many un-impossible versions of this story. It had disappeared too fast anyway to read any familiarity in the human shade of the hairless paws, the flick of the tail, the hue of the fur, the blurred saddle of the blood spot on the back.

She hadn't even gotten a good look at it. How could she think she'd seen blood?

*

Lying down in her room that afternoon, Irene felt like a bunglingly picked lock. Her thoughts—had Dr. Bishop loosed them somehow, in spite of Irene?—circled from Dr. Bishop to the mouse to Dr. Bishop again, and all her muscles were sore, as if she'd been fending something off. Had she actually tensed her body while she was answering Dr. Bishop's questions? It was the middle of this day, these were the brightest hours it would offer, and here Irene was, lying around in the dark like an ill person, waiting for motion she was starting to know would not be coming, not this time either. If she did too much more of this, she thought she might actually lose her mind.

So she decided to get up. Set out. Wend down stairs and down halls a little, just to move, because *she* could move, at least. Just to feel more like a self she recognized.

As she crept through this house, into places where she had no business being, Irene could have sworn she felt the walls lean toward her ever so slightly.

She went down to the first floor, took the hallway opposite the one that led to the dining room and ballroom, and passed the doctors' study door, which was closed. A ways down the hall she started turning handles. Most of the doors were locked, but she kept turning, and whenever one gave she pushed her way in. All were empty. A sitting room with a ceiling dark and polished as a floor, a carpet with an intricately dizzying design, and furniture arranged in visitation patterns: social clusters of easy chairs and sofas that seemed to have been whispering right before she entered. A music room where a grand piano presided like a cranky aunt, lid up. Did someone here play?

Along the back wall of this room, Irene saw, or thought she saw, the scurrying mouse again—more of the wrong movement, seen instead of felt.

She walked right out and shut the door behind her.

Books clogged the next unlocked room. In the middle of the floor lay a bearskin rug, mouth snarling, showing all its teeth— the bear might have been flattened by all the books before some- body replaced them. From above the mantel presided a portrait of a gray-haired, puff-chested man in a dark suit, striking the pose of a classical king, contrapposto, the better to look like all the other rulers of all the prior realms. No doubt he was one of Dr. Bishop's ancestors, maybe even the builder of the bloody victorious ball- room and the banquet hall and this room too, this whole mam- moth house. He had very light blue eyes just like Dr. Bishop's, Irene saw, before she turned her back on him.

The surprise of a conservatory next, a room made of win- dows to hoard the light the women were all deprived of, teeming with plants that someone must come in to water and tend. Irene stood in the center, breathing in the plant smell, the dirt smell, the heat like a rushed, imported summer. What was it about plants indoors that made them look so strange? Bright lilies hung in bas- kets from the rafters and dangled their fleshy lips: they proved as thick and rubbery as they looked when she touched them. Orchids contorted themselves in pots on the sills, making their beautiful, nonsensical shapes, every edge frilled. Great fountains of ferns frothed in large pots on the floor, and spiky, giant greenery she couldn't name, sharp enough, it looked, to cut.

This room of plants felt like a secret the house had been trying to keep from her, and she liked that she'd discovered it. But sweat beaded on Irene's upper lip. She wiped it away. Did all this light in fact feel jarring? Could it be hurting the weight somehow? She left, to be *on the safe side.*

Next, another sitting room, this one all in blue where the last one had been gold. Maybe there'd prove to be a variation in every color. Maybe the portrait king had walked down these halls at some point naming colors for other people to build rooms around. Far too many rooms in this house, and Irene was seeing only a small number of them. Imagine how much was inside all the locked ones. How many high-arched windows with heavy, closed curtains, and cold fireplaces of all shapes and sizes like portals to other places, and hard sofas, unread books, stopped clocks.

How many places for ever more failed women to eventually fill.

At the end of the hall Irene found a dim veranda, like a half-closed eye, with winter's last gray snowdrift still slumped against its back corner. She grasped the railing and gazed out across the broad lawn. George was somewhere on the other end of all this space. Doing what? She hated that she had no answer, that she was back to a life in which she didn't know. But in twenty-five weeks Irene would get to leave here and rejoin him.

Or sooner if everything went wrong, if the stirring she was waiting for never came.

I'm doing my best, she thought at George, *I swear I am,* and wondered if it was true.

When Irene came back inside, Margaret was watching her from partway down the hall.

"What are you doing, Irene?" Margaret said.

"Just checking the weather. I lose any sense of what it's like outside, don't you? We might as well be in a hole in the ground."

Margaret shrugged. "We aren't supposed to be wandering around, you know. And it's nicer inside anyway." She curled her arms protectively around herself as if she were cold, though her face was flushed.

"Margaret, have you been crying?"

Irene noticed suddenly—it was the suggestion of crying, maybe, that made her see—that Margaret wasn't actually all that thick at the middle, where her hands rested. Not nearly as thick as Pearl, though the two of them were at almost the exact same point.

"I just had my therapy session with Dr. Bishop," Margaret said. "It's *hard* talking about everything, isn't it? But good. I feel so much better after."

"Really?"

"You don't?"

"I've only been to one. Maybe it takes a while."

"I felt better right away. I wonder if you aren't opening yourself up to it."

"Margaret, there's no gold star to be awarded here," Irene said. "There's just do our babies live or don't they."

Margaret gave an irritated little shake of her head and turned to go.

*

For a number of days then, Irene tried to settle in, the way she was supposed to. She had her daily examinations every late morning, during which she tried to read Dr. Hall's face for signs. Better than endlessly reading the heavy quiet at her own middle, or seeing and then losing sight of a mouse out of the corner of her eye. Dr. Hall kept smiling at her, which she tried to find reassuring. She had therapy with Dr. Bishop every other early afternoon and took a kind of pleasure in pushing Dr. Bishop's voice to the point of just-audible frustration, making the unnervingly controlled mirror-face pinch, giving some of her own misery to this double of herself to carry instead.

"Why are you toying with her, though?" George said on the phone.

"I don't know, to pass the time," Irene said.

"You must be able to find other ways of doing that." George's voice held real impatience, and Irene thought about trying to tell him about time here, about the long rests after lunch, how strange the dark was, the stasis that came from always occupying the same somnolent gloom. But George never got upset with her, almost never. She didn't say it.

The first of April arrived. At the end of breakfast, the doctor and doctor appeared in the doorway. "We have something new for you all today, ladies," Dr. Hall said.

"What kind of thing?" Irene asked.

"A spring addition to our schedule—you'll see."

You'll see, on this day, sounded like a threat. Irene would have liked to point this out to someone, but only if that someone were George. One April Fool's Day in high school he'd painted her bicycle blue, for a trick but also because he knew it was her favorite color. She'd put pepper in his water cup at lunch. They weren't the same, she knew that.

The women were sent up to their rooms for their coats. Then they all filed out into the pale sunshine, blinking like surfaced deep-sea creatures. "This way," Dr. Bishop said. She and Dr. Hall set off. With their white coats hidden under outercoats, they might have been any couple out for a stroll.

To the side of the house, right where the lawn's manicuring ended—just past the end of one of the two enormous wings—dirt had been plowed up neatly in rows and enclosed with a small wire fence. It looked as if the house's massive arm had scraped this raw patch into the earth.

"Gardening!" Dr. Hall proclaimed. "We'll be growing our own vegetables this spring, and you all get to do the planting and tending. You'll garden every Tuesday and Thursday morning." The same block as calisthenics on Mondays and Wednesdays. The doctors had probably sketched the calendar out atop one of their matching desks, taking pleasure in the symmetry of the programming blocks just as they must take pleasure in the symmetry of the desks themselves, and rooms, and wings.

Rosy-cheeked in the cold, Dr. Bishop held Dr. Hall's arm. She looked, touching him, like a woman in love with every last choice she had ever made. "There's something about coaxing one's own food out of the ground, don't you think?" she said. "It's the kind of experience we've lost to our supermarkets and all those frozen cubed bits of things. We're reconnecting our ties to nature here."

"It seems a little too cold still for planting, doesn't it?" Margaret said—tentatively, but a challenge was a challenge. Was Irene rubbing off? She hadn't meant to.

"This is the right time for the hardiest early-spring vegetables. Your broccolis, your cauliflowers," said Dr. Hall.

Margaret was about to say something more, but Dr. Bishop spoke first. "Phillips has already tilled, so your work today will be nice and easy. We'll distribute the seedlings, and you'll just press them into the soil and pat them down," she said.

They all went into the enclosure, which gave Irene the feeling of being herded. They each knelt before a patch. The ground was cold, hard, but Irene imagined the meat of her knees softening and loosening the dirt. Still, the gardener must have had a time, making such deep black fresh-turned gashes, and Irene wondered what he thought of the pack of them. There he was, moving silently in their midst to distribute the pots: when he handed Irene hers, he was already looking ahead down the row.

"Any advice, Phillips?" Dr. Bishop asked.

Grudgingly, Phillips said, "Use your fingers to get beneath the roots in the pot, all the way down. Don't rip any. Then you can lift or you can tip out onto your hand. When you plant, space them out. Make sure you cover the roots."

Irene pushed her fingers into the pot. The dirt was warmer than the air—these plants must have been raised inside some greenhouse and just brought out. The whole root structure came out in a clump, full of bright white thready veins so slight it seemed impossible they could hold that fist-sized mass of earth in place between them. She put the plant into the ground, cringing on its behalf at the cold. Then she patted until it could hold up its own head, with those too-large leaves.

Dirt stuffed her nails now. Not giving them gloves had been a choice, probably, so they could feel nature unmediated.

"They'll die, mark my words, I hate to say it," Margaret said, softly but smugly. In the patch of ground to Irene's side she was planting something with many small shoots instead of Irene's single, reedy ones. "I'm a gardener, at home."

Of course Margaret was. "It won't make a great picture for all of us if they freeze and shrivel up," Irene said.

"This is the very earliest edge of when it's possible to plant, even broccoli."

"That's what you have there?"

Margaret gave her seedlings a dismissive look. "In a manner of speaking. My broccoli at home is famous. That and my zucchini, and my roses."

Irene imagined Margaret planting, pruning, fostering, trying to fill up her yard so it would look like a page from the storybooks in which the happy mothers gardened. Trying to produce enough to occupy all her empty space.

Pearl, past Margaret in the line, said, "I never seem to get anywhere with roses. We get too many aphids."

"Oh but Pearl, you just use white vinegar! Try it, once you're home. It'll change your life."

Irene placed this tone Margaret was using as the same one she'd heard for years from women with children, telling her how simple it was to fix her troubles right up with all the remedies she should try straightaway, all the things that had worked for them. "Aren't you a font of wisdom," Irene said.

"I'll try it, if I have the time," Pearl said. "Joe doesn't like me out there too much."

She said his name as if afraid of being overheard. Irene felt she was learning some things about Joe.

"I end up supplying the whole neighborhood. Not this year, though—I'm busy growing something else." Margaret put a hand to her belly. The right shape but—yes, Irene saw again—so small. What was Margaret feeling there? Was she feeling anything?

(Why had Irene still felt nothing? When would it be too late, finally, to keep hoping this time?)

Pearl brushed dirt off her hands and reached for another seedling. "You know," she said, "without the coat, I keep looking up and seeing Dr. Bishop out of the corner of my eye and thinking she's you, Irene. Isn't that funny? You know, how did Irene get all the way over there?"

Irene would have liked to be over there. Anywhere else, really.

When Dr. Bishop's roaming circuit brought her near, Irene asked, "What's this one, Doctor?"

Dr. Bishop peered. "That's the cabbage."

The walls of the garden Irene had discovered were visible over Dr. Bishop's shoulder, farther back, past where the line of the mowing stopped. They looked almost like rubble, the way they were losing bricks from their tops and sides irregularly, making a shape that both drew Irene's gaze and unsettled her. Irene pointed toward them. "Why not just have us garden in there?"

Dr. Bishop followed the line of Irene's eyes. "Oh, it would have been weeks of work to clear enough ground."

"Nobody uses it?"

"Not in years. Never, properly speaking. My grandfather put it in when he built the house, it was the kind of fashionable thing he liked, but I don't think anyone ever really took to it, not even him. My father always said it was my grandfather's attempt to wall off nature for himself, and he lost interest as soon as he figured out he could only get part of it inside." Her tone in speaking about her father was reproving, but Irene thought there was some buried fondness to it too. "I used to play there as a girl, when I didn't want to be found."

"Your grandfather's the one who built this place?"

"That's right."

Irene bet he was the light-eyed king from the portrait she'd discovered, then.

"What was he like?"

"He died before I was born, but by all accounts he was a real"— she paused—"force." Dr. Bishop looked past Irene, down the line of other women. "Well, keep up the good work, Mrs. Willard." She strolled on.

Irene looked down and brushed off some dirt that had fallen onto her cabbage leaf. "Godspeed," she whispered to it.

Pearl chuckled, though Irene hadn't meant to be heard, then looked back down at her own plant. "May you grow nice and strong until we can eat you," she said.

"The metaphor does break down a little there."

When they were finally allowed to leave their enclosure, the women all held the aching smalls of their backs. They made their way back to the house, more slowly than they'd walked away from it. Inside the main doors, Irene saw Dr. Bishop touch Margaret's elbow and steer her off to the side, up the stairs.

Maybe Margaret was getting an extra of those sessions she loved so much. Maybe Dr. Bishop had noticed how she was taking to them. In any case, it was none of Irene's business. Irene didn't really know Margaret at all.

*

During afternoon rest time, Irene stole out of the house. Back to the garden, because this morning had reminded her it was a place she could revisit, and because she was tired of thinking about the strange, bloody half-glimpsed mouse and wondering if she'd see it again at any moment. This kind of waiting, at least, she could take steps to end: she would find the mouse corpse and look at it long enough to take the mystery out of it for herself, make a picture like an end-stop she could call up behind her eyes whenever the question came to her.

Irene turned the rhythm of her breath into a tuneless little song as she walked. She passed the seedlings, tiny in their rows, and gave them a wave. They looked all right so far, she thought.

There was a spring to the ivy when she pulled it back from the garden gate—she hadn't noticed that the last time. Everything inside was still hopeless gray, hopeless brown, but when she broke a twig, tentative green veined its center. Maybe Margaret would turn out to be wrong, maybe it was late enough to plant after all.

She could still see the top of the house from in here, looming from above the wall like an enormous beached ship. No one inside would be able to see her, though; she was too far away, well guarded from any sight line even if the windows had been uncovered. The garden walls, the bricks, were a thousand variegated shades of red. Concrete balustrades ran along their tops, making Irene think of play soldiers stationed at intervals along a rampart, some of them crumbling now, some of them missing, the ones still in place patchy with lichen and the sun. The ivy climbed through all of it, trying to pull it down.

Had the child Dr. Bishop pulled at this ivy and poked at this dirt with sticks? Or maybe she'd never done childish things: maybe playing for her had been dissecting the seedpods of plants, the innards of dead beetles, the legs of grasshoppers, to see how they worked and how they were fitted together, something she wouldn't have been able to tell without taking them apart. If she'd found a mouse, she might have dissected even that.

Irene wished she knew. It felt as if knowing what Dr. Bishop had done then would help Irene know better what Dr. Bishop was doing now.

She neared the fountain. Such a small creature, that mouse. Such a small brain. What had it thought as it tried again and again to run up the unrunnable sides? It probably hadn't thought at all, only felt. The slipping of its pads on dirty marble, the tipping point, and the plummeting. It could have plummeted itself bloody, trying over and over, its little mind capable only of that one message: *run-run-run-run-run*. Irene regretted now covering the dead mouse with the leaf as if trying to hide it, as if it were something shameful. Better to have left it to the honest openness of its own rotting—because of course the mouse would be festering by now. If the leaf was still there, she would remove it, though she knew she'd have to turn away. Smells brought heaves so readily, and might all the way up until the baby came, according to Dr. Hall.

But Irene had come to the fountain and the leaf wasn't here, the mouse wasn't here. Not on the ground either. Like a dark twist on some nursery rhyme: *The mouse corpse fled, halloo, hullay / It left for good today, today.* Irene sat down on the fountain's edge, rough, catching at her stockings, the concrete here too having worn to unevenness. She held her kneecaps, sinking the pads of her fingers into that new plumping (that also would keep on as long as the baby did, probably), the skin still stained with dirt beneath her stockings from the morning's work.

So she'd set the mouse out on the brim, and something had found it and eaten it, that was all. Yes, she'd wanted a good look at it, to fix it stationary in her mind again, but the fact that it wasn't here didn't mean it had gone to the house to haunt her by running through room after room. No call here for Dr. Bishop's *irrational leaps.* It had just been eaten: that was what made sense. Something had scented it in the air. That sweetish, fruity rotting smell. Followed the smell to the fountain brim, sidled right up, seized the mouse, and gulped it down in all its festering, reeking.

Irene could taste it.

Bile filled her throat. She leaned over and retched into the fountain, and kept retching, as if her body could never be empty enough. She held the crouch for a time when the last wave dissipated, waiting—more waiting—to see if another was coming.

After enough time had passed that she felt safe, Irene stood slowly, took a shallow breath, and wiped her tearing eyes. Spit once into the bushes to clear the taste. Then she left the garden. Her legs had mostly stopped shaking by the time she was passing through the house's mouth-door. She walked toward the staircase, which would carry her to her room and more endless rest.

But low down along the wall of the foyer, a dark fleck of motion stopped her. She turned toward it and caught an almost clear glimpse of the mouse with its blood saddle before it turned the corner into the hallway.

No, Irene thought, *no, no.*

She set off after.

She hurried. When she turned the corner there was another disappearing flash of it, turning out of the hall. She turned too. No mouse in sight, just the book room from before, with its bearskin rug and its portrait. Irene took a breath. She tried imagining the child Dr. Bishop in here, in front of her.

And this time she found she could do it. When you watch and wait long enough, maybe, you see things in the end. Because there she was, on the bearskin rug before the fire, beneath the portrait, sitting on her father's lap. She had that gleaming-bright hair already. The same face that was, already, like Irene's face, until you looked closer. She was thumping her heels in fancy shoes against the floor. Her father was talking to her, telling her stories. Irene listened too. She wanted to catch whatever he might be saying about princesses, gold, unicorns. Dragons.

"Louey-Lou, what you *think* you're thinking is only an eensy-teensy tip of the iceberg," this father told his daughter, and put his hand lightly on her head. "Most of your mind is like a dark room. Inside that room is the key."

"Where's your room, Daddy?" the girl asked.

He laughed. "That's the whole point, Louey, no one can get into their room by themselves, and anyway, we wouldn't have the foggiest idea how to understand what's in there."

The girl reached up to touch her father's temples, pressed her fingers to the sides of his laughing-crying eyes. "Then how do you fix it?"

"A special kind of doctor called a psychoanalyst helps you."

"Who's your doctor, Daddy?"

"Me? Oh, honey, I wasn't talking about me. I was just talking. I'm a hopeless case, I'm afraid—he made sure of that." Her father nodded to the king in the portrait.

The little girl followed his eyes and was quiet for a moment. "Wasn't he a nice man?"

"He was the very opposite of a nice man. *If I say it, I do it.*

That's what he always said." The father's voice dropped and growled for the words, his mouth twisted, as if he were pretending to be an ogre in a story. "He never cared about who he had to flatten to do what he wanted. He *wanted* to flatten them."

The little girl's stricken face.

A woman came into the room then, to the side of Irene, quavering about something Irene couldn't hear.

The father rose, singing, to go.

Don't leave her there, Irene wanted to shout. The little girl with her eyes on the portrait, spread on the bearskin like an offering. How could her father not see what he was doing, leaving her there that way?

And since Irene was the one who was imagining all of this, why couldn't she stop him from doing it?

Then the father cast a glance over his shoulder. He looked for long enough to show Irene that he did see, he knew what he was doing, bringing a child into this house, leaving her in his place. Irene watched him watching and knew that he too almost expected the man in the portrait to move, at any moment, toward the girl.

What would the grandfather do with her? What did he want? The sort of man who would build a garden so he could wall off nature itself, mark it as his—what would he do with a girl?

Fear spread sickly across the back of Irene's neck, and she closed her eyes, because she didn't want to watch whatever this was. *When I open my eyes again I'll see the mouse, that's all I'll see, no child Dr. Bishop no father no portrait,* she thought. *I'll be able to tell it's just an ordinary mouse with no blood on it at all. That's what will happen next.*

Inside the dark, quiet moment she'd made, a series of small twitches played against the wall of her lower abdomen. A feeling she would never have felt if she hadn't created this stillness for it. The sensation was like a deep and tiny tail, flicking, then flicking past.

A flesh-colored tail.

Then a tiny tapping like the tentative touch of the smallest paws, one, then two, trying to run.

Little mouse.

It was alive in there. It was really alive.

Irene opened her eyes. The room was empty.

MOTH

5

To bed, to bed, to see if she could fall asleep and dream something simpler. It was early, but surely no one would tell Irene it was too early to lie down when that was all they ever wanted her to do.

She tried having a talk with herself there in the dark. The important thing that had happened, the real thing, was the moving she'd felt. The proof of life, the quickening, here in this place where everything had been slowed to a stop. The rest of it wasn't real and meant nothing. Maybe the shots they were giving her or the too-much quiet or even the pregnancy itself or all of them together were making her see things.

She laid her hand on the hardness between her hip bones, under the blankets.

Little mouse, are you making me see things that aren't there?

Was that an answer, that feeling like a twitch deep inside, or just a twitch? From the little mouse's body or her own? How terrible not to feel sure. How unfair that even the feeling she'd been waiting for, now that it had come, turned out to be only a new question.

Out into the hall, then, to telephone George. The telephone had been set up at the end of the hallway on a small table, with an armchair before it. Irene gave the operator her and George's number. When things frightened her it had always been George she called. Once from a pay phone late at night, walking with some people she'd met at a party whom she'd suddenly understood she didn't like at all, and George had come to get her, right away; another time from her own house, after her mother had screamed at her, *Why do you say such awful things?* And Irene had screamed back, *Why do you say anything at all, no one ever wants to hear it, why don't you just stop?* Once from her brother's house when in the middle of dinner her sister-in-law had touched her own curved belly and, Irene had felt sure, looked directly at Irene, on purpose, while she did.

And once too from the back office of a store in town where the manager had brought Irene and left her alone to make her call, the little silver-backed hairbrush centered on his desk like some spiky marine creature. Saying into the receiver, *I don't know why I took it, I don't want it, we don't need it, not anymore, I just couldn't stop myself somehow,* and George asking for the manager to be put on the phone. The manager nodding as he listened.

After he hung up, the man had closed his hand over Irene's and looked at her tragically and said that she was free to go, that he understood. Irene had wanted to spring at him across the desk and claw his eyes out.

But now Irene wanted George to say to her some version of whatever he'd said to that man, whatever explanation he'd given for how Irene had turned unrecognizable, irrational, hysterical, but in a temporary and expected way. She wanted him to talk her back into understanding herself. She asked to be connected and listened to the ringing of the line. Would she tell George the baby had moved? Not yet, she thought. She wanted to feel surer first, and less afraid of the way the movements had come to her.

The ringing was going on longer than she'd expected. Maybe she herself would answer, the Irene of before all this, and current Irene would have to figure out how to tell past Irene about what was coming.

"George Willard speaking," George said.

For a bad second, Irene wasn't sure she recognized his voice.

"It's me."

"Reny! You all right?"

The worry made him hers again. Irene pressed her lips right up against the receiver. "Course, I just wanted to talk to you, is that allowed?"

"Oh, well, good." He exhaled a laugh and the phone caught it like a burst of static. Irene closed her eyes and tried to feel that puff of air on her cheek. "So, then, how are you doing there? With Tweedledee and Tweedledum, MDs?"

"Honestly? I'm crawling out of my skin."

"Poor Reny. It's not forever, though."

"Tell me about you. What did you do today?"

"Let's see. I got into the office early—easier to get out of the house in the mornings without you here, I have to say."

"*I* never stopped you leaving."

"You make it so I don't want to go, same difference. So I spend the whole morning on these files Anderson botched the day before, and he comes into my office positive it can't have been his fault . . ."

Irene relaxed her back against the chair and listened to George talking. She let her head tip back to rest too and brought the hand that wasn't holding the phone to her belly again. Another tiny half-movement she couldn't be sure if she'd felt or imagined. *Can you hear him?* The little mouse might be able to hear what George was doing to Irene's body anyway. It would feel the way he slowed her down and washed her out. Such a lovely wash, the sound of him. Irene wished it would never ever stop.

"You're all right, though, really?" George said.

"Sure," Irene said.

"And what have you been doing?"

Irene was aware suddenly of the watchful stillness of the house around her. Was it listening?

If she said what she'd called him to say, what would he hear, and what would he do? This was different from the hairbrush, she saw. This wasn't just a strange, momentary impulse. This might scare him enough that he'd come here and take her home, and then they'd both lose everything.

"Nothing much, really," Irene told him.

Saying it to George made it feel true, or approaching truth. And so George continued telling her about what he'd done.

*

Irene made a rule that when she entered a room or when she sat inside one, she wouldn't look below eye level. No reason to look down at the floor, along walls, into corners. No reason to walk into empty rooms that weren't hers. With how dim everything was in this place—enough to dim a person's thinking, let alone her sight—of course her eyes played tricks, but what trick could matter compared to her mission here? *Fool me once,* she recited to herself. She ate her meals like a good little soldier. She rested. Calisthenics-ized. Weeded the garden patch, where the weeds were growing faster than the seedlings were. She listened to Margaret's stories about her nephews and to Pearl's worries about what Joe had said on the telephone (did they think it meant something that he'd had dinner with their neighbors the Portmans and Mrs. Portman's unmarried sister? "Oh please, you're not dead," Irene told her). She had another shot from Dr. Hall, another therapy session with Dr. Bishop, in which the doctor seemed to be angling to find out if Irene wished she had more female friends.

"Why would I ever want that?" Irene had asked—though she was trying to be more unobjectionable and obedient, in case she'd somehow brought the mouse and the vision upon herself.

Dr. Bishop sighed.

Irene hadn't told either doctor that she'd thought she'd been feeling movements. She hadn't told anyone. She wasn't sure enough yet: there'd been more stirrings, but they were still mere suggestions of feeling. And she worried about the images the feelings trailed, which she knew weren't the right ones. The possible sweep of a tiny tail, the smallest twitch of the smallest paw.

Two new women arrived, which wasn't the ceremony the leavings were: new arrivals were just introduced at dinner. After these dinners, sometimes, the doctors gathered them all to listen to the radio together. Symphonies, radio plays. One night a young man with a very red, sweaty face came in person to read to them from a hobby history he was writing of the Berkshires. They were given to understand he was a descendant of another of these big estates. He delivered a long, admiring passage about Henry Knox and the Revolutionary War and the *noble train of artillery,* which had carried the spoils of Fort Ticonderoga to armies in Boston through the Berkshire region in the dead of winter. "Those courageous men," he read, his voice climbing to a startling pitch, "those heroes, laboring to bring their iron cannon and their shells through the punishing snow, over hill and through icy river, to win them their freedom—what astonishment would they feel if they were to see the civilized retreats their descendants would erect on that same ground!" He listed the names and characters associated with these *great houses*—that was what he kept calling them. When he came to *the residence of the Bishop family, built by John Bishop,* Dr. Bishop stood and spun in space, as if the house were a dress she was wearing.

But I saw, Irene wanted to tell her, *I think I saw, I think I know what he was. How can you smile?*

Foolishness to believe she could know such a thing. Why couldn't she stop believing it?

A week passed.

Word carried down the halls on a Tuesday that Marian Henth had gone up to the third floor, then that she'd had her baby. All was well. The little troupe of supporting doctors and their attendant nurses had come onstage only briefly and gone off again, no longer needed. The women spread this news, and the way they said Marian's name was saturated with an envy so feverish it became, almost, hatred. "I wonder what *she* was feeling while we all slept last night," Pearl said.

(Marian had felt as if she were conducting some great force through her body, like a slowed-down, repeated lightning strike.)

Marian and her baby were up on the third floor recovering, the two of them, for one day, two days, four, and there was a new spring in Dr. Hall's step and a triumphant flush in Dr. Bishop's cheek.

Then came the morning when Marian descended the stairs to leave them all behind forever. Irene knew to be part of the swarm in the foyer this time. She wanted to get a good, full look at her, this newly besainted, this woman freshly raised up into the world of mothers, who proved that moving that way was possible. She wanted a look at the baby that had moved her. The twenty or so women waited below while Marian took her display-walk down, all of them inhabiting a version of the patterns the house had been designed for: Marian had turned herself into their debutante, the belle of this ball, and they were all spectating. Irene felt the woman beside her—Nancy Montgomery, seven months along, prone to vibrating like a tuning fork in sympathy with any external excitement—shifting back and forth and brushing against Irene's arm, too keyed up to stand still.

A small, dark, shadowy flickering along the far wall caught the corner of Irene's eye, but she fixed that eye on the new mother instead. Marian's plain face looked pale and thin, and new light came from it. Her dress hung loose over her lumpy front. She held her husband's arm and picked her way down the display-stair with the care of a person walking on a ship's deck or slippery stones, but her care wasn't the same as shyness. What a wide staircase it was, what a vast curve Marian confidently commanded. Dr. Hall went down before her (to catch if she dropped?) and Dr. Bishop behind (to pull back if she slipped?).

The doctors raised their eyes to the group in a pleased way. *You see?*

There in the crook of Marian's arms: the baby.

Marian was close enough now for them to see that the baby was moving its little legs inside the blanket. Its little fists, pulled free from the blanket's folds. The movements seemed random and unintentional as twitches. Its face was red, its eyes were shut, its mouth squinched and gathered and released, and it made a sound. Not a cry, but a sort of grating, a sort of squawk.

Marian paused for a moment at the bottom of the stairs to regard her admirers. Dorothy Steadman, next most pregnant, was trying to stand closest, but Marian gave her nothing special, not now. Because Dorothy was like the rest of them, offstage where Marian was on.

The baby made its sound again, and Marian swung him gently in her arms. "He's hungry," she said, as if she knew. Did she know? "He's always hungry."

What did *always* mean in reference to something that had been alive so short a time?

"*Oh,*" Nancy Montgomery said.

"Oh."

"Oh."

They were looking at the baby, not at Marian at all. They had all drawn in without meaning to, Irene along with the others. They encircled this baby and bent toward him as if toward an irresistible smell.

Pearl said softly, "He's *precious.*"

Marian beamed the way you do when you acknowledge a compliment's truth. For yes, the baby was indisputably precious. Look at the way they were all standing.

Marian's husband gave an impatient smile and put his hand to her back. "We better get him home."

Wise man—if they stayed here any longer, Irene thought she and the other women might pluck this baby right out of Marian's arms to devour him. Couldn't Marian sense the threat? Why would she linger?

But Marian looked at the women as they stared at her baby, and Irene saw that she understood perfectly. She was holding what they'd all wanted for years and years, right in front of them— and she was doing it on purpose, gorging herself on their greed. Who could blame her? How often in life did a person get to taste a moment like this one from the desirable side?

"Good luck, ladies," Marian said, with a sweet mother smile.

Irene filled with enough anger to knock her over.

The new family walked through the door and drove away.

*

Four days after Marian left them, a quiet woman named Sally Pettiner, who'd been at the house for only two weeks, didn't appear at breakfast. An uneasy murmuring rose up from the tables.

"Did she . . . ?" Pearl said.

"She could be on bed rest upstairs," said Margaret, her fingers fidgeting on the handle of her knife.

"Let's ask the doctors," Irene said.

"It's none of our business, it has nothing to do with us," Margaret said.

"Well, I'm asking."

Somehow, though, when the doctors came and sat in their places along the room's edge, Irene didn't ask after all.

*

(Sally felt almost nothing when it slipped from her, had felt all the pain before and after, and was sure the disaster lay in the way feeling and event hadn't matched up.)

*

It was difficult for Irene to keep track of time in this house. Now, mid-April already, spring was arriving while for her nothing much changed. Every couple of days she felt another small mouse-flicker inside her, never pronounced enough to make her certain, and could that mean something? She still hadn't told, still hadn't asked.

The days were empty enough that she left too early to get to the few places she needed to go. She arrived for her therapy with Dr. Bishop one afternoon while the session before hers was still happening, and she could hear voices through the door, which had been left ajar—maybe it was stuffy in there.

"I've been thinking you're exactly right about Rebecca."

Irene recognized Margaret's voice.

"I must resent her most out of all my sisters because I love her best. She always was my favorite. I couldn't help it. She was the most beautiful baby you've ever seen."

Irene sat on one of the three chairs that had been lined up in the hallway outside this door. She wasn't doing anything wrong by sitting here. It wasn't her fault if she could hear—if they cared, they should be quieter.

"Tell me more about what she looked like as a baby."

So this was what Dr. Bishop sounded like when therapy was going the way she'd intended. When she was pleased with her plans, the same plans that were doing such frightening things to Irene's thoughts. Irene shifted on the hard chair, which was like the one she might have sat in at the doctors' Boston offices during that first appointment; in addition to being uncomfortable, its spindly lines had the wrong scale for this hallway. Irene was surprised the house hadn't simply chewed it up and spit it out.

A dark scurrying caught her eye at the end of the hall, and she twitched her face away.

"She had these big pools of blue eyes. I remember thinking that even at eight years old, that now I knew what books meant about *the pools of her eyes*. And these rosy, plump cheeks. Just stuffed full of joy."

"Do you know who that sounds like to me?"

"Who?"

"You sound a little like you're describing yourself, Margaret."

"Ohhhhhh," Margaret breathed, as if Dr. Bishop had pulled a curtain back to show her something that had been hidden. "You know, she *does* look a little like me. Much prettier, of course, but Rebecca and I both take after Mother, that's what people say. Rebecca's like a beautiful revision of myself."

"Interesting," Dr. Bishop said. "Do you feel you need revising?"

"I suppose so." Tears warped Margaret's voice. "I *love* Rebecca of course, but I think I've always hated her too."

A pause, in which Irene imagined Dr. Bishop leaning over the back of the couch to get a better look at Margaret's face, at her experiment's progress.

Margaret blew her nose. "Even talking about the ugly things helps somehow. Why is that?"

"Do you know what Freud said about women, Margaret? He gave a lecture, a very famous lecture, on femininity, and he said, *You are yourselves the problem.* That always interested me, that and how my obstetrics professors in school were saying the same thing, in their way. A hopeless thing is certainly hopeless if everyone decides it is. That's what I think. When Dr. Hall and I did our study and realized what the drug might allow us to do, I also knew this work, what you and I are doing now, would have to be part of things."

"Well, I've definitely been feeling better. Much better actually, lately," Margaret said. "Would you say I'm looking better, Doctor?" Naked pleading suddenly in the words.

"Oh yes, I think so." Irene could hear the guardedness. Surely Margaret could.

"You know, I keep trying to tell Irene how much this part can help."

After the shock of hearing her own name, Irene found she understood. Margaret was trying to establish a contrast, to convince the doctor and herself that she was exemplary enough to be sure, if anyone could be sure, to leave here with a baby.

"Really?" Dr. Bishop said.

"I do worry for Irene a little."

"Let's keep your focus on your own progress, Margaret."

"Of course."

Irene stood. She walked to the door. "Knock knock," she said, and pushed it right open.

Margaret rose with a flustered smile, wondering, Irene could tell, how much Irene had heard. "Time already?"

"Just about," Dr. Bishop said calmly. She kept any wondering to herself. "Come in, Irene."

Irene drew herself to the side. "Please, Margaret first. We'd better allow the treated to leave the room before the untreated enter."

Margaret shook her head. "It really might help you to take all this a little more seriously." That tone again, and a look thrown over her shoulder—*what did I tell you?*—toward the doctor as she prepared to go past.

"Oh?" Irene said. She let her eyes drift and hang for a long, scornful beat on Margaret's middle.

The house held them all in its stillness for a moment.

"Mrs. Willard," Dr. Bishop said sharply, as wild devastation came over Margaret's face.

I'm sorry, Irene almost said, because she was. What she'd said hadn't really been about Margaret at all. She'd wanted to punish her and Dr. Bishop a little for the pleasure they were taking in themselves, that was all.

Margaret whirled to Dr. Bishop. "Is it all over? I'll be like Sally for sure, won't I? Doctor, it's hopeless, isn't it, and you just don't want to tell me."

Dr. Bishop looked at Irene for a moment. Irene felt scalded.

Then the doctor crossed the room to take Margaret's hand. "No. Margaret, no, of course, I would never let you have hope if it were hopeless." She met Margaret's eyes and spoke steadily. "I will always tell you what you need to know. If there were no hope, you would need to know. Wouldn't you?"

"Yes."

"There we are, then."

"You promise?" Margaret said.

"I promise."

Margaret's face smoothed. She nodded, then turned to go. As she passed Irene, she said, "You're *horrible*."

Irene sat on the sofa. Dr. Bishop took her time closing the door behind Margaret. Irene had made her think twice about leaving doors open.

When the doctor came back around to her chair—ready, Irene could see, with her reprimand—Irene said, "Should you really have promised her like that?" because it seemed important to speak first.

"I didn't promise her she'd have a healthy delivery. No one can do that. I just promised I'd tell her the truth."

"I don't think that's what she heard."

"Let's talk about what *you* said, Irene," said Dr. Bishop. "I'm wondering how you feel about what you just did."

Irene felt better, now that Margaret was out of the room, now that she didn't have to look at Margaret's face. "I don't think I'm the one doing anything here," she said.

"Mrs. Crowe might disagree."

"I'm not responsible for how she feels. Who is she to me? And anyway, *I'm* not sticking her with needles, locking her in here to talk to me all the time."

Making her see and hear impossible things that might be there or might not be.

Dr. Bishop watched Irene in a way that suggested she could wait and make Irene wait with her for as long as necessary.

Irene sighed. "I didn't mean to make her really unhappy. I don't especially like her, but I don't have anything against her. I just say things."

"What are you thinking before you say a thing like what you just said?"

"The thing comes to me, I say it, that's all."

"Lie back, please," Dr. Bishop told her.

"I'm getting very good at lying down in this place." Irene laid herself flat and folded her hands on her belly. The little mouse gave a little stirring, she thought.

Dr. Bishop, now invisible behind the sofa's back, said, "We'll try a dream analysis today. Please tell me as much as you can remember about a vivid dream you've had. Every detail you can recall."

Irene knew right away which dream she should tell Dr. Bishop about: the one she'd had over and over while George was gone, of climbing the stairs of her house and opening her bedroom door to find paint or ink, dark and black, all over the room. The first time just on the carpet, the next time on the carpet and some of the walls, then all the walls, then all the walls and the desk. The floor and all the walls and the desk and the bed. The last time there'd been paint coming out from under the door before she'd even opened it. She didn't want the paint on her—if she touched it she'd never get it off her again—but she was going into the room, she didn't seem to have a choice, and she would have to touch it. She knew somehow, with shame, that all the paint had come from her at some earlier point she couldn't remember, like she was some squeezed squid. The dream told her that even if it took a war to create the distance, George was lucky to be well away, because even a war could not be so corrupting as she was. You could wash a war off you. So she'd thought then, anyway.

But talking about something like this dream, what good could it do anyone? Anyway, she'd woken up before touching the paint, at the last possible minute, every time.

There was also the way she'd walked into a room of this house and seen a girl offered up by her father to the portrait king, and the way she kept seeing mice in the shadows, and if those weren't dreams, then what were they? They were certainly this doctor's fault, whatever they were, and that Irene was also desperate to stay here made it worse.

"You know, I think this house gives me strange dreams," she said. "Funny feelings, this house, this garden. Don't you find that?"

"It's just a house, just a garden," Dr. Bishop said.

"I bet you had some strange dreams, growing up here."

"No stranger than the dreams I'd have had anywhere else, I'm sure."

"Did you have nightmares about your grandfather, I wonder?"

"What an odd question."

"I don't think you get to build a house like this by being nice."

Dr. Bishop gave a startled laugh. "That's probably true. No, I don't think he *was* very nice—from what my father said I always felt lucky I never knew him. I don't recall any dreams about him, though it's true I've always been able to imagine him exactly."

It's the house, Irene wanted to say. *You're living inside him here.* It worried her, how she could think that without even feeling certain of what it meant.

"Does it give you a funny feeling to come from a man like that?" Irene said.

"Well, I'm taking what he built and using it for something good now."

"I wonder if it's that easy."

"Easy? No. Now let's get to your dream, please."

"There *is* a particular dream I've had lots of times," Irene said.

"A recurring dream, that's interesting," said Dr. Bishop. "Tell me about it. Try to relive it as you describe it to me."

"I'm in the house where I grew up, sitting in the living room, and suddenly there's a man at the door. He's dressed all in black. I can't see his face. The door is locked but he's coming in anyway."

"How do you feel, then, in the dream?"

"Afraid, so afraid! So I run out the back door, and I run, and I run, and I look back, and he's chasing me. So I try to run, I try to keep running, but you know, I find that no matter how hard I try, *my legs won't move at all.*"

Irene couldn't resist sitting up for a moment so she could see this land.

"Never heard that one before, have you, Doctor? Tell me, whatever can it mean?"

Dr. Bishop breathed in deeply, breathed out. "If you're quite finished, then, Irene," she said.

*

A few days later, Irene found a large dusky-brown moth on her windowsill. It must have been drawn to her lamp, having crushed its way through some tiny gap in the window frame. She wondered whether moths had any kind of last-second realization about the costs of their appetites before the end. This one might have: it lay only partly at peace, its wings halfway between folded and extended, the edges of one of them ragged. When she pushed it with a fingertip, testing the depth of its death, she saw the dusty scrim its throes had left on the white paint. All was still, now. All the thread-legs stuck up at angles, and the head, the antennae, the mashed wings.

An idea came to Irene. A test.

Keeping her fingertips as light as she could, she pinched the moth and lifted it and slipped it into her pocket.

Through George's whole time overseas, Irene had kept in her pocket an ordinary white button from one of his shirts. She wore only her dresses with pockets and explained to no one, not even herself, why she'd abandoned the others. The button waited on her bedside table at night while she slept, where it could watch her like an eye. All day, while she went about her life, she imagined the warm darkness the button was seeing. She set herself a rule then too: whenever she thought about George she had to flip the button over in her fingers, once and only once, to change its view. If it had been looking in, toward the flesh of her hip, now it would look out, toward him, and vice versa. In this way the button made a live line of connection between them even when his letters dwindled—and they did dwindle and almost stop, a thing she wouldn't have believed, that George should almost completely cease writing to her a few months into the war, as if she and their marriage and their entire life had stopped existing for him.

Irene had no sense, then, of what the button might prefigure. How could she have known that one day she would look back and envy herself for having carried a hidden thing she could simply touch when a thought of it rippled her mind? She and George had been married only six months when he was deployed, and when he left, Irene had never been pregnant. She'd vaguely expected that someday pregnancy would come with the automatic ease she'd thought then it mostly always came with. Yes, she'd known of barren women, but they were pitiful and uniformly old, and it had never really occurred to her that they'd been young once. Why should she have guessed they had anything to do with her?

Once George was home again, Irene had asked him about the letters. She'd been lying on their bed—after the third time, maybe, or the fourth—feeling deflated and achy in that way she always did for a while. Staring at their ceiling, listening to the sounds of George moving around their bedroom, she'd begun to wonder if there might be some hidden rotten heart to the two of them that could explain what was happening, and so she'd asked.

"I'm sorry," George said.

"I just want to know what happened. Did you think you might want a different wife when you got home?"

George looked away. "I didn't know what I would want."

Irene's stomach swooped like she'd fallen.

"I didn't mean it like that," George said quickly. "It's hard to explain. I wasn't a person. I was just feelings: hungry, thirsty, scared, tired. I was trying not to have thoughts, and I couldn't write to you without thinking."

"You made *me* think a lot, not writing."

"Well, Irene." It was the angriest she'd ever heard her name sound in his mouth. "I guess I figured you could manage."

Irene only barely had. Some of her friends had walked around with their most recent letters from their husbands where she kept her button. She wouldn't have wanted letters like theirs, full of a stiff performance she and George had never had with each other—mediocre letters through and through—but why should these other women get letters when she got none? Still, George was right, she understood, that this was nothing compared to what he must have been seeing, which he'd refused to tell her about, the only thing he'd ever really refused her in all the time she'd known him. Maybe it was this refusal, and her failure to be the kind of wife who could have surmounted it, that had poisoned them and was poisoning them still. Or maybe Irene and everything inside her had always been poisonous.

Dr. Bishop would like her thinking this way. She would consider this rich and promising ground to explore.

Irene left the house. She passed the planted seedlings. They hadn't grown much, not that she could tell, but then it had only been a couple of weeks. At least they didn't look dead.

Outside the garden gate, she felt gingerly again for the moth. So different from the button—funny how well her fingers remembered that button still, round and smooth as a coin, a little smaller and lighter, but not as light as she might have expected, only very subtly foreign currency. The moth, on the other hand, felt flimsy and soft, prone to crumbling. It might have been a large deposit of lint.

Ivy scrabbled at her hand as she reached for the handle. The gate was heavy in its motion; though it looked delicate, all those elaborate scrolls and curlicues, it was still iron. It swung with a humanlike moan. Had it made that sound other times? She ducked her head beneath the trailing, clutching branches. All remained leafless within, but green nubbins were starting to fleck the twigs in places. Inside the fountain she saw that this week's rain had turned the vomit she'd left indistinguishable from the rest of the scum at the bottom.

By putting the moth just where she'd put the mouse, by seeing what came next, Irene might determine something about which pieces of this impossibility were really happening. She lifted the moth from her pocket as carefully as a wishing eyelash and tipped it onto the rim. Wing dust on the tips of her fingers, right where, after one of them—the second? the fourth?—blood had caked and dried without her noticing, and she hadn't found it until hours later, like evidence of a crime committed by or visited upon her. It had been, both. Would it matter if Irene had further crumpled the moth's wings? Were there rules about what could inflict damage if that damage were to be repaired? She straightened the moth, in case, putting it in a just-alighted position before covering it the way she'd covered the mouse, with another old leaf she found at her feet.

She wiped her palms. This was ridiculous. "Ridiculous," she said to herself, and saw her mother's face, her mother's mouth, the particular purse it took on in saying this word to and at Irene when, as a tiny girl, Irene had required dragging back from lake edges, street curbs, rims of heights; from the thresholds of all the worlds not intended for her. She supposed it was fear that had turned her mother's mouth in on itself. It had looked like rage. Her mother had needed to change the words only slightly when Irene grew and the problems became ones of impropriety and cruelty and volume, because these too had been worlds Irene had wanted. For what? She'd never been sure, only suspicious that life held something no one was offering her, and that if she pushed hard enough on its surfaces eventually one would give.

Now one had. This world she was in, though, Irene had never wanted it. She'd wanted a baby, yes. She was still mostly sure of wanting one. But feeling the little mouse move, she kept filling with fear—because of the wrongness of the image, because the feeling still wasn't definite, but not only for these reasons. If it survived, after all, it would become a child, and children could die; then a person, and people could die. Irene would be in charge of its limits as her mother had been in charge of hers. She would love it, she knew that, but how could she be trusted to pull anyone else back when she herself had always needed someone to stop her?

Now she was here, in the space that opened when she wasn't stopped. She looked around the border of the garden: she'd trespassed inside this circle—just leaving brown behind for green, like the moment when a wave begins to tip over—only because she'd found it and the door had opened when she pushed. A whole enclosed world where she had no business being. That it would be better to leave this place alone seemed true, and irrelevant, as such truths always felt to her.

So Irene would make her little test. She would leave her offering on the fountain rim and see what happened.

Before she left the garden, Irene looped back to weight down the moth and leaf with a stone so sharp and pyramidal she'd be sure to know it again when she returned, if she did.

6

The seedlings died in the end. "It's unfortunate," said Dr. Bishop briskly from the head of one of the dinner tables. The doctors stood there together to deliver the news. "Phillips says we had a late hard freeze, later than anyone could have expected. Not to worry, though, he's tilled the rows again, they'll be all ready for pansies and snapdragons in another couple of weeks, and a variety of vegetables this time too."

"Who wants to grow broccoli anyway?" Dr. Hall said.

Laughter from the three tables.

Irene wished she'd gotten to see the seedlings before they were plowed up and taken away. Had her little shoots frozen hard and stiff like wires? Or had they drooped and splayed on the dirt?

"A few last reminders about tomorrow," Dr. Hall said.

Tomorrow, the last Sunday in April, was the husbands' visiting day. The women had held it up before themselves for weeks, and now it was upon them. (This week made week twenty for Irene, halfway to her unimaginable baby, and had once seemed as if it would never come.)

Dr. Hall laid out the rules. They'd have the husbands for the whole day, or as much of the day as both parties desired. They'd be allowed to take them wherever they wished. "Just remember to maintain your pelvic rest, that's all we ask. Enjoy each other, but not too much," Dr. Hall said genially. Next to Irene, Pearl's cheeks flared.

Irene wondered if she'd be able to stop herself from pushing

George down on her bed. This last week or two she'd craved him as ravenously as she suddenly craved food, and in her dreams, his hands and his mouth were on her. She'd had these kinds of dreams while he was overseas too—the dreams were about George, but she carried the feelings they gave her into her waking life, looking around for the few men who were still left and watching them. She hadn't ever done anything real with those feelings, though she'd come close, relatively close, once. She'd never told George, because it hadn't seemed to matter anymore after he got home. But who knew now what had mattered, what had affected the *maternal environment*.

Drs. Bishop and Hall strolled amongst the tables to survey intake of this food no one could possibly want to eat, even if Irene was hungrier than she'd ever been.

"It goes without saying, about the unfortunate symbolism of the seedlings, doesn't it?" Irene said to Dr. Bishop once she was close enough.

"It does indeed, Mrs. Willard," said Dr. Bishop. She'd laid a crispness in her voice, like laying down a sheet and tucking it tight.

"We'll replant them, Lou." Dr. Hall touched Dr. Bishop's wrist.

Irene saw the grateful smile she gave him, for the touch of his skin. But she also thought she saw how things had gone for the two of them: her furious working toward where she wanted to go; his easy, unconscious force, like a broad river. All her paddling and all his drifting and here they both were, in just the same place.

If I'm honest, I didn't picture it lasting, George's mother had said to Irene once, a few months before the wedding, while they'd washed the dinner dishes together. *The two of you are so different. It was all well and good for a while, that's what I thought, and eventually it'd run its course and you'd go your separate ways.*

Irene had told her, *We don't have separate ways.*

These doctors had given them some, though.

When the doctors were out of earshot, Margaret said, "Didn't I say those plants would die?"

"Credit where credit is due," Irene said, to encourage this little flare of self-pride. Margaret seemed generally to be wilting too, as the days passed. She hadn't even changed her dress for dinner tonight—it was the same shapeless baggy blue thing she'd been wearing earlier—or neatened her hair, and she'd appeared late, after they'd already started on their watery soup. Irene had watched her sidle in, then kept watching the doorway.

Yes, there was Dr. Bishop, a moment later.

"Margaret, right before dinner, were you off somewhere with Dr. Bishop?" Irene said now.

"No business of yours," Margaret said.

"All right, what *happened* between you two?" Pearl said, glancing from Margaret to Irene.

"Nothing, Pearl."

"Like nothing happened with you and Dr. Bishop before dinner?" said Pearl.

Margaret sighed. "Dr. Bishop was just giving me an examination."

"At this time of day?" said Irene.

"I asked her to. I worry, that's all."

"We all worry," Pearl said.

This was true. Irene felt movements more often now, but still nothing she could feel completely sure of—whispers of a feeling, hints of it, like the currents made by someone's hand a little ways from yours underwater. What was that worth?

And she'd been too afraid so far to go back to the garden and check on what had happened to the moth. She'd walked that way once but turned back before she reached the gate.

Margaret slumped inside her terrible dress. She took an extra-big bite of her pork, chewed. "Dinner tonight isn't half bad, don't you think?"

That night in Irene's room, a dark shape scampered beneath

her window. She didn't try for a clear glimpse of it, wasn't going to try anymore for glimpses of things she didn't want to see. Instead she would focus on what was real, fill herself up with it so there was no room left for what wasn't. George was coming here tomorrow. That was real. She closed her eyes, turned over, and imagined touching George's arm, warm under her fingers.

She could let George help her, maybe. She could take him with her to the garden, show him the moth, and tell him everything. Then she'd be able to stop thinking about it and just grow their child. That was what she would do.

*

In the morning, Irene waited in the dining room with a hollow feeling below her ribs, as if the man coming to meet her were not George at all, or as if she might be stood up.

"Why so nervous?" Pearl said to her, jouncing her own leg.

Irene tapped Pearl's knee and Pearl laughed.

Around them, other women were pretending to eat, sliding neatly into their roles of wives awaiting the husbands they'd all been missing, the way they so often slid into the roles their doctors assigned: obediently they performed calisthenics time, radio time, gardening time. This, now, was husbands time. Nancy Montgomery knocked her water glass over and it spilled into her lap, where it darkened the shelf made by the upper curve of her belly. Nancy laughed, and Beatrice Loomis, next to her, pressed her napkin there, laughing too. Beatrice was a practical-seeming woman who took this sort of thing in stride, about seven months along, like Nancy. They'd mostly sorted themselves into camps by progression, as if positioning themselves along the pages of a medical book like the one the doctors were surely planning to write about them in the end. Irene had been Margaret and Pearl's nearest match, that was all.

Mrs. Conrad came to the door every once in a while to call a name. She seemed a little bored—not part of this current of anticipation, having presumably left her own husband at home in bed this morning, where she left him every other morning too. Roger, his name was Roger; Irene had ascertained this by asking directly while Mrs. Conrad readied the room for one of her examinations, though Mrs. Conrad said, then, "Mrs. Willard, I think it might be better if we kept ourselves to ourselves a little." The words gave Irene a better sense of Mrs. Conrad than she'd had up until that point: there'd have been a childhood in some homely little suburb where her mother used this adage for distance from neighbors she didn't like. Mrs. Conrad's finesse must have come only later.

There was no order to the husbands' arrivals. The men had been told they could come anytime this morning, so nobody knew when hers would get there. Each woman leapt up when her name was called, then caught and slowed herself.

Mrs. Conrad appeared. "Mrs. Loomis!" she said.

Beatrice dropped her napkin and left Nancy half mopped up, with a quick apologetic glance behind.

"It's like they've put us in a holding tank," Irene said.

"No, it's like they've asked us to wait in a dining room," said Margaret.

"Testy! Looking forward to your husband's visit?" Irene said, before she remembered she was trying to be nicer. All morning Margaret had been spearing her food with vicious ticks of the tines against the plate and answering questions with monosyllables, dreading, Irene imagined, what her husband would see about her size.

"Of course I am."

And she might be, even if she was dreading it too; maybe she felt for her husband some portion of what Irene felt for George. Though Irene knew most people didn't make their homes of another person as she had. Getting married was just part of the way most people shaped the passage of time, a step to be taken on the way to other steps: You took them because what were you supposed to do, stand still? They were all here now because the next steps had thus far eluded them. But children hadn't occurred to Irene at her wedding to George, and she didn't think they'd occurred to him either. She'd watched his eyes on her face, and there'd been no room in those eyes for anybody else. Before the war, if they'd failed as they had, Irene felt sure it wouldn't have mattered much. It was only after that George had begun to need children as ballast or an anchor, weight he might pile to prevent himself from being swept away. Irene doubted that was really how children would work, but she needed most to give him what he needed.

She brought her hands to the little mouse. In response—had it felt her hand?—it pulled its tail along her from the inside, longer and more forcefully than it had done yet. A motion pronounced enough that for the first time she felt sure, completely sure, that it had happened.

"What?" Pearl said.

"Nothing." The movement had been Irene and George's. Only theirs. Maybe it knew he was coming. What did the rest of anything matter, visions, mice, moths, gardens? This was Irene and George's, and she could tell him today.

She kept her hand where it was. *Just wait, little mouse. Wait till you see what it's like to have him love you.* That part of things at least she'd done right. She could tell Pearl and Margaret knew she was keeping something from them, but that was just fine. What did she owe them?

There, over by the window—was that a moth drifting darkly?

Her eyes darted after it but found nothing; her heart sped. The little mouse—she wished that weren't how she kept thinking of it—tapped her.

"Let's go wait in the foyer," Irene said.

"We're supposed to stay here," said Margaret.

"It's not a rule. We aren't a secret. We all have our clothes on. Let's go where we'll see them coming."

Pearl stood, and Margaret too, and they walked together out past Mrs. Conrad, who'd come to the doorway again to call someone. "Where are you three off to?" she asked, creasing the perfect pale plane of her forehead.

"We're just going to wait out here," Irene said, and see, Mrs. Conrad didn't stop them.

They sat down in the foyer on a velvet settee the poisonous green of some spilled potion. Irene imagined she could feel ghost air, wafted in on long-ago gowns, in the slippery nap beneath her palms. Sun fell pleasantly on their backs, on their shoulders, because the drapes had been opened today in honor of the husbands' visit, but Irene wished they were still closed—she worried that even George might not believe her about this place without proof.

They'd lined themselves up like mannequins in a storefront: one, two, three. Which, sir?

"What's wrong with me?" said Pearl. "It's just Joe coming. I see Joe every day, most of the time."

"This isn't most of the time, though, is it?" said Margaret. "I wish . . ." She trailed off.

Irene said, "What?"

"I don't know. Victor didn't want me to come here, that's all."

"Why not?" Pearl said.

"He kept saying *maybe enough is enough.* Finally I had to tell him that enough will never be enough, not for this."

"Joe would have sent me to the moon if he'd had to."

Irene looked at Pearl, and Pearl's face closed.

"I mean I wanted to come, of course."

An arrival interrupted them, a man none of them knew. They were watching him walk off down the hall with Mrs. Conrad when the door opened again, and Margaret leapt to her feet at the sight of the next arrival, coming through the door in an abashed way. He looked like a bank teller. Perhaps he was a bank teller, Irene didn't know.

"Yours?" Irene said to Margaret, as a joke.

Margaret hurried toward her husband. "*There* you are."

"Here I am." Victor kissed her and drew back to survey. "You're looking well." But his voice was too bright.

There was an awful pause in which Irene was aware of Victor's measuring eyes on Margaret's belly.

"The doctors are really pleased with her," Irene said. She wasn't sure whether to approach, so she stood but hovered. "With her progress."

"You can ask them, Victor," Margaret said. "You can ask them yourself, it's like Irene says, that's Irene." The gratitude coming off Margaret made Irene unsteady and seasick. Why had Irene said anything? In speaking she'd assumed a kind of responsibility.

"Nice to meet you, Irene," Victor said. He gave her a thin smile that left her unsure if he'd believed her.

Margaret led him off with her, up the stairs.

Pearl's husband appeared not long after. He was thicker, a little mean-looking. "Am I late?" he said when he saw them waiting. He didn't seem to know what to do with his hands.

Pearl fluttered over to him, and Joe's hands found a place then on the mound of her belly. "Well," he said, and grinned. "Well."

Pearl flushed. She put her hands on top of his. "I don't think I'd realized how big I'd gotten," she said. Her smile looked like it hurt, it was so wide.

Then there was only Irene, last lone mannequin. She crossed one leg over the other. The other over the first.

"Still waiting?" she heard behind her.

Dr. Bishop floated down the stairs in her white coat, hand on the dark carved banister, as if stroking the strange beast of this house.

"Not now, please," Irene said.

"Not now what?" Dr. Bishop sat beside Irene.

"Go ahead and report me for disobedience for leaving the dining room, if you want," Irene said. She wanted to scream. She would do anything not to be found by George with Dr. Bishop in attendance on her, which would seem to suggest she needed extra supervision. And George must be nearly here. Where was he?

"*Disobedience*—I suppose that's the word for it, for you. Report you to whom, I wonder?"

"You like that, don't you? That you're in charge."

"It's not a matter of liking. I do take some pleasure in using my parents' house for this—they'd have hated it—but that isn't really what matters to me. I'm pursuing a solution. I saw a problem, I saw how that problem might be fixed, I implemented what I'd seen."

"We sure are grateful."

"I don't do it for that either. I do it to solve the problem." Dr. Bishop shrugged in the sunlight, which caught in her sandy eyelashes, paler too than Irene's. Maybe the brightness hurt her eyes, that light color; maybe she was doing all the drape-pulling for herself. "Anyway, how are you feeling this morning, Irene?"

"I felt it move before, in the dining room. I've been feeling something for a little while now, but not like this."

As soon as she'd spoken, Irene felt furious at both herself and Dr. Bishop. She'd wanted to save this for George, and she hadn't managed to wait for him. Why had she told? How had Dr. Bishop managed to make her?

"That must be a good sign, don't you think?" she said.

"Oh yes."

"Maybe I'm becoming a better maternal environment."

"Maybe so," Dr. Bishop said.

What guarded attention the doctor gave this, the problem she was solving. Irene couldn't stand it. "Maybe, maybe. What are we even doing here, if that's all you can say? When will you be able to tell me something real?"

Dr. Bishop raised her eyebrows. "For my purposes, we'll know something when you deliver and your baby breathes. But you? If you're looking for certainty, Irene, you may have undertaken the wrong project."

Irene stared in shock into that face so like her own.

"Irene?"

There was George.

Irene was running toward him in the doorway without even deciding to move. Before she touched him she stopped to look, to take in his face, the particular slope of his mouth, his wet eyes.

"How did I not see you come in?" she said.

"You seemed awfully absorbed."

Irene clutched him to prove to herself he was really there, then pulled back and turned to the side to display her middle. "How am I doing?" She was making a joke of it, but of course it wasn't a joke, it was the hardest part of their lives, and she was watching him seriously and hating herself again for her need.

"Oh, Reny," he said, his mouth trembling.

So she knew for sure that this was the furthest, the closest, she'd yet come.

"Mr. Willard, welcome back."

Irene had forgotten all about Dr. Bishop. She spun as if caught by her mother with George after a dance, as had actually happened once.

George cleared his throat. "Thank you, Doctor. Reny hasn't been causing any trouble, I hope?"

"George," said Irene. He wasn't her jovial uncle, and he knew how she felt about Dr. Bishop. Why would he ask her a thing like that?

"She's been doing nicely," Dr. Bishop told him. "I'll let you two enjoy your time." She moved off toward her study.

"And stay there," Irene said, once Dr. Bishop had turned the corner.

"You still don't like her?"

Had he thought she might? Had he thought her feelings about Dr. Bishop were something she'd get over? She looked at her George, in all his fragile eagerness. The foyer seemed to loom around them, and she felt aware of their failure to fill this setting of the new mothers' crowded farewell scenes. Just her and George here at the bottom of the empty stairs, inside a lot of dead space.

"I'll tell you more once we're away," Irene said, and pulled him through the door.

But then she couldn't tell George anything, because his elation made him talk and talk. "My mother came over for Easter," he said as they crossed the lawn, in a tone that made Irene expect he'd say next, *You remember my mother?* "She made this huge ham, you should have seen it—hulking—just for the two of us. She seemed surprised when we sat down, like she'd been planning on a whole tableful and only just realized we were by ourselves."

Irene knew what she'd have said if she'd been present: *Are we expecting someone?* George's father, dead three years now, had loved ham, and she'd have regretted the words as soon as they were out, though she and George's mother didn't like each other. Here at the house-hospital they'd had ham for Easter too, but it had been too unsalted to be convincing, and nobody had said much else about the holiday, which felt jinxed, charged as it was with ideas of children and egg hunts.

"She says to tell you she's thinking of you all the time."

"Since when has your mother ever thought of me all the time?"

"Since you've been in the process of giving her a grandchild, I think."

"Well, I've been at that for a while now, haven't I?"

"Reny, don't."

"I know, I'm supposed to be *keeping calm,* they keep telling us that."

George's hand was there on her middle again. Her skin relaxed under the weight. He said, "It's so strange in the house without you."

"It's strange *here.* It's the strangest place I've ever been. They're the strangest people." She couldn't resist checking to see if Dr. Bishop had come back out to trail them, though she'd said worse to Dr. Bishop's face.

"We knew that, didn't we?"

"*You* don't know anything," she said savagely.

He took her hand. "Sorry."

This was how she and George had survived so well for so long.

"It's just so much more than you can tell at first," Irene said. "She's really in charge of everything. She must have found him somewhere along the way and thought she'd use him to hold all this up, like a piece of furniture. Dr. Table. Dr. Ottoman. She lived here as a child, and it's like she pulled everything that's happened since straight out of her brain."

She startled herself with how sure she felt about all of this, as if Dr. Bishop herself had told it to her.

George turned to look at the house. "How does a girl who grows up here end up a doctor?"

"I don't think easily." Irene thought of the cast of Dr. Bishop's mouth in saying *my parents' house,* and the care in her little-girl hands, touching her father's face, and the way he'd left her there on that bearskin. "But now she has it, everything she ever wanted. She's *loving* it."

"Loving what?"

"What she's doing to us."

"Well, you would hope she'd love that, wouldn't you?"

"It's not the helping she loves, it's being the one to prove all the points and ask all the questions," Irene said.

"Irene, she isn't holding you hostage."

"Isn't she?"

They were quiet for a minute. Irene slipped a little on loose ground, and George caught her by the arm. "What sorts of things have you been telling her?" he said anxiously.

Surely he knew better than to think Irene might uncover some feeling other than loving him. She squeezed his hand. "All about how *awful* you are to me."

He stopped and pulled her to him and kissed her then, long. The taste of his mouth, somehow she'd almost forgotten it, and it set her whole hungry body humming.

They moved past the corner of the house, where she could see those walls again. She held George's hand. Yes, with him beside her Irene thought she could be brave enough to check the moth. She didn't need to dread absurdities anymore. She could make the whole thing into another joke, tell him how crazy she'd gone here in this manor, crazy enough to dream while she was awake—*treat a girl like a shut-away and you get a shut-away*—and take off the rock and the leaf and hand the dead moth to him. *A souvenir of me, to hold you.* She could almost see it in his palm, its wings perhaps detached by now. She would watch while he put it in his pocket, and he could take it away with him and keep it there as she'd kept the button. If she asked him to, he would.

Then, in the garden, where after all no one ever came, she might kiss him as long as she liked with no one watching, no one tromping too loudly down the hall outside. *Pelvic rest* would be nothing but a nonsensical, powerless phrase. She'd be her old self again.

But now that she'd brought George abreast of the ivy and the wrought-iron gate, its curlicues looked sharper than she'd remembered, like teeth almost, and she wondered suddenly why she'd ever gone inside such a place, and if it might be better to keep walking and tell George nothing about the garden at all.

George would get to go home after this, though, leave her alone to keep wondering.

"Come in here a second," she said. "I want to show you something." She checked again behind her for Dr. Bishop.

George followed her through the gate. She turned to watch him emerge through the ivy, which trailed its fingers covetously through his hair, and she thought of ripping that ivy out roots and all. Through, he shook leaves from his cuffs. "I hope this is good," he said, and laughed.

Good Irene wasn't sure of.

She closed in on the fountain. There was the leaf, there the rock, still in place—what did that mean? Did it mean anything? She sat.

George perched uncertainly next to her. "It's eerie in here," he said. "Why would they leave it like this?"

"I think everyone's forgotten about it."

"A whole garden?" George said.

People forgot larger things, Irene thought. Look at George now, all over his face a pure happiness made possible only by forgetting.

But he was waiting for her to explain.

"Something happened when I first came in here," she said.

"What?" George said quickly, eyes on her belly.

She saw that he expected whatever she was about to say would be about the little mouse. He thought she was going to tell him she'd sensed its heart stopping, its fingers failing to form, to flex, its eyes failing to blink or failing ever to open, its feet failing to kick or failing to become feet in the first place. And she would give anything to stop George from imagining any of that. George, who'd seen nightmares enough already and come back to her afterward wanting just this one thing, which she hadn't been able to give him. Who'd always been more than she deserved. Who'd scooped her out of that pond while they were courting and pressed her to his heart as if she were some remnant of a fairy tale, found to his tremendous luck, and said, *You're so warm,* and for once in her life she hadn't been able to think of a word to say in response. When she'd kissed him that day she'd thought—she remembered thinking—she'd remember his taste until she died. Had she died?

Whatever this garden was or wasn't, it would give George more questions than he must already have about her. How could she ever have thought she might be able to tell him?

No, Irene was alone in this. Even George couldn't change that.

"It's not really even worth saying," she said.

A stirring played gently against her insides. "Quick," she said, and grabbed George's hand and pressed it hard to her stomach. A twitch, another twitch. "It's only very small so far, I don't know if you can feel it."

He waited, studiously, to feel the thing she'd meant and failed to keep only for them.

Twitch, twitch, twitch. Finally she watched the feeling dawn in his expression.

"I *think* I felt—"

"Yes!"

"Amazing," he said, and of course it was. Whatever else was true, that was true too: this was the most amazing thing that had ever happened to them.

They waited, George pushing on her belly with an alertness like he was listening to a very precious and very faraway sound, until the movements stopped.

"Oh, wow," George said, and wiped his eyes on his sleeve.

She kissed him. "I'm not sure what I was thinking, bringing you in here. It's awful. I hate it. Let's keep walking."

She stood, and then he did, and they walked, and she held his hand tight to hoard the warmth of him, but all the while in her head the word repeated, *alone, alone, alone.*

*

George left after four hours of talking and careful touching over clothes, the way they'd touched when they'd first started dating. One more fold-over of time, here in this liminal house. He drove off, and Irene waved until she couldn't see his car.

Bereftness came to her first.

Then immediately, again, a thrill of dread that made her clutch her arms. She thought of that leaf, still in place—now she knew it was, having seen—and what was or wasn't under it. This was a feeling she knew well, the same one that had sent her so many times, over years now, to the washroom to check if there was blood in her underclothes after she *might* have felt wetness, she *thought* she'd felt it, she'd *probably* not felt it but should check, to be sure.

She would hurry in and tug them down with shaking hands. For those moments between the impulse to look and the view of the blood or not-blood, both states were real. She'd both lost it and not lost it. The thing was both alive and not alive. Efforts to resist these checkings were like holding her breath. The question wasn't whether she'd give in but when.

Having George here had changed nothing. Somehow she'd thought, she'd really thought, it would.

No sense in putting off any longer what she knew now she had to do. There was perhaps an hour until dinner, until anyone would miss her. Irene went back to her room. She draped a sweater over her shoulders in the matronly way she could remember her mother doing any chilly evening. *There's a bite in the air,* her mother would say, and Irene would wonder what she was talking about, all those nights when her own skin had felt kissed by the cool, and why if her mother wanted the sweater she didn't just put her arms inside it. Now she understood how sometimes arms needed their freedom for nervous motions. She strolled back down the steps with a deliberate, lazy danglet before each foot landed and out the front door. Instead of cutting too direct a path in the direction of the garden, she made herself meander, closer to this tree, farther from that one, and tipped her head back as if she were dreamy, staring into the sky. For Dr. Bishop, she was staging this one-woman show, in case the doctor was looking through one of the windows right now, or in some way using a window as an eye.

Why had Dr. Bishop come downstairs to sit beside Irene today anyway?

Irene put grace in her steps.

Her heart thudded thickly, and she laid a hand on her stomach, because this wasn't staying calm, was it? *I'm sorry for the upset, little mouse, we're fine.* But the little mouse would know the truth, because she was sending the blood pounding through both their ears. She wasn't used to having her lies known from the inside. Maybe she hadn't ever replaced the button and pocket with something else, just turned herself into the pocket—either empty or full, no third option. A pocket, in and of itself, was nothing at all.

The ivy seemed to have grown even since this afternoon. The leaves scratched against her hands and face as she ducked through. Inside, the quiet blanketed her, the eerie fading quality of the light. She regarded the fountain. How strange that Dr. Bishop's grandfather had chosen a cherub of all things for the center of this particular garden, at this particular house—almost like he'd had a premonition. The cherub's whimsical bent-armed posture was meant to charm, but the expression ruined the effect, the blankness of those pupil-less eyes.

Irene closed the space between herself and the pyramidal rock she'd left on the fountain's edge. In the moment before she lifted the leaf off, of course she knew beneath she would find the dead and waiting moth or else she would find its absence, which would mean nothing except that she would keep seeing the moth as well as the mouse in the corners of rooms.

Irene lifted the leaf. There was the moth, perched just as she'd left it. Bigger than she'd remembered but otherwise exactly the same. The end.

Then the moth twitched its wings and rose.

It drifted close to her face, closer, and brushed her lips fleshily— had it taken on bulk somehow? She flinched back and saw the large, ragged wings with, yes, real meat on them, those particular torn edges she'd learned, jittering like sparking nerves lighting up and going dark, light and dark and light. It brushed past her, flying on, unevenly, irregularly, climbing and dipping.

She turned to follow its flight, but already it was gone, it had gone, she'd seen and felt it only for that instant, only just long enough to know she had.

Twitching at her middle again, but no, it wasn't twitching now, it was brushing, the wet brushing of large wings, the moth's wings, inside her. Opening and closing and opening hard, with real force, dragging along her whole interior breadth.

Little moth.

Irene squeezed her eyes shut, long, and opened them again, on a garden that wasn't empty anymore.

The man from the previous dream, Dr. Bishop's father, stood by the fountain.

He was as solid-looking as Irene's own hands, which she held in front of her as if to stop him from being there. He wasn't looking at Irene, though. "*You* would know," he was saying to a woman who stood there too, very close to him. He was holding her hand. He looked older than he had the last time.

"*Archie.*" The woman wore a blue dress and had stylishly curled hair. "Where've you brought me anyway? I would say it's beautiful but."

Both of them so real, their motion and words stealing Irene's own.

"It's sure nice to escape a minute."

"From your Betsy and my Walter, you mean," the woman said in a perfected bored-sounding voice.

"Where *is* Walter?"

"Probably sitting somewhere and eating—it's his favorite thing."

"You miss a lot that way, just sitting down."

"You do."

They were drawing closer together.

"And where's your little girl gotten to?" the woman asked. "I know I should know her name."

"Louisa. Lou. Oh, who knows where."

"I hope you won't mind my saying so, but I'm afraid she'll be no great beauty. That age, you start to be able to tell."

"A funny little nothing, isn't she? Not much to her. Not like present company," the man said.

"Oh, you."

Their voices were softening and blurring. Irene could see the two of them and somehow see herself too, standing there in her sweater, stupid fragment of the wrong time.

But she wasn't the only one watching. Behind her Irene could see that the gate she'd closed when she came in was open again, and that the girl who had been Dr. Bishop stood without being noticed, except now by Irene, learning about her father and about the world. Looking so much like Irene herself, wearing the same expression Irene wore, as she watched her father prove himself willing to pay with her for what he wanted. And what he wanted, really, was the winning itself: look at his hands on that woman's waist, look how he pulled her to him. This beloved father no different really from the portrait king, both of them unable to understand what she wanted to do and be in the world—no, worse, neither of them caring enough even to see that they didn't understand.

I'll show you, Irene could feel the girl thinking at both of them.

Here the grandfather was too, as if Irene had called him here by thinking of him, free of his painting as she'd known he could be, watching from along the garden wall with approval, watching his son eat.

"You know I said to myself I wanted you the very first time I saw you?" the father crooned to the woman.

If I say it, I do it, said the grandfather, though only Irene could hear him, in, yes, the ogre-voice his son had used for him the last time. He gazed on the scene from the same pose he struck in his portrait. But then he turned his head.

He saw Irene. She saw him see.

Could he tell Irene and Dr. Bishop apart? What would it mean if he couldn't? What might he do?

His cheek's sheen: that wasn't the gloss of paint, as she'd thought, but the moistness of decay.

Irene whirled, finally. She ran for the gate, to put space between herself and that appetite. No girl stood in her way, just as, when she looked back, no man and no woman and no grandfather were behind her. But it was also true that she didn't have to open the gate—she ran right through an already open space.

If the little moth was still moving, she couldn't tell; all she could feel was the larger frantic motion of her own body, running away.

SNAKE

7

Irene continued to feel as if she were floating about a foot above herself, watching herself seem to walk down halls and eat dinner like a woman inside a regular day while all along her mind whirled and fluttered—it couldn't have happened, it had happened; it couldn't have been real, nothing here was real; she was losing her mind, she was growing her little moth, maybe both had to happen at once, how could she stand it? That might be a moth, that speck of motion high up in a corner of the foyer's vaulted ceiling as she passed through, and she looked in another direction. No one around her seemed to notice anything unusual about her. If that was a moth's wing brushing against her insides, no one else could tell. The night nearly bested her, all that quiet, every part of her still except that part of her middle that seemed never to be still now—too much of what she'd wished for—but in the end she fell asleep.

Her first thought on waking was to wonder what the little moth had been doing all those sleeping hours.

That morning after breakfast, Mrs. Conrad came to the door and called Irene's name and also Beatrice's and Margaret's.

"What's this?" Irene said. It shouldn't have been her examination time until early afternoon.

"The doctor wants to see all of you."

Did the doctor know somehow what Irene had been doing and what had been happening to her? But surely not, if she was calling these other names too.

"You never do know what's coming here," Beatrice said.

Irene thought she caught a faint frown of concern on Margaret's face before she smoothed it.

In the therapy room, Dr. Bishop sat them all on the couch. She put Beatrice in between Margaret and Irene.

"Too cramped for lying down today, I guess," Irene said.

"I thought we'd try a group session," Dr. Bishop said, careful, Irene thought, to give them all the same amount of eye contact. Maybe having Irene do therapy with these other, more obedient women was an effort to bring her to heel, or maybe the doctor wanted to watch Irene and Margaret together, with the buffer of Beatrice, so she could make sure Irene was behaving herself. "And did we all enjoy our visits with our husbands?"

Margaret and Beatrice murmured assent. "We certainly did," Irene said.

Dr. Bishop came to sit then in a chair beside the couch, so they were all in the same line. Irene, closest to her, could smell again that rosy perfume, the kind Dr. Bishop's mother would probably have approved of, even if she'd approved of little else about this daughter. The tentacles of mothers reached. Irene gestured toward the stack of cards Dr. Bishop held. "What's that, a tarot deck? My roommate in college used to practice on me." These cards seemed too big for tarot really, but they too trailed mystery.

"Of course not," Dr. Bishop said. "This is called the Rorschach test. It's a therapeutic tool. We'll leaf through the plates, one at a time. Each has an inkblot in an abstract pattern that's open to interpretation, and for each card, each of you will tell us what you see. Giving the test in a group this way is an experiment—but I think one with potential benefits. I'm hoping both your answers and your reactions to one another's answers might be revealing."

"Why are you sitting over here with us?" Irene said. "Are you playing too?"

She took some pleasure from Beatrice and Margaret's surprise at the way she spoke to the doctor.

"The examiner's face can react and give unintended encouragement or discouragement." As if Dr. Bishop ever gave anything away she didn't mean to.

Dr. Bishop set the stack of plates down on the table and turned over the first one. Irene took in a long breath.

That inkblot was a moth. Wings outstretched in midflight.

Within, her own little moth's wings spread wide.

"What do you see here?" Dr. Bishop asked. "Each of you, take a moment to get an answer or two in mind before speaking."

But what other answers could there be?

Dr. Bishop gave them a nod to start, and Margaret said, "I see a cat's face. See, there are the eyes, there are the ears, there's its mouth."

She was pointing to parts that were clearly not what she was calling them. Irene waited for someone to snort, but Dr. Bishop just nodded some more and wrote on her notepad, which she'd positioned so none of them could see it.

"Oh yes, I can see that," Beatrice said. "To me, though, it looks like two angels with their hands raised, here."

Irene's turn to speak had come. She looked from the moth to Dr. Bishop. "I see a bat. Is that right?"

"*Right* isn't really relevant here."

"Somebody obviously planned it to be a bat: here are its ears, and here is its nose, and here's its little face."

Dr. Bishop wrote more of her secretive notes. "What expression would you say its little face is wearing?"

"Oh, I see. I might almost be talking about a *baby,* is that what you noticed? This particular bat-baby looks fairly happy to me. See, he's almost smiling."

As Irene spoke, her little moth was opening and closing its wings, as if in response to her lie. She worried that the motions were visible somehow through her skin and her clothes, or that they were reverberating in her face.

The next plate, blessedly, looked nothing at all like a moth, and

Irene felt her whole body relax. Margaret mentioned a cow, and Beatrice, an animal with four legs, she couldn't be sure what kind.

"Aren't we going to talk about the red? The blood?" Irene asked.

"Blood, Irene?" said Dr. Bishop. "Interesting."

"Oh please, it's *red*, and it's the only color they've used, they knew what they were doing."

Beatrice looked horrified. Margaret stared fixedly at the ceiling. But Irene knew this time she was just the only one to say aloud what they were all thinking, given why they were here.

"Go ahead and write it down on your paper if you'd like, Doctor, because of course the red does make me think of blood. Other than that, what I see are two little elf-men, wearing red hats. Touching palm to palm like they're maybe playing some kind of game."

Some women around a cooking pot next, though Margaret thought they were men carrying something, and Beatrice thought she might see a child wearing a bow. Then one they both thought was an animal skin, where Irene saw instead a reclining man, viewed from below and from the foot of the bed so the soles of his feet loomed large.

But the fourth plate was another moth. There wasn't anything else it could be this time—Irene couldn't even think of a lie. Its wings were indisputably moth wings, folded in where the last moth's wings had been extended. It even had antennae.

"A moth," Irene said. "But everyone must see that, don't they?"

"I would say this one's more like a bat, actually," said Beatrice.

"Oh, or a dragonfly!" Margaret said.

Heat rose to Irene's cheeks. She glanced at Dr. Bishop, who was looking straight at her. The little moth gave a series of twitches, first in the middle of Irene's abdomen and then to one side, as if trying to take flight.

"What do *you* think, Doctor?" she said. "What do you see? It's amazing how we all see such different things. I guess that's true in life too, isn't it? Dr. Bishop, only you could look at this house and see a hospital, a hospital just for us, that's what I think."

"What are you doing, Irene?" Beatrice asked.

What Irene was doing: trying to find out, as best she could, how much Dr. Bishop might know.

"I just wonder why that should be. What special magic made our doctor see that."

Dr. Bishop laughed. "Magic? I go in more for science, Irene." Her eyes were open, scornful but direct for once.

"Tell me about the science again, then. Tell me about the drug."

"The drug, as you all know, because we've been through this"—Dr. Bishop smiled for the group—"is a synthetic estrogen. It was discovered by a Swiss doctor who had, pardon my saying so, no sense at all of its potential. Our work, Dr. Hall's and mine, let us see how it could be used to help women with your particular complications."

"Here."

"Well, yes, here," the doctor said, puzzled.

She didn't know. Irene saw that no matter what had happened to the doctor inside that walled space in her life, she really didn't know about the garden, not the way Irene did. She looked only forward, while the garden's happenings swirled in an eddy off to the side. There were things here she had never seen.

So Irene was alone—again, still—with what she'd found, alone to think about what it might mean and how it could be.

Dr. Bishop tapped the cards with a sharp sound on the table to line them up. "All right, next card," she said.

*

That night turned out to be the one that bested Irene. The moth cards had left her unable to stop picturing the small twitches she felt as insect legs and antennae, prickling their way along her inner walls, feeling blindly in between wing sweeps. There was a horror to this feeling now that she had these images for it. She wanted to dig the thing inside her out—or with one hand she wanted to do this, while with the other she wanted to keep the little moth safe as safe could be and let the twitchings grow until they were all she could feel.

The world out here, little moth, it turns out I don't understand even the things I thought I understood about it.

And then: *But maybe I could use even what I don't understand. If I had to.*

For you, maybe I could.

Irene went out for the washroom after midnight, just when Margaret was emerging from her own bedroom with a teary face. "What is it?" Margaret asked Irene quickly, so there must have been stains of some kind on Irene's face too.

Irene thought of saying, *Nothing*, and turning back into her bedroom. But what would she do with the quiet in there? Her fear and Margaret's had swelled in a single wave that had carried them both out into the hall at this moment, and that synchronization must hold some significance. Her feelings about Margaret—about all these women—didn't matter. No, she hadn't chosen them, but here they all were, and they had things in common that she would never share with another soul.

What if she tried telling them what she hadn't been able to tell George?

"Let's wake Pearl up. I think I only have it in me to say it once," Irene said.

So they unearthed Pearl, blinking, from her quilts, and Irene pulled them into her room and sat them down on her bed. Of course the house wasn't listening. Of course she didn't need to whisper so it wouldn't be able to hear.

"Are you all right, Irene?" Pearl said.

"You've seen that garden out back behind the house, with walls all around? Have either of you been inside?"

Both women shook their heads. "What were you doing back there?" said Margaret.

"It's a real mess, this garden. The first time I went in I found a dead mouse, and I covered it up with a leaf—just to hide it, or something, I don't know. When I went back, the mouse was gone. Which, of course, anything could explain that. But then the same thing happened with a dead moth, except the moth—this is the part I have to tell you—the moth *wasn't* gone. It was still there. But it wasn't dead anymore."

"What does that mean?" Pearl said.

"When I went back and moved the leaf—this was yesterday— the moth flew up, right at my face." Irene touched the place where that dusty flutter had brushed her lips. She looked at Pearl, then at Margaret. They squinted at her. "There's no reason for you to believe me," she said.

Margaret huffed. "Irene, you're really something. I don't understand you. I mean, I can see this is scratching some itch for you, but I've been having a time, I really have, and here you are, trying to make us believe this story as, what, a joke?"

"I haven't been kind to you, I know that."

"That's true," said Pearl, and put her hand on Margaret's.

"It's a thing I do, like a habit. I'm sorry."

Margaret stared at the floor. "I hate this place. I feel scared all the time. Having Victor here made it worse—having him look at me like that. Do you know the doctor's started giving me more injections?"

Irene made even her breathing quiet, as if any sudden move or word might make Margaret stop talking.

"More than we're supposed to have? Which doctor?" Pearl said.

Irene already knew.

"Dr. Bishop. But there is no *supposed to*, Pearl, they're the ones who decide everything. She said I might just need a little more of the drug than expected, that's all." Margaret's voice tried for lightness. "She didn't want to at first, she said it would interfere with the experiment—she was the one who brought it up, but then she tried to change her mind. I said I didn't care about her experiment, and how could she expect me to, and in the end she said all right. As long as I promised not to mention it to Dr. Hall, she'd do it."

Dr. Bishop, who hated to lose, forever taking whatever actions were possible. Dr. Hall making careful choices about what he wanted to know. Because doing something had always been the wiser course for one, who'd had to prove her right to everything she wanted; while doing nothing had been wiser for the other, to whom, in exchange for all of that nothing, so much had always been handed.

"Do you think she's right? Do you think this could fix it?" Margaret said. "Do you think things could still turn out all right for me?"

"Of course," Pearl said, looking to Irene helplessly.

Irene sighed. "Sure. But I don't know, extra injections? That doesn't seem like the best sign."

"But don't you think more—"

"I don't even mean just for you, Margaret. Maybe it shows they don't really know anything, if they're still changing their minds."

"She keeps saying I'm not that small, it's not that bad. She's the doctor here, not you." Margaret looked furious.

"You asked us, Margaret—I'm just answering. Changing course in the middle of the plan like that, it makes me worry. Doesn't it suggest there's something wrong with the plan?"

This, what Irene was doing, felt familiar. This was the feeling of taking the reins, preparing to steer. Irene knew just what to do next. She looked at Pearl.

"Next thing you know," she said, "the doctors are on the phone to our husbands, telling them they have to come get us because it's all gone wrong."

Yes, the sound of *husband* did what she'd expected to Pearl's face.

"All I'm saying is, I think it's to our advantage to learn as much as we can about everything here, as fast as we can. So come. Just come with me and let me show you."

"Whatever you're talking about, it has nothing to do with us, though," Margaret said.

"What if it could, if we need it to?" Irene knelt before Margaret, but her own belly had grown too fast for her mental sense of her shape to adjust, and she tipped forward before she caught herself on the floor. She touched Margaret's knees.

She couldn't be alone with this anymore.

"Let me just show you. That's all I'm asking. Please."

*

In the morning, after breakfast, in the window before any of them was due for her examination, they crept out of the house. Irene led Pearl and Margaret across the lawn, feeling their reluctance in the way they trailed her. She'd made them come, but she couldn't make them believe what she'd said.

Not until she got them inside.

They reached the gate and she pulled them with her through the ivy. Something about its touch, its spring, its strength, made her suspect it might begin to twine around her hands and wrists. The other two also flinched away from its touch, she saw. They followed her toward the fountain. And there they were, occupying this center together.

Pearl said, "It's very abandoned-feeling, isn't it?"

"Because it's abandoned, no mystery there," Margaret said. She brushed at her arms. "Where were these supposedly dead things, Irene?"

"The mouse was right at the bottom." Irene gestured. She watched the others look down into the dry leaves.

Margaret shuddered. "You touched it?"

"I used a stick. I lifted it out and put it right here." She hovered her fingers above the place.

"And then you put a leaf on top of it."

"Right."

"The moth, you put it right in the same spot?" Pearl asked.

"I don't know if that matters."

"What exactly are you saying? Matters to *what?*" Margaret said.

"I guess we'll see, won't we?" said Irene.

"Stop, we aren't supposed to argue," Pearl said. She stepped forward with her hand on her stomach—that besting gesture.

Irene touched her own stomach too without quite meaning to do it. *Can you hear us in there, little moth?*

"We aren't supposed to be doing any of this," Margaret said. "Running around, making ourselves nervous, putting ourselves through nonsense. I'm going back."

"Wait, Margaret," Pearl said, louder. "Irene could be right."

Margaret had begun to turn back for the gate, but she wheeled on Pearl. *"Right?"*

Pearl's cheeks were flushed. "Not about whatever she's saying about this place, probably, but about the doctors. I've tried to believe them, I've tried to be sure, but I mean, they're doing a lot of things to us without exactly saying why, aren't they? And still changing it all as they go. Sometimes I think it feels like just another set of ideas to try out. I've tried lots of other ideas before."

"Haven't we all?" said Irene. "I used to walk exactly twice around the block each day, no more and no less."

"I drank bottles of cod-liver oil," Pearl said. "I spent most of the six months before I came here lying around with my feet up. I've started wondering how different this is really."

"I can't *believe* you, Pearl." Margaret sounded as if she'd had the wind knocked out of her. She sat down on the brim of the fountain. "Of course it's different. They've figured it out, they've learned how to stop it."

"Is that what Sally would say? Or Samantha? Margaret, what if the doctors don't actually know what they're doing? What if they're only seeing what will happen?" Irene said.

"We've gotten further than ever before, there's your proof."

"So far. But some women just . . . can't," said Pearl. "That's always been the way it is."

"No," Margaret said. She shook her head and closed in on Pearl. "That's the most hurtful thing you could possibly say to me. It shouldn't be allowed, to say that here."

"I'm saying it to all of us, Margaret," Pearl said, her voice quivering. "I'm just starting to think they're acting like they know more than they do, trying to get us to believe they have the solution when really it just might not be something they can fix."

Yes, that was it. This garden, what Irene seemed to be discovering about it—it didn't feel much more impossible than everything else.

And if it *was* happening, really happening, and the other promises broke . . .

Irene didn't and wouldn't finish the thought. She would just take this first step, that was all.

"What has any of us ever known about anything?" she said. "Let's just see what we can find out."

They set off in search of dead things. Another moth, maybe, or a dried-up worm, or even a bird fallen too early from its nest. But five minutes turned up nothing. Living things were everywhere— the garden teemed with them now that it was late April, really spring; even the dirt had that rich, wet living smell—but not dead ones. Irene overturned a loose brick to spill a colony of ants over the buckling pathway. Margaret poked some leaves with a stick and shrieked when a bumblebee trundled loudly forth.

"I can't *find* anything," Pearl said.

Out of necessity, then, they adjusted their rules: find a thing that could be killed.

This was easier. Margaret found and cupped between her palms a scrabbling black beetle so shiny it looked polished. Irene watched Pearl pin a salamander's tail beneath the toe of her shoe before releasing it with a strange quiet in her face. What she arrived with: a roly-poly curled tight as a fist.

Beneath a rock, Irene discovered a tiny garter snake, caught it behind the head the way her brothers had taught her, and carried it to the fountain's edge, while its dangling tail made wild shapes in the air. The others looked at her in shock, but she shrugged. She'd have carried the salamander too, if she'd been the one to find it.

She took a rock and smashed the snake's head, once, twice, three times before it stopped moving. She handed the rock to Pearl, who handed it to Margaret.

When they were sure all three were really dead—the snake limp, the roly-poly's curl released, the beetle crushed sticky and flat inside its shattered shell—they adjusted their positions on the same part of the fountain's lip, in case this was in fact some requirement. Three things in a line. Each covered hers with a leaf and then a weighting stone.

"Now what, Irene?" said Margaret.

"Now we just wait, I guess," said Irene, as if they didn't know that waiting, always, was the hardest thing a person could ask herself to do.

*

Irene had hoped Pearl and Margaret would make her feel better, but she found they made her own waiting worse. She didn't like the emphasis of all their stolen glances while they counted down the strange biblical clock they had designed.

Three days, because this was how long Irene had accidentally waited with the moth, and that might *matter* somehow.

Meanwhile, Irene saw the mouse once again, running along the floor of her closet when she opened the door, and the moth twice, up near the curtains in the talk-session room, then floating in the middle of the hallway. There they were, her creature's various selves, carrying their chill across her shoulder blades. She blinked and held her breath, and they were gone. But inside her the little moth kept stretching the parts of itself that might be wings.

At least she hadn't opened her eyes on another dark ancestral fragment from Dr. Bishop's life. She couldn't quite tell the others about that piece, not yet.

She waited, through these days, through meals and sessions, through a new arrival (a woman with a loud laugh whose name, Lucy, Irene kept forgetting). Through an evening talk from a Freudian expert on hypnosis who'd met Dr. Bishop during her psychoanalysis studies in Europe and was now giving an American lecture tour. The women sat in the bloody ballroom in rows while Dr. Bahr told them in his thick accent how deeply he approved of the treatment they were receiving. "What productive timing, to delve into the psyche at a point of such upheaval. Particularly the feminine psyche, with its tendency toward greater, pardon me, confusion."

Dr. Bishop looked at him.

"A general rule only, Dr. Bishop, of course. What you're doing here is groundbreaking, truly groundbreaking. Your patients should feel very proud to be a part of it."

But we're the ground, Irene thought.

Two mornings after she and Margaret and Pearl had killed their creatures, Irene almost walked to a different breakfast table— maybe she'd sit beside Dorothy, ready to pop, instead. Dorothy gave her a little welcoming nod, and Irene nodded back, then thought better: next to Dorothy she'd have to listen to a lot of buzzy baby plans, and anyway, decamping wouldn't stop the waiting. She turned at the last minute for her expected place. Neither Pearl nor Margaret greeted her or acknowledged in any way that she'd nearly shunned them, though she knew they'd seen.

Margaret took a sip of her coffee. "Let's just go check today," she said.

"It isn't time yet," said Pearl.

"Why wait, though? Why are we doing this to ourselves?"

"We did *all* of it to ourselves," Irene said, but of course the rest of this had partly happened to them.

"I'm going now."

Pearl grabbed Margaret's wrist. "Don't."

"If you go, Margaret, Pearl and I will try again, and we won't invite you," Irene said.

Margaret stood so fast she shoved her chair back. She fled the room noisily, and Irene watched the doctors noticing. Dr. Bishop made her way over, the way she must have once navigated throngs at dinner parties in this room. "Everything all right?"

"Fine," Irene said.

"Why did Mrs. Crowe run off just now?"

"We had a little tiff," said Pearl.

"None of you should be letting yourselves get upset."

"All right, then, next time we won't let ourselves," Irene said. She felt all the fury of her wait boil forth, ready to pour onto Dr. Bishop. For telling them over and over that they just had to follow her rules and they would be safe, for trying to make them believe safety was possible for them.

"You might also take some responsibility for each other. Consider your effects."

How dare she use that preachy voice? This woman had only grown Irene's terror larger. "Have you considered your effects, Dr. Bishop?" Irene said.

"Irene," Pearl said. She put her hand on Irene's wrist, saw what this did to Irene's face, and took her hand away again. "We're sorry, Dr. Bishop," she said. "We'll make it up with Margaret."

"Good," Dr. Bishop said.

Screaming made them all jump then, even Dr. Bishop. The sound had a watery quality, like a scream into a full glass. Irene's eyes went first to where Margaret had disappeared. But Dorothy Steadman stood up, clutching her enormous stomach and screaming a word now, *no,* and *no* again. They all could see the blood that filled her chair.

8

Where did you go to deliver a dead baby? The answer here, as in other hospitals, seemed to be the same place you went to deliver a living one. The doctors whisked Dorothy up to the third floor. The remaining women, left behind, pushed themselves out to the perimeters of the room, holding their mouths.

"Don't *say* that, *dead,* we don't *know* that," Pearl told Irene, who could hear that she was about to cry.

Their eyes moved to Dorothy's bloody chair.

Pearl gave a shake of her head that turned into a shake of her shoulders. She approached the chair, shook out a napkin, and laid it down over the seat. Irene tried not to look to see if the blood was seeping up where the napkin touched to make a blot shape in which she might see mice or moths or snakes. Within her the little moth beat its wings furiously. Whatever else it was, her creature wasn't dead.

She imagined what was happening to Dorothy up on the third floor. It would be worse because the baby was bigger, but still much like what she herself had felt with the others, probably, just more.

Mrs. Conrad came into the room awkwardly—it was clear she'd been sent. "All right, let's all go back to our rooms now. Examinations are going to be a little delayed, so let's wait where you'll be more comfortable."

"A *little delayed?*" Irene said.

Mrs. Conrad looked at Irene as if to say that none of this was her fault.

Upstairs, Irene and Pearl found Margaret, puffy-faced, hovering on the second-floor landing. "What's going on?"

"It's Dorothy." Pearl took in a trembling breath and touched Margaret's hand. "It's bad, I think."

Margaret shook her head. She looked defenseless, agonized, the way Irene felt every time she saw something she didn't want to see in this house. Irene was tired of feeling that way.

She didn't turn toward her room. She kept climbing, up toward the third floor.

"Where are you going?" Pearl whispered.

Irene pointed up, where she might learn what she didn't trust anyone here to tell her. Her head was already partly in the third floor's air. She waved a silent hand to say they should come along.

This floor looked vertiginously like the second, where they slept and were examined and had their therapy, as if they'd never left their hallway at all, as if under their feet this house were doubling and redoubling itself. The hush, though, was different, a frightening quiet that, once you were paying attention, wasn't perfect, because there were noises someone was trying to stifle. Voices. People speaking quietly and urgently. And lower, anguished sounds.

Partway down the row, a door opened. Dr. Bishop hurried out, into another room, without seeing them, then out again with a bag. Irene wondered what was in there: sharp silver instruments or the set of inkblots, needles or cloths to put over the eyes. Before Dr. Bishop reentered the room where Dorothy must be, she stood for a moment and squared her shoulders. Irene felt the movement in the muscles high up in her own back.

Then Dr. Bishop went back in, armed with all that resolve they'd watched her summon.

"Move aside, please," said somebody from behind. An unfamiliar man in a white coat brushed past—but not entirely unfamiliar, because Irene placed him after a moment as one of the doctors Dr. Bishop had led into the ballroom during her first calisthenics class. He was in a hurry, but he stopped short for a moment to look at them. He was the one, Irene remembered, who'd squinted with such skepticism.

"You three shouldn't be here for this," he told them sternly. "She's in a real mess now, Dr. Petticoats. This is no place for you."

It wasn't.

They hurried back down the stairs to their nearly identical floor, before what was happening to Dorothy could catch them.

*

(Dorothy had the feeling she'd waded out too deep and let herself get washed out to sea, away from the ground she'd been standing on. The hot flood was coming out of her still. She was afraid to look, so she didn't, but even with her eyes closed she could see red, red, red, flooding the sheets, flooding her vision, blurring Dr. Bishop's face, which hovered above her, saying, "Scopolamine," not to Dorothy but to the other white-coated figures in the periphery. Dorothy wanted to answer anyway, to say no, to tell the doctors she had to stay awake. If she didn't the red would swallow her, didn't they see? But it was too late. They hadn't asked her, and the swallowing was done.)

*

By lunch the doctors still hadn't reappeared. No one had been given her regular examination. The gait of the whole house seemed to have been broken; even the food, meat loaf with a thin gravy that tasted of sweat, was cold.

But Mrs. Conrad came as the plates were being cleared to tell the women it was gardening time.

"Gardening, today?" Margaret said.

"It's Thursday, so you garden," Mrs. Conrad said.

"Is this a requirement?" said Pearl.

"I'm just doing what I was asked," Mrs. Conrad said with irritation, and Irene realized that even if Mrs. Conrad were willing to be warmer, Irene would have come by now to hate her—for being spared what they were feeling, and what Dorothy was.

Mrs. Conrad didn't follow them outside, only to the doors, so she could report that they'd gone where she'd sent them. Maybe the doctors needed to do something to Dorothy that would make her scream even louder, and that was why gardening time was being observed, to get the rest of them out of the way where they wouldn't hear. Or maybe the baby or Dorothy or both had died and would be taken from the house while the women couldn't see.

They went out and sat in their rows before the new seedlings they were to plant today. Their hands were slow with the digging. The little moth flexed its wings against the insides of Irene's stomach.

As they worked, Irene and Margaret and Pearl tried not to look at one another, and they kept their bodies turned away from the garden walls in the distance.

*

The doctors finally reemerged partway through dinner. They weren't rumpled, no blood was visible on their coats, but they couldn't hide their faces. The women greeted them by going silent and putting down their silverware. No one had been eating much anyway. Dorothy's stained chair had been taken out, but they'd left a space for it at the table, like a missing tooth.

The doctors stepped together to the front of the room. "We wanted to address what happened this morning," Dr. Hall said.

The women waited in the charged air. They would probably work hard to believe, now, almost anything the doctors told them. That Dorothy had been a witch, that her child had been a changeling, that Dorothy had drunk, before coming to this house, from a poisoned well, or fallen earlier down a deep, dark hole, or breathed the wrong air in a separate, distant place. Any of those, or all of them, was the explanation—those events belonging to a time distinct from this one. So the rest of them didn't need to fear it had anything at all to do with them.

Even Irene would try to believe it.

"Dorothy's all right, first of all—first things first. She's resting now. Recovering well, all things considered."

The room let out some of its breath, but it was also true that nobody looked very surprised. All of them knew firsthand the dumb, cruel resilience of their own bodies. Every time, hadn't they rested and recovered and become almost as good as new again? Apart from their memories, anyway. Irene felt the women around her coming back into those bodies now, shifting with impatience. Their eyes narrowed. Dr. Hall hadn't in fact tackled the first thing.

"And?" said Irene.

Some of the others nodded.

"Sadly, Dorothy has had a stillbirth."

"How did it happen?" said Lucy Smallman.

At this, Dr. Hall seemed wrongfooted: usually they asked their questions of him with more deference. "That's a difficult question to fully answer, I'm afraid. Stillbirths have happened as long as births have."

Dr. Bishop inclined her head at him, but he shrugged, as if to ask her, *What more do you want me to say?* So Dr. Bishop stepped forward.

"There are some things we know, of course," she said. "Dorothy experienced what's called a partial placental abruption—this happens when the placenta pulls away from the wall of the womb and causes bleeding."

Irene thought about Dorothy's chair and its pool. She brought her hand to her belly, imagining that inner tearing away.

"But what would cause that?" said Pearl.

"Just an accident, a kind of natural fluke," Dr. Hall said. "A series of unlucky anatomical occurrences. You can think of it as a falling of dominoes in just the wrong way. Dorothy didn't do anything to make it happen, and she couldn't have done anything to stop it—but you should know that really it's quite rare. It happens in only a tiny fraction of a fraction of pregnancies. There's no reason for any of you to worry about something so unlikely."

"Do those kinds of fractions apply to us, though?" said Irene.

"Right."

Margaret was the one who'd spoken, though Irene could tell the doctors hadn't placed the voice from the way their eyes spun searchingly. Irene felt so proud that it had been Margaret.

"Actually, your pregnancies are far *more* monitored and tended than most," Dr. Bishop said. "I do know you all must be frightened. But really, what happened to Dorothy and her fetus—"

"Her *baby*," said Margaret. This time the doctors could tell the voice was hers.

Dr. Bishop made a small movement, as if adjusting her balance. "You're right, Mrs. Crowe. Her baby, then. Which is related to the point I was going to make: our treatment here is designed to prevent *miscarriage,* a loss much earlier in the pregnancy. A stillbirth isn't the same. We do of course hope we can help maintain health for both mother and child all the way up to delivery, but even given this tragedy, you must see that many things went right with Dorothy's pregnancy in order for her to make it so far."

"Dr. Bishop, are you trying to say you fixed her?" Irene said.

"I'm trying to tell you there's no reason to assume that what happened had any connection to her treatment."

"Did you tell Dorothy that?" Margaret said. Her eyes glittered, though her voice was still soft. "Did it make her feel better?"

"We feel for Dorothy, of course, tremendously," Dr. Bishop said. "I know you all do too. That's why we're telling you all of this. We didn't want you to be left with only rumors. We thought you deserved to know."

"*Thank* you, Doctor," said Irene.

"There are things we can't control," Dr. Bishop said, straightening up. She swept her gaze over the women's stomachs, even Irene's, as if surveying a cache of possessions. "But I promise you, here, we do control every last thing we can."

*

"Was that how you wanted things to go, you and Dr. Hall, with your Dorothy talk?" Irene asked Dr. Bishop during her therapy session the following morning.

"It's worth remembering, Irene, that what *we* want is only to keep *you* healthy and safe."

"We seemed to surprise Dr. Hall a little."

"This is all quite different from his previous interactions with patients."

Irene imagined Dr. Hall with those previous patients: a touch on the shoulder here, a smile there, perhaps an offhand remark about the weather, then a hand on the knee, only to steer it into the proper position—a hand under which women's legs would have relaxed like horses' flanks.

"Free association now, Irene," Dr. Bishop said briskly. "We'll begin with the word *stoop*."

"I think of a house, which makes me think of Dorothy leaving this house. When will that be?"

"Sometime in the next few days, probably. Let's try the word *grass*."

"Babies buried under."

The garden, the grass in the garden, hiding what?

"How about *smooth*."

"Baby skin. Skin of Dorothy's—"

"Enough," Dr. Bishop said.

It had a very final sound.

"I don't have to keep going?"

"I don't think *we* should keep going. You and I will have to continue to meet, that's our protocol, but I don't see much point in continuing to go through the motions of this therapy together, do you? It's certainly not getting us anywhere."

This was on some level what Irene had been trying to make happen, but there was terror in hearing Dr. Bishop say it, when her next sentence might be: *Actually, why don't you just go home.* A groveling apology was rising to Irene's lips—she would say anything to get to stay; the only thing she was more afraid of than staying was leaving—but Dr. Bishop stood. She walked to her desk.

"One more thing."

From a drawer she took out a syringe.

Irene looked at it there in her hand. Its simple, straightforward shape: clear in its intentions.

Irene should have expected this. In light of Dorothy, of course Dr. Bishop would be rushing to shore up every wall. She would be making the same calculation about all of them that she'd already made about Margaret, because she saw every one of them now as a vulnerable point.

Or only Irene?

"You're taking matters into your own hands?" Irene said.

"Everything here is in my hands."

"Are you doing this for everybody?"

"I can't discuss other patients, Irene."

Does Dr. Hall know? Irene might have said.

But if Dr. Bishop said *no,* said *on second thought,* said *maybe, after all,* and put the syringe away again, and something happened afterward to the little moth—what then? Irene would have to know for the rest of her life that there'd been an action to take, that it had been offered to her, and that she hadn't taken it.

When Dr. Bishop drew closer, bent her mirror-face down and in, and reached for Irene's arm, Irene swore she could smell Dorothy's iron-y, musky blood on her hands, whose skin was, in fact, very smooth.

*

Irene and Margaret and Pearl gathered at two o'clock in the afternoon, the least suspicious, most sun-drenched hour.

"Time to check on our risen creatures," Margaret said. "As if they need a precise amount of baking in the miracle oven."

But Margaret could say whatever she wanted—Irene knew she wouldn't back out now, not for anything.

As they walked, Pearl said, "Do you think they'll tell the husbands about what happened with Dorothy?"

"I don't think they'd ever choose to."

Pearl gave a little reassured nod. "I don't think so either. Maybe they won't. I just—things are better when Joe isn't worrying."

Quiet fell for a minute. Irene imagined the world inside Pearl's house, the currents of Joe's feelings swirling, Pearl with her finger to the wind.

Then Margaret said, very quietly, "Am I next?"

"What?" Pearl said.

"Do you think what happened to Dorothy will happen to me now? I can't take it, not again."

Irene was glad Margaret hadn't seen that pool of blood in the chair and so at least didn't have to imagine it when she asked herself this question.

"Of *course* it won't," Pearl said.

Irene said, "It could be any of us next, Margaret."

Margaret laughed angrily. "Irene, you aren't much for reassuring a person."

But in spite of themselves they'd come to the gate, ivy so thick across it you could barely tell an entrance existed. Irene imagined the ivy overtaking the walls, the gate, swallowing all the empty open space inside, eating the whole landscape.

Without looking at Margaret and Pearl, she pushed the ivy out of the way—like arms now, some of its dangling sections felt as thick as arms—and went in. They followed. All of them held back inside the gate, watching the fountain in fear.

"It won't mean anything if they aren't there," Margaret said.

"That's what I told myself before," Irene told her.

"It's nature. Things eat things. Even ants could have done it."

Irene thought she could actually smell the fountain, brackish and watery, though it looked to have been dry so long.

"Sure, if they're just gone, but the moth wasn't gone," she said. "It was there. It was there and alive again."

"A different moth."

"Beneath the same leaf and rock? It just flew itself into place?"

"Come on, before we lose our minds," said Pearl.

They could see before they reached the lip that their three rocks and leaves were where they'd left them.

"I can't stand to look," Pearl said.

But they went, they lifted.

And the beetle scuttled, the snake curved, the roly-poly scurried and then closed in on itself again, with the speed impossible things have when they happen, rolling forward frictionless over all the flattened rules.

Their hands went to their mouths at the same moment, as if together they made one woman. A woman with a just-now-changing shape, who was trying not to scream, who had grown new limbs to prevent herself from screaming through all her mouths.

The things tumbled one-two-three off the edge of the fountain to the ground and kept moving. The snake pulled Irene's eyes toward the rose bramble, where it disappeared. But the grandfather from the portrait in the bearskin room was there instead, surveying them from the garden's edge like a rotten-faced king, wrapped in the ivy, wearing it all like a cape, only that ruined face exposed, sunken and grayish, skin sloughing the way wet fabric sloughs.

He was alive and rotting. He looked at each of the three women in turn, but he looked at Irene the longest. The others weren't looking at him—why weren't they? Why should Irene be the only one? His face, she did not want to look at it. His eyes moved across her; she could feel them on her, crawling.

This garden is mine, his wet ogre-voice growled, and Irene shrank from it. But even through her terror, she wondered: Was it, really? He'd wanted it to be; he'd put walls around it to make it his. But maybe in overgrowing itself, the garden had been telling him *no.*

All of you are here in my garden, so all of you are mine, mark my words. If I say it, I do it. All of you and everything you carry.

Everything they carried. What was that?

The snake she'd killed had gone, but within Irene the coiling, writhing, of her little snake remained.

The scrabbling of beetle feet.

The roly-poly's spinning.

She saw that the others had their hands at their bellies too, staring at the places where their creatures had disappeared.

9

At dinner, Margaret sat on the other side of the dining room, as far as she could get from Irene and Pearl. She snuck away as soon as she'd eaten. Dr. Bishop's eyes followed her out, but the doctor didn't give chase.

Irene and Pearl did. They went to Margaret's door and knocked. Silence.

"Open up!" Irene said. To Pearl: "We have to make her open up."

Margaret had kept repeating *God, God, God* over and over as they'd run from the garden, so finally Irene had said, *What do you want Him to do?* and then Margaret stopped talking. Still, all three of them held hands as they ran—trying to keep one another on their feet and be sure they all made it out and away—and Irene had felt like they were together. But they'd let go to climb the steps to the house, then the stairs to their separate beds. The one body they'd made together had come apart.

Irene put her hand flat to Margaret's door now. They couldn't be sure Margaret was inside, but where on earth else could Margaret be? Irene tried to sense Margaret through her palm, pressed to the wood. Like putting her hand to her belly. The little snake rolled, as if it had heard her thoughts—making a sick, dizzy feeling in Irene's stomach—and was still again.

"We know you're in there, Margaret—we have to talk about it."

"*We* could just talk about it," Pearl said. She turned to Irene, eyes welling.

Too much feeling, at too close a range. Irene looked quickly away.

"I don't understand what I saw," Pearl said, "or what I *think* I saw, because I can't really have seen it, I must have just thought I did." She was running her finger over her lips repeatedly as if wiping them, still trying not to cry.

"Pearl, we were *all* there, we *all* saw," said Irene. Because that was one explanation she didn't have anymore: that she was privately seeing wrong, or privately losing her mind.

Was that a beetle scrabbling at the edge of the carpet at the far end of the hall? A shiny bit of darkness, moving fast. Irene turned to look full-on. Nothing. Had Pearl seen it? Irene peered at her and Pearl's eyes darted from hers, but then Pearl's eyes often did.

In bringing the others into this with her, it seemed Irene had only multiplied the strangenesses within, the strangenesses without. She'd hoped Pearl and Margaret would somehow save her from this. Instead they made new tethers to the impossible things she'd seen, because they'd all seen them.

Now there were new questions about what to do next.

"I need a little time, all right?" Margaret said through the door. She sounded more muffled than the wood could account for, as if she might be speaking into a pile of clothing. "I need a night, a rest."

"What's a rest going to do?" Irene said.

"There has to be something that explains it," Pearl said. "If we can talk about it, I'm sure we can figure it out."

"I don't think we're going to be able to figure out a way it didn't happen, if that's what you're hoping," Irene said. "Just how to think about it, maybe."

"We'll talk *soon*," Margaret said in a firm, unanswerable voice.

That night, inside Irene, the little snake seemed to wake. It began its writhing somersaults. She pressed her fingers to that place and felt the snake press up against them. Then the tail became small prickling legs, became a rolling, became a mouse tail and then a snake tail again, became paws, became wings. She'd had no idea love could swirl with horror this way.

George would be lying in his dark bed too. She wondered if he was still sleeping on his side the way she was even in this new bed, if he too was still turned toward the space where her body would be if it weren't elsewhere, or if he'd claimed the whole middle for himself. He felt so far away he might have been impossible too, another dream she'd had.

A sound at the window. A very small sound. A dull, slight tapping against the glass. She couldn't see that far, it was much too dark, but she could see what was making the sound anyway, just as she could see the little snake writhing inside her: hearing and feeling could spill over into seeing when what they told you mattered enough. So Irene could see a moth, a particular moth with ragged wings, bouncing against the glass.

Not to come in—it was in already. Not to go out either. Just to feel for the borders of its new world.

Irene slid her finger up and down the dark line that had appeared some weeks before on the bulge of her lower abdomen, a deep bruisy, autumnal red brown that she could also see without any need for vision. The *linea nigra*, Dr. Hall had called it. A line, a border. An underscoring of a place that could be torn if the future made tearing necessary. If what was in wanted to be out badly enough.

*

Margaret sat with Irene and Pearl again the next morning at breakfast and met their eyes over the table. She looked exhausted and pale. They ate—they all knew by now it was important to eat—their dry, thick toast and their mushed apples the color of weak tea. Had Irene eaten anything at dinner the night before? She couldn't remember. She took another bite of her toast and swallowed. "Where should we go to talk?" she whispered.

And Margaret simply stood and left the room.

For the next several days, this was how things went. Margaret didn't avoid them—she sat with them, walked with them, ate with them—and she would talk with them about any number of small, everyday things in an almost normal tone of voice, but as soon as Irene or Pearl tried to bring up what had happened, Margaret left without a word. If they tried chasing her, she walked to her room and shut her door in their very faces.

"We'll give her some more time," Pearl said, outside the closed door, in a soothing tone, or maybe a self-soothing one. "It might even be better if we don't dwell on it."

"It's not some bad feeling, Pearl."

But Pearl was already walking away.

One of these evenings, another of Dr. Bishop's experts arrived to present. This one was a woman in her sixties with silver curls. She hadn't merited the ballroom: they gathered to listen to her in the gold sitting room, where she sat in a chair before their small circle of sofas.

"This is Nurse Smith," Dr. Bishop told them. "You may have seen her in the house from time to time to help with our deliveries. She's here now to provide an overview of infant care."

Some of the women flinched—this counting of unhatched chickens.

Dr. Bishop said, "We felt this might be helpful. Aside from preparing you for what's to come, Nurse Smith's information will give you something specific to picture, during your time with us, as you imagine your future life with your child. You should all be trying to fill yourselves with these kinds of positive images."

She gave Nurse Smith a nod, and Nurse Smith reached underneath her chair and brought forth a doll. It was made of plastic, smaller than a real baby, with rosy lips and cheeks. Its rubbery arms swung on hinges. It wore a diaper, nothing else. Margaret, Irene saw, couldn't take her eyes off it.

"I'll demonstrate diapering first," said Nurse Smith.

She showed them the right angle for the pins. She showed them good bottle-feeding technique and how to cock the baby up over a shoulder to force the gas out. How to swaddle and bathe and rock.

"But I already know all this," Margaret said. "Dr. Bishop, you know I'm the oldest of four sisters. I don't remember a time when I didn't know all of this."

"Well, good for you, Mrs. Crowe." Dr. Bishop's voice was sharp. "But there are others here who aren't as familiar, and even you might benefit from the reminder. Really, I wish you would all stop fighting plans that are only for your own good."

The doll lay forgotten facedown on Nurse Smith's lap, its plastic buttocks shining with diaper cream. Everyone stared at Dr. Bishop's flushed face, so strange without its veneer of control, like the face of a woman they'd never met.

Things here weren't turning out the way Dr. Bishop had wanted. What did that mean for them? And what would she do about it, next? She who was so used to doing.

*

The following week, at gardening time, while the women weeded the rows of vegetables and flowers they had planted outside, Irene asked the question she couldn't stop thinking about. "Dr. Hall," she said as he passed, "what happened to Dorothy's baby?"

She had to shield her eyes to see his face, looming above her like something in a dream, blocking the sun. "What do you mean, Mrs. Willard? We told you, the baby was stillborn."

Margaret and Pearl kept pulling the weeds, but Irene could feel them listening. Dr. Bishop, on the other side of the patch, began to notice the conversation. She still didn't seem to like it when Dr. Hall talked too long to Irene.

"I know. I meant the actual . . . body. What happened to it?"

Dr. Hall looked in Dr. Bishop's direction, as if he'd have liked to wait for guidance. "Well, it's been released to the family."

Too late, then, in any case. Too late absolutely.

Dr. Bishop came and took Dr. Hall's arm. They strolled away.

"I know why you asked that, Irene," Margaret said softly. "I'd been thinking about it too. I think—"

"*Stop,*" Pearl said, "don't." She had her face averted, tipped down toward her garden plot.

"Pearl—"

"I don't want to hear it. It's too horrible."

The sun lay heavy across Irene's back. The snake wriggled in the new shape her crouched position had made for it inside, different from the shapes it was used to. Beneath Irene's fingers, the stalks of the weeds and the stalks of the intentional plants felt the same. She and Margaret and Pearl heaped the ripped-up shoots, a pile of white string, stitches all pulled out.

A car drove up to the house. Its tires on the gravel made a sound like chewing up little bones. It stopped beside the front door.

"Keep up the good work!" said Dr. Bishop, so Irene understood that they weren't supposed to pay this car any heed.

A man emerged and stood uncertainly.

The doctors set off across the lawn toward him. Dr. Bishop waved from a distance. The man waved back. When they reached him Dr. Hall shook his hand, then gripped his shoulder, and then Dr. Bishop shook too. They went into the house.

"That's Dorothy's husband—I remember him from visit days," Pearl said.

Irene stopped weeding and waited. Would Dorothy walk out or be carried? Would she acknowledge them? Curse them? The snake spun and Irene sucked in air.

A few minutes later, there was Dorothy, walking, holding her husband's arm. She looked even smaller than Irene remembered. Her hair was down and lank on her shoulders—had no one styled it?

"Oh, she looks so strange," Pearl whispered. "I remember feeling like that, like how she looks."

Irene knew what she meant. That feeling of being a person whose outside no longer had importance.

"It's even worse for her, though. She's going to feel like this forever," said Margaret.

Irene raised her arm in a wave. Dorothy saw her, Irene could tell—she paused, turned in her direction—but didn't wave back. She thought of that happy nod Dorothy had given her the morning of the catastrophe and felt like crying: Why hadn't she sat beside Dorothy and let her enjoy her boastful digs one last time? Irene wanted to run across the lawn to her and ask her all the things she wondered before Dorothy was carried off and out of her reach: Had she seen her baby before they took it away? Had she held it and looked at its face, and what had it looked like? What had happened to her up there on the third floor exactly, and had it felt like the other times, or more like some terrible variation of giving birth?

Though, of course, how could Dorothy know that?

Dorothy stood without moving for a moment, looking at Irene, who still had her arm raised. Then she climbed into the car. It drove off while the doctors watched. Irene lowered her arm. The big muscle was a little sore where Dr. Bishop had injected her.

"Dr. Bishop seems to have decided I also need more shots," she said to Margaret and Pearl.

"Me too," Pearl said, and Irene let out a breath. Though really, why should she be relieved? This meant only that Dr. Bishop was unsure about all of them.

Relief and then sadness passed over Margaret's face too.

"Everyone now, I guess," Irene said.

"It doesn't have to mean what you said before, though, Irene," said Pearl, shoving her hands into gardening gloves.

They worked for another twenty minutes, until Phillips, who'd been left in charge, released them. They trooped back into the house, and Irene pulled the others aside. "Come this way. There are open rooms down the hall sometimes."

But today the pattern of the doors seemed to have shifted: the first handles she tried, some of which Irene knew had yielded before beneath her hand, resisted her stiffly, as if the whole house were one vast lock and somebody had changed its combination. She had the feeling that when one finally gave, it might open on a distant landscape: the swing of the door would reveal a stretch of grass, a lecture hall, a seashore, the office of one of the doctors they'd all seen before these, one of their own living rooms with all three of their surprised husbands lined up inside: *We weren't expecting you so soon.*

Or another of her glimpses of Dr. Bishop's history, like a pocket of weather—if it *was* Dr. Bishop's history Irene had been seeing, really, and not some heightened or fabricated version of it. The vision would knock Irene still on the threshold, and the others would either see it or not, but certainly they'd know Irene had seen something. Then she'd have to tell them, wouldn't she? That something seemed to want to plant her inside Dr. Bishop's life, here in this house.

Can you see it too? she'd have to ask.

She thought she knew the answer, though. She was the only one with the mirror-face, wasn't she? Only she fit into some hole Dr. Bishop had left behind when she'd grown up and left this place, maybe—or the fit was near enough.

When the door to the blue parlor did finally open, though, that was all it was, only the blue parlor with its furniture inhabitants that seemed to have stopped some whispered conversation moments before. Irene pulled the others through, checking the hall behind. They sat, Irene and Pearl on the sofa and Margaret on a chair that faced it. The room had the faint odor of fabric left too long in an airless place.

"So are you finally ready to talk to us now, Margaret?" Irene said.

"Not really, but seeing Dorothy like that—I know we have to."

"I don't think we have to get into—I mean, what I've been thinking is maybe we could all have imagined it somehow," Pearl said, speaking very quickly. "I've heard about things like that. Groups of people, women usually, just sort of, you know, gripped by something. All completely convinced, when really it isn't there."

"We're well past that, Pearl, don't you think?" Margaret said.

Pearl slumped.

Margaret drummed her fingertips on the sofa's arm. "At first I thought I just couldn't get Dorothy's baby out of my head because it's such a terrible thing. But that wasn't the whole reason, I realized. It was because I was trying to figure out what we do next."

"Do?" said Pearl.

Before answering, Margaret bit down so hard Irene could see the big knots of her jaw muscles. "It's too late for Dorothy, but it might not be too late for us, if we can learn some things. If everything does go the worst possible way, maybe we could use this, if it does what we think it does."

"How?" whispered Pearl.

"We could take . . . what comes out." Margaret's face went red, but she persevered. "We could take it and put it there, and the garden might finish it, give it the rest of what it needs. Bring it back. Oh, don't look at me that way—it must have occurred to you both."

"The doctors would stop us," Pearl said.

"Maybe not," said Irene. "I don't think they know about the garden. I don't think all this fits with what they understand, with their synthetic estrogen and no salt and therapy." She put on Dr. Bishop's voice for the list of methods, the way the father had put on the grandfather's voice, and she saw Pearl wince. "I think the garden is separate from them, from what they know. But still, it might not work, Margaret. Babies aren't beetles or mice."

"That's what I was thinking too. So I think we have to try something else."

"What are you talking about?" Irene said.

"So far we know almost nothing about this: how it happens, or what it can and can't do. All we know is that it seems to work on very small things."

All three of them put their hands to their stomachs—even Margaret's wasn't small, not really, even if smaller than it should be.

"You want to try with a *big* dead thing? What are you proposing, Margaret? A stabbing, a shooting?" There was a wild laughter in Pearl's voice. "This is all too crazy, isn't it?"

"Easy for you to say," Margaret said.

Because it was Margaret whose fear was the largest, who had felt the questions these doctors had left unanswered in the shape of her own body when she smoothed her dresses over it. She'd done every last thing she was supposed to do and carried with her the constant proof that none of it had been enough. She'd taken on the doctors' plans ferociously. Now, Irene saw, she would take on a new plan in the same way.

"Margaret, any of us could be the one who needs it," Irene said. Pearl gave a strange gulping cry. "Or maybe not, it could be that what the doctors are doing is working just fine, that's also true. We aren't giving up on their plans, Pearl—why should we? We'll just do this too. Don't we need to know? We can't be finding out only when we need it if it'll work."

The clock on the mantel struck, making them jump. Five chimes, though it was nowhere near five o'clock.

"Right, because if we don't figure it out, if we don't have a plan already when—if—it turns out we need it," Margaret said, "it'll be too late."

Those words they'd heard plenty of times: *too late,* and also *too early.* Each a way of saying *nothing to be done.* What if now there was, at last, something?

"How do we get something bigger to use, though?" Irene said.

Pearl tapped her fingers on her kneecaps. Irene thought next she might say, *You two do what you want, I can't be part of this.*

But she said, "Joe does some trapping, he and his brother.

He keeps traps all piled up in our shed. I could call and tell him there's something getting into the flower gardens here. I could have him drop one off the next time he goes to visit his mother. This wouldn't be far out of his way."

"Won't he ask questions?" Irene said.

"I don't think he'll wonder much. Joe loves to be the one who has the thing people need."

"What would we catch, do you think?" Margaret said, pale.

"There are a lot of things around here. A raccoon, maybe, or a possum, or a groundhog. It wouldn't really matter, would it?"

No. The size mattered, that was all.

10

Pearl called and asked Joe, who said sure, he'd bring a trap, he'd tell her when. "Soon, though?" Margaret kept asking.

Irene understood—Margaret was twenty-nine weeks now but still looked only slightly bigger than when Irene had met her.

"I'll tell you as soon as I know, as soon as he tells me."

Back to waiting, then.

Not long after, the doctors surprised the women with an announcement. A day trip. The lakeshore—now that it was warm, almost June, almost summer. "For pleasure!" Dr. Bishop said. Really for boosting their morale, Irene and everyone else knew. But in spite of themselves they were boosted, they soared on summery swells of excitement: they would be leaving the house for a whole day.

They woke early on the morning of the trip to get ready. They put on dresses with wispier fabric than usual, in lighter colors—Irene's was her lightest blue—and pinned back their hair, and carried layers for the lake breeze, in case it was stiff. They pretended as they went down the stairs that they would meet not the doctors and the other members of their coven but their husbands. They could be going on holiday with their husbands, whose arms they could hold to walk, with whom they could talk about next summer, and the way next summer they'd have their babies with them, by then solid and in the world enough to grab up fistfuls of lake dirt, could they imagine? They could—had—and at the same time couldn't at all.

Out on the front steps, Irene, Pearl, and Margaret hung back from the others, not enough so any of them would notice. The sun felt hot on the top of Irene's head already on the steps' baking white expanse. A thick warmth crept into the rooms of the house these days, even with the curtains drawn—the breezes from the open windows behind them got caught in the fabric, setting the thick, heavy damask swaying like the skirts of waltzing women, while inside the real women, expanding, bulging, sweated in humid low light. At night Irene's sheets went damp as soon as they touched the skin of her arms and legs. She reached up now to pat her baking hair. This summer would just keep getting hotter as she kept growing. The changing of seasons made her feel the quantity of outside-world time she was missing, sealed away in this place as if under glass.

"It's all right for us to go and leave the garden, you think?" said Margaret.

"Oh, I'm sure," murmured Pearl.

"*I* don't know," said Irene.

At the bottom of the front stairs a line of five cars waited like a small stationary parade. The drivers were both of the doctors, Mrs. Conrad, Phillips, and another man Irene had seen working the grounds in front.

"It's like we're being taken on a summer-camp outing," Irene said.

"You went to summer camp too?" said Margaret. "Wasn't it magical?"

Irene grimaced at her. Margaret looked awful, haunted, but her face creased with joy at the memory of summer camp, which Irene, who'd gone only once, at about twelve, had found intolerable. Margaret might have been at the very same camp, organizing fireside sing-alongs and neatly, intensely crafting while Irene smoldered and swatted mosquitoes off her legs, back then so skinny she'd hated having to expose them. When Irene had refused to go back the next year and her mother had pitched her voice into its wailing key about this, having cherished her freedom from Irene's constant biting presence, her father cleared his throat and said the place cost too much anyway. That had been the end of trying to turn Irene into a more cooperative and group-oriented girl. Maybe all this, now, was some punishment for her failure to ever sew herself nicely into the fabric of things.

Irene, Pearl, and Margaret ended up in Dr. Hall's car, with Irene in the passenger seat. She hadn't climbed into a car for weeks, and her legs nearly buckled as she lowered her new weight. Dr. Hall waited for Dr. Bishop to pull her car out ahead of him with his hands at ten and two. In their way they were appealing hands, square and capable, beneath the knuckles a few red-blond hairs sparkling. Irene imagined them on Dr. Bishop's face, with its lines like her own face, and ducked her head down.

"Isn't *this* an event, leaving the house and everything," Dr. Hall said.

Sarcasm from Dr. Hall was a surprise. Irene wondered if the strain on their plans here was fraying his mood. "Well, it's all up to you, isn't it?" she said. "We could do more excursions, if you're antsy."

"We like to be careful with all of you."

Dr. Bishop's car began to move, and Dr. Hall moved theirs after.

"But now it suddenly seems important to keep us happy? Why-ever should that be?"

In the back seat Pearl and Margaret raised their eyebrows.

"Really we just thought it'd be nice to give everyone a little break," Dr. Hall said, backing again into resolute cheer. "You'll see, it's a special place."

"Do you go to this spot often, Doctor?" said Margaret.

"We try for at least once a year. It's special to us. Lou—Dr. Bishop—first brought me not long after we met."

They were far enough away from the house-hospital now that when Irene looked for it over her shoulder she found it had been swallowed by a tall, dark row of trees. You wouldn't know it was there at all. Out here, in the sunshine, this was a regular day. Trees, a road, occasionally a smallish farmhouse set back in fields.

"How *did* you two meet?" Pearl asked Dr. Hall.

"Medical school. Our very first week, though she doesn't remember me from then." Something private and distant was happening to his expression. Irene wanted inside whatever he was seeing—she wanted to know everything she could about Dr. Bishop, so that she could stand inside another vision, if another happened, and feel confident about which of the two of them she was.

"She must have stood out. There can't have been many women," Irene said.

"Just her." He pattered his fingers in a trill on the wheel. "But I'd have noticed her even if there had been others. She was right in the front row, with her notebook and a set of pens lined up, like she thought she might need more than one pen in a hurry. All her hair was bundled back, like she was hoping no one would notice she wasn't a boy."

Like, like—did Dr. Hall know anything actual about his wife?

"She looked at the professor, nobody else—really the rest of us might as well not have been there."

"And she was so beautiful you fell straight in love."

Here Irene turned the brunt of her own similar face on him.

"Well, yes," Dr. Hall said. "But also I'd never seen anybody focus like that. Look at only one thing for so long."

Irene could see both of them in that room: young Dr. Bishop staring at the chalkboard with the full force and panic of her desire; young Dr. Hall imagining what it would feel like to have her stare at him instead.

The little snake writhed. Irene put her fingers to her belly, which was tight as a drum.

"How lovely," Pearl said.

"Anyway. Lou has nice memories of swimming at this lake with her father. He wasn't with us anymore, sadly, by the time I met Lou."

"He was dead, you mean," Irene said.

Margaret, of course, inhaled sharply, but it was true. And Irene had seen enough to feel she knew some things about that father.

They drove in silence then. Irene fell asleep against the car window and woke to a hot sore cheek, a stiff neck, the little snake twisting, and, through the windshield, a pocket of silvery water rimmed by dark trees.

"Here we are," announced Dr. Hall.

They climbed out into the heat. Dr. Bishop stood already at the start of the path, facing back toward them. "Be careful, please," she said. "The ground's a bit uneven, but there's a pretty beach up ahead." She strode off, too quickly at first: Irene watched her remember and slow herself. The waddling women followed. Tree roots here, loose stones. They picked their way with caution. Beatrice Loomis, who was very big now, extended her broad hands to either side as she moved, as if she were touching an invisible shelf in the air that might allow her to catch herself if she stumbled.

The beach was nice, though. It was really just a lawn, no actual sand, but it was broad, a vivid green, and lined with white Adirondack chairs. A white gazebo perched in the middle, showpiece-y and delicate as a wedding-cake topper. The grass made a carpet of space that stilled the eye before it met the water, which shivered light across itself. Into the lake stretched a wide dock, with small, wavering canoes tethered to its sides. "No boating please, ladies—there's a little chop today—and no real swimming," said Dr. Bishop. "Just enjoy the fresh air."

They hadn't brought their swimsuits to the hospital with them anyway. Their swimsuits wouldn't even have fit them.

Margaret went to sit in the gazebo: "This sun, I'll fry like an egg!" Irene suspected her of fearing, still, too much light and agitation, not because she really believed the doctors anymore but because she feared everything. Pearl and Irene settled themselves into Adirondack chairs. The tipped-back angle was difficult in their new bodies, and when Irene tried to hold herself upright enough to look at Pearl, she found her stomach muscles didn't seem to be available to her. Pearl too shifted restlessly.

Inside Irene the little snake uncoiled itself as if stretching. Their levels of comfort and activity seemed inversely proportional so much of the time. Would this be true once it was out in the world too? It had always been true for Irene and her own mother: when her mother wanted to sit, Irene wanted to move, and when her mother was trying to move her somewhere, it was usually against Irene's will.

Pearl stared into the sky. "Do you think we could have *made* it happen somehow? By needing things to stay alive so badly. What if that just, I don't know, spilled over?"

Irene considered. Some needs might be too great for bodies, some bodies anyway, to contain. Her own most of all, maybe. She'd been the one who started it.

"What if we did?" she said. "It doesn't change anything. We still have to figure out what to do next."

"I guess that's right."

Irene leaned her head back too to stare at the sky, which was the kind of blue that stings the eyes and then reveals all the little cells floating inside them. Small rings with darker circles at their centers, one or two waving wormlike things. As bulky as she felt now, she was still made of many layers of nearly transparent material, and so was the little snake. Add up enough thinnesses and you get a thickness.

Were the little snake's eyes still closed? Did it have real eyes yet?

"We used to take a lake vacation, every summer, with Joe's sister and her husband," Pearl said. "I looked forward to it for months ahead of time. She's really funny, Betty is, and her husband's so nice. We'd play cards and drink and go swimming in the dark."

Pearl's past tense had a final ring. "Why'd you stop?" Irene said.

"They had a baby boy. Then another baby boy."

"And stopped taking vacations?"

"No, they probably still take those trips. Joe just stopped wanting us to go along. He told me work was busy." Pearl shifted again. Irene wanted to tell her it was hopeless, there was no way to get comfortable, but Pearl was crying a little, so Irene stayed quiet. "But I know really it was that he couldn't stand it anymore, them fussing over their baby while we stood around and held it sometimes and pretended to think it was so wonderful, so adorable, when what we were thinking the whole time was *Why not us?* Joe just—he always wanted a big pack of boys. I understood in a way, but I was so angry at him for being the one to decide we should stop going. As if he were the one it was all hurting most."

Irene thought of George's expression when he carried her to the car to drive her to the hospital the second time. She'd looked up at the underside of his chin, at his face, which was wet, and said, *Why are you crying?*

Irene reached over and put a hand on Pearl's stomach. Pearl's eyes flew open. "Well, it's a good thing you're having a baby now, then," Irene said.

Under her fingers, Pearl's stomach felt as firm as underripe fruit. Irene's own stomach felt just like this.

Did Margaret's?

Irene took her hand back. "I can't stand these chairs. I'm going to walk." She hoisted herself up, out.

She felt the doctors' eyes on her from their own chairs as she neared the lip where the lake and land met, but she didn't turn her head. Maybe she should climb into a canoe and start paddling to see what they might do about it. Though she wouldn't be very fast away, with how long it would take to lower herself in.

The weather-beaten boards of the dock creaked pleasingly underfoot, and the lake glinted and shadowed through the gaps between. At the end of the dock Irene made a clumsy move to sitting, took off her slide shoes, and let drop her bare, pale feet. The shocking cold of the water ached deep in her bones, but the lapping noises it made as she swished her feet back and forth were appetizing, and the smell too, that good lake-y smell that made you think of clean depth. Irene was thirsty and hot. She wished they'd brought something to drink; maybe they had, maybe in a moment she'd go and ask them.

When Irene cast a glance over her shoulder, she found that Dr. Bishop had moved while she'd had her back turned and stood at the water's edge. The lake spread itself between her on the shore and Irene on the dock, one bit of a huge, unreadable inkblot. Dr. Bishop's eyes tick-tick-ticked over the women, hanging on Irene for an extra beat each time: she was counting them, maybe. Studying them. Seeing what they looked like here in this new place, like putting a new dress in a new light to check the color.

Dr. Hall shifted in the background: leaned his head back in his chair, which he seemed to find comfortable enough, extended his legs, and closed his eyes.

Irene faced the water again. A moment later she could feel someone's approaching footsteps in the motion of the boards beneath her. *Dr. Bishop,* she thought, and turned, to be ready, but she found instead a plump older woman with a stiff-looking iron-gray permanent.

"Mind if I join you?" the woman said. She was already lowering herself.

Irene looked at the lake, to discourage friendliness. But the woman gave one of those appreciative sighs that told Irene the conversation would be continuing. She said, "If you don't mind my asking, are you all here together, like some sort of club?"

Irene had encountered this problem before: when you separated yourself off, people thought you'd be grateful to talk to them because they were saving you from your aloneness. This woman waited to hear news she could go home and share: *You'll never guess what was going on out at the lake today.*

"That's right, we're a club," Irene said. "We get together to be pregnant."

The woman's expression furrowed. Irene felt the little electricity of pleasure that came from saying a needly thing. She looked back again and saw Dr. Bishop watching her closely, and was she leaning slightly forward? Why should Dr. Bishop be nervous? Irene wondered again exactly whom she'd told and not told about what she was doing, and how much rushing she had done, how much keeping quiet, to start seeing if her idea would work as fast as she could.

"I'm teasing. We're patients at a hospital not too far from here. We came with our doctors, two of them, they're married."

"Married doctors!"

"That's her, right there, and he's back behind."

Irene made sure Dr. Bishop could see her pointing.

"Isn't that something," the woman said, looking at Dr. Bishop with unabashed curiosity. "I have four children myself."

Irene dreaded what would follow. *I saw the doctor only at the very end. Why the need for such a fuss?* Or *What's wrong with all of you?*

"It might have been nice to have . . . others with me. It was lonely." The woman let out a bark of laughter. "After the babies too."

"But you have them, your children," Irene said.

Below her, there in the lake—was something stirring, a snake-like something? Irene fought the urge to pull her feet back up.

She hadn't considered that the visions might follow her here.

"Well, they aren't children anymore, all grown. Two are still nearby, one's out in Montana, and one's down in New York, and it's hard to get much time with any of them. Funny how they leave you—for a long time it doesn't seem like they ever will. You can't really prepare yourself, no matter how people tell you ahead of time." The woman kicked her feet. "The water *is* cold, isn't it?"

Movement in the periphery caught Irene's eye: Dr. Bishop was walking out onto the dock now. She wanted to check what Irene had been saying. She would try, probably, to bring her back to shore. Already Irene could almost feel Dr. Bishop's fingers on her upper arm, closing over the injection site, and could hear the crisp greeting she'd give this stranger while she pulled Irene away.

So Irene threw herself forward.

She imagined the woman flinching behind her, Dr. Bishop too, as if the water had come up over their faces. Against Irene's face, the lake felt as startling as she had wanted. Its cold possessed her and brushed her eyelids and lips and woke her up and set her straight and sent her back where she'd wanted to be, in memory: swimming with George in that pond off the back road past his house, where they weren't supposed to go because it belonged to somebody—alone together and naked, as of course they weren't supposed to be either. They seemed almost never to go swimming at the right season, mostly spring or fall instead, so the water was always freezing. His beautiful body had cut through it, chasing hers. Her own body turned beautiful too as his nearness transfigured it. She'd used its power on them both. Neither of them had seemed to feel any failures coiled and waiting at the center of her.

Irene came up and breathed, ducked under again, and swooshed her arms. Green plants drifted in the shivery light below. She could touch the bottom here if she needed to, but she didn't. Being in the water in clothes felt strange, but her buoyancy counterbalanced the extra drag some: the little snake in its cushion of water thrust her up from below, so that she lay almost flat on the surface while she swam.

She pulled herself onward until she was out too deep to touch. Only then did she let herself turn to look back, though she'd been able to hear them all along.

Lined up on the shore, all the women and Dr. Hall were shouting at her, and Dr. Bishop and the woman stranger waved from the dock. The doctors had raised their arms high above their heads, and some of the women had their hands at their mouths.

Irene spun around again to fix her eyes on the opposite shore. Maybe she should keep swimming until she reached it. See what it had to offer.

Instead she tipped herself back, spread her arms, and floated easily. Was this how the little snake felt? She swept her arms back and forth. No wonder it wriggled and bumped against her. She could imagine the frustrations of meeting your liquid world's solid edges, keeping you back and in. Would George recognize her body if he were here with her? Would he chase it through the water like a prize? They were both chasing the little snake now. She put her hands to her belly and found she could float pretty well even without her arms' ballast. She closed her eyes.

Their shouts still reached her, though. She would hate the feel of them hauling her by the elbows out of this delicious drift, if they came out here in a boat to fetch her, as they might feel the need to do soon. She sighed and dove under to swish herself forward one more time.

And the snake was there. In the water with her. Off to the side, twisting like a plant amongst plants in all that green light, except it was too dark a shape, too full of its own movement.

Her whole skin shrank, and she swished herself backward, but when she turned her head toward it, of course it had gone. The plants where it had been were hazy and dim with particulates.

Her heart was starting to slow again when swimming through those plants was something else: Dr. Bishop as a girl, deep under the water, all pale lit-up skin, cutting through the weeds, using her hands to part them. Swimming very fast, away from something. Fear in her haste.

Swimming, also, straight for Irene.

Her hands, why were they extended?

Irene whirled and swam toward shore. At any moment she knew the girl Dr. Bishop would close her grip around Irene's ankles and pull her back and down, deeper. Drowning Irene because she was drowning. Keeping Irene for her past self instead of her present one.

Irene swam as high in the water as she could, with a fast, jerky crawl. When finally she was shallow enough to stand, she lurched to her feet.

Everyone stopped shouting as she approached and stood still, watching her. The feel of gravity was deadening. Irene couldn't believe she'd been walking around with all this weight.

Her panic, though, began to leave her, out again in the sunshine.

Dr. Bishop waded into the water herself to put a hand on Irene's elbow. "What are you *doing?*" she whispered. She gripped tight, as tight as Irene had known either version of her would, steering Irene in.

"I got warm, so I thought I'd swim."

"In your clothes?"

"I didn't have my bathing suit, did I?"

"I told you no swimming."

"Wish we had a towel," Dr. Hall said. He swiveled his head around as if it might turn out there was one here after all, someplace. His hair looked as if he'd been rumpling it in terror. Had they thought she would drown? Of course she'd thought so too, for a moment.

"We didn't expect to need one," said Dr. Bishop.

"Just goes to show," Irene said. She wrung out some of her wispy summer skirt. Her whole dress had gone transparent and clung now to the peachy globe of her stomach, her newly protruding belly button fixing them like a watchful eye. She put her shoulders back to aim it at them all. She felt better now, good almost in her coolness, in her tingling skin.

"Why don't you go sit in the sun to dry off?" Dr. Bishop said. "We don't need you shivering the whole drive home."

Over Dr. Bishop's shoulder, the gray-haired woman stranger stared.

Irene found a sunny patch of lawn and sat. She gathered her hair and squeezed water from it over one shoulder, so drops scattered in the grass. The attention of the others began to drift.

After a minute Pearl and Margaret, wearing tense, grave expressions, came to sit beside her.

"Yes?" Irene said.

"What *was* that? You're not—are you feeling all right?" said Pearl.

Irene let out a burst of laughter. "You're worrying I'm losing my mind? I just wanted to swim, that's all, I swear."

Pearl took a breath. "I wondered. Because I've been feeling strange. A little strange. Neither of you has?"

Eagerness welled in Irene. "How do you mean?"

Margaret looked away, at the water.

"You're going to make me say it?" Pearl said. "Fine. I've been thinking I see them sometimes, the things we put in the garden. Only ever for a second, as I'm walking around and doing other things. Never long enough to be sure."

So there it was. Proof that Irene had done to them what had been done to her, and that the garden was invading them too. Whatever the cost of their discovery, now they were all paying it. Irene looked at Pearl's teary face. She knew what that felt like, to believe you'd crossed into a frightening new country alone. She'd brought the two of them along with her because she hadn't been able to bear that feeling. She hadn't meant to do this to them; she had meant to, of course she had; both were true.

"So have I," she said.

Next she almost said, *And what about the doctor, Dr. Bishop, and the father, and the grandfather? Have you been seeing them too?*

Something stopped her, just in time.

"Margaret?" Pearl asked.

Margaret was pulling at the grass beneath her hands, stretching it long, combing it. "It doesn't *matter,*" Margaret said. "Who cares what I see? Nothing I could see could matter. Nothing could stop me, not if it works."

"But what does it mean?" Pearl said. "Are they even really alive?"

"We can't know, I guess," Irene said, "since we can't really see."

"We aren't seeing everything, that's all," Margaret said fiercely. "They're alive. They're moving, aren't they? That's enough."

And Irene nodded, because she remembered the terror of stillness.

POSSUM

11

The doctors didn't seem to want much to do with the women that evening, and they didn't come to breakfast in the morning. Irene sipped her meager cup of coffee and raised her eyebrows at Margaret and Pearl, who raised them back. What if the doctors had stolen off in the night? They could have waited until the house was still and silent and then risen to shove clothing into bags, tiptoe down the stairs, and drive off into other lives, leaving their white coats behind forever. It might not have seemed like their worst idea. Dr. Bishop might decide to be done with this project, now that it was unfolding in ways she couldn't steer.

Part of Irene liked the prospect of having bested Dr. Bishop in this way, having showed her finally, with that swim. But what would she and all the left-behind women do? Everything that had been set in motion here would keep moving whether or not the doctors were at the head of it, like a driverless cart rolling downhill.

Mrs. Conrad came to the door then to announce calisthenics as usual.

Their time in the ballroom also went, at first, like always. Dr. Hall appeared (still present after all, then) and led the exercises from the front of the room, looking only a little tired and wary, and Mrs. Conrad controlled the music as smoothly as a fancy piece of machinery. The women did their stretching, reaching, pulling, breathing. The room warmed by the second. The more of Irene's body there was, the hotter she seemed to get. Reddish light came off the blood-colored walls and bathed the women, like—no other way of seeing it—they were all together in a huge womb. Irene's little snake was lulled into stillness by her motion. Irene's mind too was lulled. For a while she stopped thinking and just moved as instructed.

Dr. Bishop entered partway through. She went to a wall and leaned, and when Dr. Hall saw her, there was a hitch in his gaze. So he didn't know why she'd come either.

She let him finish. Only when he clapped and told the women they were done did Dr. Bishop say, "While you're all here, I'd like to try another brief exercise."

"Be my guest, Dr. Bishop," Dr. Hall said, and made way for her.

Though really wasn't he her guest here and everywhere in this house?

Dr. Bishop took the front of the room. Their troubles lately seemed to have left more marks on her than on Dr. Hall: her face was drawn, with translucent purple moons beneath her eyes. Irene had seen the first glimpses of those shadows beneath her own eyes too after bad nights. Age surfacing. Her mother had them permanently.

Dr. Bishop's eyes passed over Irene's face. Irene wondered if she could sense that some version of her past self, that vision girl, had wanted to drag Irene down to the lake's cold bottom.

Dr. Bishop said, "If you could all make a line, one line, and take the hands of the women on either side of you. Good. Please close your eyes."

To Irene, closing herself into that darkness felt like laying herself out on the couch. She shut her eyes to the sneaky, imperceptibly open position she'd discovered in childhood to let her check that the people around her were doing what they'd been told—she wasn't going to be the only one. Quick turns to the right and the left showed that Margaret and Pearl, at least, seemed to be obeying. Margaret's hand was warmer and moister than Pearl's.

When Irene glanced forward again she saw that Dr. Bishop was looking right at her, so she shut her eyes all the way.

"Now breathe in, then out, slowly. In, two, three, out, two, three. In, two, three, out, two, three."

Irene breathed. Even the darkness had a warm red tint, like being inside a body. Could the little snake open what it had for eyes? Was there light to be had through Irene's abdomen the way there was light to be had through her eyelids?

"I want you to imagine for me. Imagine, please, that you're standing inside your own front door."

Dr. Bishop was making an effort to reach into their minds more directly, then, maybe having learned the limits of trying to open them up and let what was inside pour out. Maybe she felt done waiting.

"You've just come back from an errand, the grocery store, if you like. Now take a step forward. One step forward, into your own home. Feel it around you."

The words made a physical pain in Irene's chest and an image of her living room inside her mind: the blue sofa set, the rug that was wearing where they walked on it most. She wanted no more visions. She thought about opening her eyes and telling Dr. Bishop she was done, but Margaret and Pearl were already stepping forward, Margaret's step larger than Pearl's, so Irene was pulled to one side.

"Who's inside your house with you? Maybe you can see your husband, or your sister, or your friend; maybe some people are over for coffee. Think about them. Visualize them. Take another step, please."

Irene did see George and her mother, sitting against opposite arms of the couch. Her mother was drinking coffee, holding the saucer under her cup like she thought she was the queen of England, and eyeing Irene's clothes. George gave Irene the biggest smile.

"You're all the way inside your house. And now that you're inside, you can hear your baby."

Irene gasped. She could feel the gasps Margaret and Pearl took beside her in the way their hands tugged.

"Your baby—upstairs, or wherever the baby's bedroom is— is waking up from its nap. It isn't crying, it's not upset. It's just making some sounds to let you know it's awake. Take another step forward, please, closer to that baby. Because your baby *needs* you."

Around her Irene could hear low half-swallowed sounds of women crying. All their steps were so big now.

"You are the one, the *only* one, who can give your baby what it needs. You are going to that baby now, to feed it. Imagine yourself feeding it. You're going to bring it what only you can. Another step now."

They took their steps. Inside Irene the little snake spun, as if to say, *Baby? What baby? I'm all that's here.*

"*You* will keep your baby alive. Do you understand? No one else can do it for you, not even me. You're here so you can learn how to do it, yes, but also *you* have to begin doing it now." Dr. Bishop's voice was getting louder. "Take another step. Feel the strength of your legs, carrying you toward your baby. Feel your arms, ready to lift and hold your baby."

Irene's legs felt tired, but it was true that they were carrying her. She tensed her arms at her sides.

"Another step. Feel your heart, your lungs, working to move you toward your baby."

In her mind, Irene had reached her house's staircase. The George on the couch watched her, still smiling, but something began to happen to his smile: it dimmed, faltered, flickered like a faulty bulb. Her mother on the couch dropped her teacup, kept hold of the saucer but at a slant. Her eyes were still on Irene. What did she see? Why was she looking at Irene like that?

What had Irene done, to make them both look at her that way?

"Feel your whole self drawing closer to your baby, this baby only you can keep alive. You will do it, won't you? You will keep that baby alive? Another step."

Where had her mother's teacup gone? Irene looked for it on the floor, but it was nowhere. The baby, where was the baby? This conjuring felt just like one of the visions now, and Irene felt the same panic grip her and move her, faster. She hurried up the stairs of her house. Would she reach her baby? Would she see it? What would it look like, what parts would it have, and would she know it on sight as hers?

"Another step. Another. Another. *You* will keep your baby alive. You *are* keeping your baby alive. Another step. Another."

"Lou," Dr. Hall's voice said.

The spell broke. They all opened their eyes.

They stood very close to Dr. Bishop now. They'd backed her right up against the far wall of the ballroom. She'd shrunk with her palms pressed to that solid surface behind her, her cheeks red, her lips shining from all the shouting, her eyes shining too. Her posture was terrified, but her expression was full of the exultation of someone who'd just won a race. Dr. Hall stood beside her with his hand on her arm.

Dr. Bishop looked toward him. Her face rearranged itself.

"All right," she said. She turned back to her women. "Remember, all of you. *You* keep your babies alive."

Here and there in the crowd surrounding Irene, she could hear the sounds of sniffling, the aftermath of tears and the continuing of them. Nobody had been ready for what Dr. Bishop had made them do.

Dr. Hall put on an unconvincing pleasant expression. "Ladies, you're free to go now."

They moved out those wide double doors. Irene smoothed her hair and saw that her hands shook.

"How could she say that to us?" Margaret said. "That it's our job? That it's our fault if it doesn't work? What are we doing here, then?" Her voice was clogged and wet.

"What can have gotten into her?" Pearl said.

"She's afraid, I think," Irene said.

"Of what? These aren't *her* babies," said Margaret.

Why are you *crying?*

"I don't think it's the babies for her. Or not mostly. The babies just prove that she's managed to do what nobody else could. She's made that the thing that counts most about herself somehow, so she can't stand the idea of losing it, and I think she's starting to be afraid, really afraid, that she will. So she's trying every last thing she can think of to make us work the way we're supposed to."

"How do you know all this, Irene?" Pearl said.

Irene thought of the girl Dr. Bishop's horrified face in the garden, of the force and fear of the girl Dr. Bishop's swimming, and then of her own. She knew because she'd seen, that was why. But she couldn't tell Margaret and Pearl how this piece of things was happening only to her, how some affinity between her and Dr. Bishop, or some mistaking, was giving her parts of this place she had no desire to possess. She looked at the floor. "I *don't* know, of course. It's just a feeling. I just think she's always wanted to get far, far away from the girl she was here and doesn't quite believe she ever will, and this was supposed to be how she did it, so it has to work."

"She chose to bring us all here, though," Margaret said.

Irene thought. "I wonder if that's because on some level she knows. Not what *we* know," she said quickly, seeing their faces. "She doesn't think that way; she'd never even think to look for the kind of thing we've seen, I'm almost sure of it. But something, enough. I wonder if her life here, even if she hated it, made her think this would be a good place for trying to make something like this, something impossible, happen."

"Don't say that, *impossible*," said Margaret tightly.

Pearl checked behind them, waited while Willa Cobb, one of the newer women, passed—Pearl gave her a smile—and then caught Margaret and Irene by the wrists and tugged them into the corner.

"I talked to Joe this morning. He says he can bring the trap Wednesday," she whispered. "But do we still want to do this? I could still tell him never mind."

"We have to," said Margaret.

"There's another question than just whether it'll work, isn't there? There's also if it works, what it might mean, what it might do, what it might actually look like."

Whether we can bear it, she meant.

"That's true," Irene said. Because there could be hauntings of different scales, like griefs of different scales. Shadows of one size a person could glimpse out of the corner of her eye and still remain herself, but other shadows could be large enough to fall across everything.

On the floor above them, a door closed. They straightened and pulled back from one another, readying themselves to be discovered, though this corner of the hallway was perfect for their secrecy—might almost have been designed for it, tucked back behind the entrance to the hall so that someone would have to be hunting for them to find them. Irene was sure other kinds of sneaking had happened here over the years: maids pushed hard to the wall by serving boys, men of the house hissing their money panic, women telling other women about losses they'd had, speaking in the whispers women had always used for delivering that news.

And the man from the portrait, that old, hungry king, slipping down the stairs to do some kind of violence somewhere. Armed with the certainty that once you built a house like this you could do what you wanted in it. Dr. Bishop, who'd never even met him, nonetheless fleeing from him, all her life here a flight. Who knew what he would do if he caught her. And yet she'd brought herself right back here to him, as they both must have known she'd have to, in the end.

The three of them waited. Once there'd been quiet for long enough that she was sure no one was coming down, Irene said, "I think that's part of why we need to do it, though, Pearl, isn't it?

Because if the worst thing happens, we have to know. We have to understand what we're choosing."

Her little snake twisted, and Irene thought how from the very first the little mouse-moth-snake had summoned images that weren't baby images when it moved. All this talk of choice when they might already have agreed to the garden's terms, somewhere along the way.

They whispered their plan through. They'd set their trap and give it a couple of nights—night was when animals were more active. "Even mine," Pearl said, and laid a hand jokingly on her belly.

Margaret gave a strained smile. Irene wondered how much Margaret's baby had been moving lately.

As she passed the telephone on the way to her room, Irene thought about calling George, to hear his voice. But she remembered the expression on the imagined George's face in their living room, while their faraway imagined baby made its sounds. The way his smile had been the one she knew only at first. The longer he'd looked, the more he'd seemed to be seeing Irene as she really was, for the first time in all his years of looking at her.

If she somehow said too much, if she gave herself away, he might come out here to drag her home, away from her only help. Or he might leave her behind forever, like a lost thing, because he'd decided that was what she was.

She walked past.

*

"Hmm," Dr. Hall said during Irene's next examination.

"What?" Irene said. Her mind had been drifting, carried on the backs of mice and moths and snakes, while he measured her belly.

Dr. Hall looked up from Irene's chart at her. "There's a bit of an unexpected pattern developing."

Not just Irene's mind but also her wrists and ankles and her whole self, every joint, snapped to attention. Her hands were on her midsection: When had she put them there? "What does that mean?"

"The fetus is nice and active, which is just what we want. But you're gaining weight in an unusual way. You *are* still gaining, but more slowly than you were. It's moved you off your curve."

Had Dr. Bishop known her injections would do this? How had she thought Dr. Hall wouldn't catch them in the end? She must have decided to act first, while she could, and handle the repercussions later—but then where was she? Why had she left Irene to face this question alone?

Or maybe it was that a snake-moth-mouse didn't weigh what a baby would have weighed.

Irene must not let Dr. Hall see, must not let him linger here, on questions that might have answers that would involve leaving the garden behind, when the very raising of the question showed she might require it.

"Can't there be variation? Surely every woman isn't exactly the same."

"No, but—"

"What about us is *usual?*"

"Well." He smiled. He resumed the examination, palpating her belly, though his hands and eyes stayed wary.

"Is it always so hot here in summer?" Irene said. She could feel her heart pounding all the way out to her fingertips.

"It is a hot one, isn't it?" he said.

*

The following morning the women had gardening time. They walked out after breakfast into the light gray mist, warm as breath, and headed for their patch.

But no one was there. The doctors beckoned to them from outside the walled garden. The gate, their gate, was open. The ivy had been pulled to the side and pinned with a stone to clear the way in.

"No," murmured Pearl.

Irene met her eyes and shook her head urgently. Margaret gripped Pearl's arm. "Don't you say a thing, Pearl. Just don't say anything and it will be fine."

So they went through the gate and into the garden like the rest of the women. Irene looked at these innocent others to know how she should hold her face. Yes, surprise was what she would feel, confusion.

And she did feel these things, she didn't even have to pretend, because since they'd last been inside, a section of the right-hand side of the garden had been cleared out and plowed up. A patch of naked dirt was left now where there'd been whole tangled thickets before.

The doctors stood with Phillips partway between the patch and the fountain. That blank-eyed cherub regarded the scene. "Our new garden!" Dr. Hall said.

"Doesn't look new," somebody said.

"New-old, then."

"What are we doing here?" said Irene.

"You were the inspiration, Mrs. Willard, actually. You asked me about this garden a while back. Remember?" said Dr. Bishop.

"But you told me it would take too much work to clear it out."

"I'm sure Phillips would say it did!" Dr. Hall clapped Phillips on the back. Phillips's face didn't change.

"We're done with the other patch?"

"Just expanding our project."

Irene suspected Dr. Bishop of chasing her desperation right into this garden, trying to find the feeling that had made her use this house for her hospital in the first place—she could sense on some level, maybe, that this feeling lived here. The world around Irene seemed to tremble. She patted her stomach—*it's all right*—trying again to lie inside her own body.

Three carts had been wheeled in, piled so full of new plants that the leaves obscured the pots beneath, making them look like portable patches of teeming ground. The women would be planting tomatoes and cucumbers today, the doctors explained. A few sunflowers and marigolds too. Irene and Margaret and Pearl went around to the far side of the patch: they could not, would not, have their backs to that fountain. Just looking at the kneeling women across from them, who had no way to keep an eye on it, made the skin at the back of Irene's neck contract.

The doctors sat on the very lip of the fountain to watch.

"Does Dr. Bishop know?" Pearl whispered.

"Hush, nobody knows anything," Irene told her.

Dr. Bishop leaned back to let the sun hit her face. Irene could almost feel it on her own cheekbones. Dr. Hall put his hand over his wife's on the fountain lip, and Irene looked down at her own hand, dirtied already. She made herself keep digging. The garden's dirt felt different somehow from the dirt in the other patch, warmer, closer to alive. But then it was almost summer, warmer and warmer every day, wasn't it?

Would the garden like this, what they were doing?

"What if this changes something?" Margaret said very softly. "What if we stop it from working right when we're about to figure it out?"

"Dr. Bishop must know," Pearl said.

"Plant your flowers, both of you," said Irene.

So they did, while the doctors watched them. The cherub watched them too from over the top of the doctors' heads. What would happen to these plants? The sunflowers might turn out towering, big as actual suns; the marigolds might bloom like wounds.

12

Pearl told them Joe changed his mind when it suited him and she'd learned never to count on anything he said, but in fact he'd left the trap right where she'd told him to: by the stand of trees at the end of the long driveway, no need to bother anyone up at the house.

They closed in on it but paused to give it a prudent space. "Well then," Irene said, because it was strange to see something whose purpose was so visible, that U of dark damage-ready metal. What animal could fail to see what this was designed for?

They had to hide it. Together they scooped and shoveled leaves and branches onto the trap until it was well covered. Irene took care to keep her fingers far from those metal teeth. They would sneak down tonight to put it somewhere promising and bait it with whatever they could secrete away. "Possums and raccoons aren't picky, they'll go for almost anything we eat, that's what Joe says," Pearl told them. She paused. "I do wonder if maybe we should wait, though. It's only four days until the husbands visit. Maybe we should do this after?"

Or maybe not at all—Irene could see Pearl still thinking it.

"No more waiting," Margaret said quietly, and what was there to say to that?

Dinner was a pale and flavorless piece of fish with moisture beaded up across it like dew, mashed potatoes the off-white of old teeth, and asparagus boiled to translucence. Irene carved off hunks of the fish, bits of the potatoes, and slid them softly from her fork's tines between the folds of the napkin she'd spread across her dress. She timed these transfers for moments when Dr. Bishop was maximally distant in her orbit of the room. The mass was disconcertingly warm in her lap.

It had long gone cold, though, by the time she decided the house was quiet enough to creep from her bedroom that night. Damp and, in a tactile way, very dead—the kind of thing you drop by instinct. Irene put it into her pocket as she went down the stairs. She was first to arrive in the foyer. First to trust the quiet, maybe, or first, only, to believe that if the doctors stopped her she could think of some way of getting free.

But Pearl and Margaret weren't far behind, each carrying her own napkin-wrapped heap. They were learning to be braver. Was Irene teaching them? She'd never meant to teach anyone anything.

They wrestled in silence with the elaborate old locks on the front door, full of scrollwork, as if the portrait king had wanted not just to demonstrate ownership but to display it. In the end they won. The night outside felt fresh on Irene's skin. The sky was so huge and black above them that she had the sense of being at the bottom of a sea. They had more trouble spotting the trap this time because of the dark and how well they'd hidden it, but they found it in the end.

Irene said, "Let's pull it by the chain, so it can't spring on us."

"It isn't set yet," Pearl said.

"Just to be sure."

"Won't it be loud?" asked Margaret.

"Nobody will hear." Irene picked up the chain and pulled it herself. It wasn't as heavy as expected, though, yes, louder than she would have liked.

"Like in a ghost story—the rattling of chains," said Margaret.

"We're the ghosts?" Pearl said.

The edge of the woods was loose and airy and maintained as part of the grounds; it didn't serve their purposes, so they passed through it quickly. Not far in, the weave of the trees became thicker. Untended underbrush began filling in the spaces between.

"Here, maybe?" said Pearl.

Irene dropped the chain.

They took their napkins full of food from their pockets. "Did Joe tell you how to bait it?" Irene asked.

"I tried to get him to explain it to me without making him think it'd be *me* doing it—just some tips for the garden man or whoever."

"So you're saying you don't know?"

"I think I do. Basically, you put the food here while the trap is open. Then you close it and arm it."

"And try not to lose a hand," Irene said.

"Oh, fine, I'll do it," Pearl said.

Irene looked at her in surprise: certainly braver. Pearl took their napkin-bundles and neared the trap. She bent awkwardly to reach, with her other hand on her belly as if to push it back and out of range. From a little distance, she dropped the food, then stood up again. Touched, actually touched, the bar with the teeth to crook it into place, and Irene couldn't stop herself from wincing. They all heard the click. A sound that implied and prepared the ear for another sound, the first of a two-beat rhythm.

"Will this work?" Margaret said.

Irene knew what she meant. It was still hard to imagine any animal could be stupid enough to trust its body anywhere near such a vicious glint, no matter how enticing the smell. The whole setup looked just like the trick it was.

"As long as there's food. They're *greedy little monsters,* Joe says."

Greedy little monster. Irene patted her belly, and the thing inside kicked her hand. Squeamishness rose, covetousness. What was her monster now? She had nightmares about its shape; she would pay any price, no matter what it was, to keep it growing.

She wondered if Dr. Hall had been saying anything to the others about *unusual patterns.* She wished there were some way to learn without having to ask.

*

Dr. Bishop met Irene at the door of the therapy room the next morning. "Come with me, Irene."

No *please*, no explanation. Irene followed the doctor down the hall. "Outside?" she said at the front door—it had been raining earlier and they hadn't had gardening time. But Dr. Bishop said nothing, just led her across the lawn then, into this day, which had cleared and which was growing hot. Irene would never get used to the mismatch of emerging from the evening-like, lamplit interior of the house into brightness.

"Where are you taking me?"

"A few different places," Dr. Bishop said.

They neared the woods, and Irene's body began to buzz. Dr. Bishop had found their trap and guessed somehow whose doing it was. Would feed Irene's arm or leg in as punishment, or if some animal was in there, would take it out and rub Irene's nose in the carcass, like she was a dog and this was her mess: *See what you've done?*

But at the end of the lawn, Dr. Bishop said, "Stop here. Look at the trees a moment."

Irene eyed them, roots to tops. The motion made her dizzy.

"How does this space make you feel, Irene? What memories does it prompt?"

"I thought you said we were done with my therapy." Their recent sessions had been just injections followed by silence, the doctor reading while Irene looked at the floor or the ceiling and hummed loudly.

"Does this look like therapy? Are you on a couch? Just humor me."

So Dr. Bishop was still looking for a new way in.

"All right. Trees make me think about climbing, though I can't say I've ever tried climbing a tree this tall. Our town didn't have any real woods left except on the very far side, past the shops.

I wasn't allowed to play there, but later on, George and I went sometimes." Pine needles prickling the skin of her back from the force of his weight on top of her. Pulling him closer, in.

Dr. Bishop made her list some words the trees made her think of and describe them as if to a person who couldn't see them. Then she led Irene onward, to the center of the great lawn in front of the house.

"Would you say you feel exposed here, Irene?"

As her answer, Irene extended her hands to indicate the empty table of the land that surrounded them.

"How do you feel about all this empty space?"

The truth was Irene hated it. When George had been overseas, she had read the papers to find mentions of battles and then gone to the library to find books with photographs of those places— she skipped past buildings, hunting for fields. She scoured every picture of a field she could find, not letting herself turn the page until she could find a hint of a hiding place somewhere: a boulder, a crevice, a dip in the land. She knew it meant nothing; she knew there were trenches and the men were blown up inside them, that death had taken on such a scale that it fell like an enormous shadow, or rose like a flood, and could find anyone anywhere. Still, she bent over the books with her eyes on whatever hidden divot and thought to George across the ocean, *Find that.* She'd come to wonder, before this hospital, if her own interior might be the same way, some scorched-earth battlefield with no places of safety to find.

She told Dr. Bishop a story about running around in her back-yard as a child and how her mother had always wanted her to put her shoes on so her feet wouldn't go rough on the bottoms.

Next Dr. Bishop led Irene to the garden.

But this Irene couldn't allow. She saw instantly: she couldn't let the doctor take her inside. It was one thing for the doctors to have them come here for gardening at regularly scheduled times—she and Margaret and Pearl could plan around that, maybe—but if

Dr. Bishop started making a habit of bringing them here whenever she wanted, she'd find them out, she'd discover what they were trying to do and why and it would all be over. If this gate opened under the doctor's hand now, this space became only hers.

And if she and Dr. Bishop went inside together, alone, Irene didn't think she had it in her to hide what she knew about this garden anyway.

"Here, Dr. Bishop? Really?" Irene said.

The doctor had been reaching through the ivy, which had fallen over the gate again, for the gate handle. She looked like a person having her hand swallowed. She turned back to Irene. "Why not?"

Irene felt herself drawing near a high ledge she'd have to leap from. "It's just—this isn't the happiest place for you, is it?"

"What?"

"I can feel it. I can feel what you felt here—just like you were having me do with the woods and the field. Do you want me to? You don't want us feeling all that, do you, when we're supposed to be keeping calm. Walking around inside and summoning all the things you felt, and seeing what you saw here?"

"I'm afraid I'm not following." But Irene saw the doctor's face sharpen, tighten. Irene's mirror-face was doing the same; she could feel the tension in her mouth, her cheeks, her forehead, bracing for a blow, even if she was the one delivering it.

"Maybe you weren't quite telling me the truth when you said no one in your family used this garden. You told me you came here to avoid being found, but maybe sometimes you weren't the only one who had that idea. Your grandfather was dead, but I wonder if your father wasn't actually a very good man either, not much better in the end, and if this is where you learned that. None of it seems like the right kind of calming feeling for me, does it?"

She wished she were able to read the doctor better, so she could know for certain if she were seeing confirmatory panic or just confusion. All she could tell for sure was that Dr. Bishop was shaking her head.

"It's bad for us to get worked up, and if it's bad for us, it's bad for your plans. After Sally and Samantha and Dorothy, especially Dorothy—"

"Stop!"

The word seemed to have escaped from Dr. Bishop. She stood white and shaking.

"I just would think you'd be more careful, so you don't end up with more incidents to report. If you even are reporting them. That's another thing I've started to wonder."

Dr. Bishop looked at Irene the way she'd looked at her father in the vision as he'd thrown her to the wolves, one of the wolves being him.

Behind Dr. Bishop the grandfather appeared, first wolf and largest, there suddenly amidst the ivy that covered the garden gate, which grew over him as if it were part of his substance. Glimpses of that mottled decaying skin between and beneath the leaves.

Which of you brought me?

Irene didn't know—it could have been either of them or both who'd done that, who'd let him live again. But Dr. Bishop wasn't looking at him; she still watched Irene; she hadn't even seen him.

The grandfather stretched out his hands toward Irene's belly.

Mine.

Cold on Irene's skin, cold, cold, spreading from her shoulders down to the center of her.

He reached toward the little snake, little moth, little mouse, the thing Irene was building of all those parts together.

I've said it. You heard me. And if I say it—

Irene closed her eyes. When she opened them the grandfather was gone.

Dr. Bishop's eyes were on her face.

What had she seen?

"For some reason the garden seems to be upsetting you, Irene," the doctor said more calmly. "We don't have to go in. I'll give you your injection and have done."

Dr. Bishop produced the syringe from a little bag she'd been carrying and held it between them cautiously. She seemed to be wondering what Irene might do.

And Irene rolled up her sleeve, offered her flesh, so that the thing within her, whatever it was and whatever it was becoming, might keep moving, at least for now.

*

Irene, Margaret, and Pearl returned that night to check the trap. Joe had said it would probably be fast—they needed it to be, if they were going to get their three-day experiment in ahead of the next gardening day, only five days from now—but they'd brought bits of their dinner with them in their pockets again in case, to freshen up the bait if another night of temptation was needed. Pot roast this time. The smell of food wafted from all of them as they hurried across the lawn.

The pot roast proved unnecessary, though. The trap had already done its work. Cinched in the middle by that vicious metal band was a possum the size of a house cat, rotund in a way that suggested it was used to eating well, splayed out limply. Its legs were extended as if it had died still thinking it might escape. The ground pillowed its cheek up so its lip lifted at one corner to reveal tiny, needly teeth. The places where the sparse light grayish hair was sparsest—the snout, the tail—were the pink of clean-scrubbed skin.

They watched the possum like it might move.

"How do we get it out, Pearl?" said Margaret.

"Joe said there's a button." Pearl inched closer to the trap. "A release. Here, here it is." She reached out and pressed something. The metal mouth of the trap sprang open. Maybe this was their problem, all of them: some version of an inner button pressed too soon every time. The metal lifted, but the cinched part of the possum stayed compressed.

"We didn't think about this part, did we? How we're going to get it there now," Pearl said.

"We'll have to carry it," Margaret said.

"Do *you* want to?"

Irene stepped forward, because she could tell Margaret would if it came to that, and Margaret looked as if she might not be able to stand one more thing. Irene shrugged her sweater off her shoulders. This sweater, a peaceful light green, had been a gift from her mother, designed like so many of her mother's gifts to make Irene more like other daughters. If only her mother could see her and this sweater now.

She got it wrapped over and then around the edges of the possum, then rolled it into her hands. Up so close, though, it smelled shockingly of rot and death, and Irene gagged and spat.

Pearl said, "They make a smell when they're afraid—Joe warned me. It's part of playing dead."

"This one's not playing."

"Maybe it was hoping for the best."

"Ugh, it's horrible." Irene tried to breathe through her mouth, but then she could taste it. The possum was sodden, soft, not as heavy as she'd expected.

"Be careful, Irene," said Margaret.

"Of what?"

"Don't they have diseases and things?"

"All wrapped up that way, it's almost like—" Pearl started.

"*Don't,*" Margaret said.

Irene held the possum at arm's length from her body. She wanted above all else not to cradle it or feel its weight as something her arms were tending, not to connect it with the kind of imagining Dr. Bishop had asked of them. That feeling in combination with the thing's deadness and its smell of rushed decay, taken in close to herself, would make her scream. As they walked, she made it her main project to hold a strip of light between the possum and her belly, so the two animals wouldn't touch. They left the trap where it was, behind them. There was nothing really to tie it to any of them if somebody found it.

At the door of the garden, Irene said, "Dr. Bishop tried to bring me here today."

"What?" Margaret said.

"During my therapy time. Some other places first, but then here. She had me walk all around the grounds, *visualizing*, she called it. I managed to stop her before she brought me in."

"Oh no," Margaret whispered.

"How can we do this without her finding out? What are we even thinking?" said Pearl.

"Wait, let's go in, let me put this down," Irene said.

Getting the possum out of the sweater was a trick. Irene put it down wrapped and did her best to slide the fabric from beneath but ended up touching it accidentally—its fur was surprisingly coarse, you could tell from the feel that it would repel moisture. She stood and brushed her hand repeatedly against her skirt. Back inside she would wash her hands in the hottest water she could stand until they were bright pink and painful; she would remember to touch no other part of herself until she had done that; she would not let herself think about her hands' pinkness in connection with the color of the possum's skin. She dangled the emptied sweater by one of its arms. If she could have burned it on the spot she would have.

"It's not sitting right," Pearl said.

The possum did look bad, with its head bent, like it was ready to turn a somersault. One paw bent beneath too.

"*I'm* not touching it again," said Irene.

"I guess it's fine," Margaret said doubtfully.

"So what do we do about Dr. Bishop?" Pearl said. "Maybe she knows everything already."

Irene could see why Pearl would think so, why she'd suspect their discovery might not be a discovery at all but something Dr. Bishop had her own plans for, plans they might already be part of, and that she might already be using this garden on them somehow. Irene was sure this wasn't the case, knew this doctor had put her faith elsewhere, even if something unconscious kept drawing her to the garden too—but it was hard to explain her knowledge to the others. "I don't think she does."

"If she comes back while it's here . . ." Margaret trailed off.

"But we didn't even make it inside today," Irene said. "I don't think the whole thing went how she'd hoped. She might never try it again." Another thing she couldn't tell them, not without making herself alone again: how she'd awakened ghosts for Dr. Bishop here, and Dr. Bishop had seemed to know it, even if Irene hadn't been able to make her look at them.

"We'll be back out here for gardening anyway." Margaret's voice trembled.

"Not until Tuesday. By then it'll have happened."

"Or *not* happened." Margaret shook her hands in the air. "What if it doesn't work?"

Irene touched her arm. "We'll just have to see."

"It has to work," Margaret said.

"We need to put leaves on top of it, I guess that might hide it, in case," said Pearl.

So they did, whole handfuls. Even Margaret settled into the task. Irene collected downed branches from some of the fruit trees to lay over top. Recent downings with the leaves still moist and alive, the fruit still green.

The fruits on the two branches were different: one a papery green pyramid that proved hollow when she prodded it, one an orb with creases scored into its top in a star shape, like the core of a sliced-through apple.

"What are these, Margaret, do you know?" Irene said.

Margaret squinted. "That's a medlar, I think, but it looks funny. And this one's maybe from a golden fountain tree? The seedpods are smaller usually, though. Over in the corner, those look like some kind of peony too, but I've never seen one with so many buds. These must be rare plants—whoever planted this garden must have collected them."

Or the garden itself had made them this way. Irene thought this but did not, could not, say it, either. What if the others grew so afraid they wanted to stop? The more she saw of this place the more afraid of it she was, and yet how could she be done with it, when the reason she would have for needing it, if she did, was the greatest terror possible?

By now they'd gotten the possum covered. The heap of leaves was too deliberate in its shape to be mere leaves up there on the rim, and the neat rows of their plantings against the right-hand wall seemed to stare.

"That isn't very good," said Pearl.

"Best we can do," Irene said.

Back in her room, Irene wadded up a skirt into a possum-sized pile, put it across the room on the desk made for ladies' letter writing, spun around twice, and tried to ascertain how likely she'd be to notice it if she didn't already know it was there. But it was impossible to tell, because she did know.

They just needed three days without being caught. Three days for their experiment to work or not work, and to cost either more or less than they could withstand paying.

13

This time Irene stayed where she was supposed to be in the dining room to wait for George, because this time she didn't actually want to see George at all. Or rather she could allow her desire for it no space: she would have to fool him into thinking she was worrying about nothing, anticipating nothing, while they were still waiting for the possum's necessary three days to pass. She would have to keep George far away from her real thoughts. She wondered if the coming deception was worrying Pearl and Margaret too, across from her at the table, eating little bits of their breakfasts, or if they were better used to keeping truths from their husbands.

She wished Dr. Bishop weren't here watching her worry. Dr. Bishop who sidled over to the wall, leaned against it, and *looked*, as if she could see inside Irene's mind.

"We're her lab animals," Irene said to Pearl and Margaret.

Along the floor beneath the windowsill, a snakelike patch of shadowy wriggling.

"Did you see that?" Irene said, softer. "The snake, there, on the floor."

Margaret and Pearl sipped their cups of coffee and turned their heads only fractionally. Dr. Bishop's attention still snapped in their direction, but they were looking at each other again by the time she was full-on facing them, the same way the creatures were always gone by the time Irene turned her head to see.

(Though the scenes she saw from Dr. Bishop's life seemed to stay put well enough, until she'd seen more than she wanted to.)

"I didn't see anything, Irene," Margaret said.

Pearl took a bite of toast and swallowed. "They're never still there, never, when I look again. I don't know why I even try."

"Same for me," said Margaret.

"It's like they're only partway there to begin with," Irene said.

"Did you know stars are like that? The dimmest ones. Victor has a telescope, but when they're very far off you can only see them out of the corner of your eye," said Margaret.

Pearl said, "Do you think that means our babies would be only partway there, if we had to do it? Just partway real?"

Irene thought about what it would be like to have babies who were visible only in the periphery, flashes of babies that vanished when their mothers turned their heads.

"No. It would be different, I know it. We'd *make* it different," Margaret said.

"Let's just see what happens with the possum," said Irene.

"Nobody's seen it yet?" said Pearl.

They shook their heads. "Maybe it hasn't worked, it was too big," Margaret said.

"Maybe, or maybe it'll take the full three days."

"I just hope nobody finds it today," Margaret said with a little twitch of her shoulders, as if the idea were too horrible to sit through. Margaret was thirty-one weeks now. There was still a heartbeat at the core of her too-small stomach, Dr. Hall found it without much trouble every time, that's what Margaret told them. But her mouth and eyes seemed to be receding into her face with the passing of weeks. More and more she had the look of a woman living through a slow nightmare.

"The weather should help us," Pearl said. Today didn't invite pleasure walking, it was true; Irene had checked first thing and been relieved to see the swollen gray sky behind her curtains.

Margaret looked down at her hands. "I'm so afraid Victor might try to take me home with him."

"Why?" Pearl said.

"If he thinks I'm still not enough bigger. If he decides he wants to talk to other doctors."

"Well, you can't let him," said Irene. "Tell him whatever you have to. Say the treatment doesn't allow for interruptions and it's something you have to finish if you've started it or it'll kill you both."

"That might even be true," Pearl said.

"Maybe he won't try, maybe it'll be fine. My mother used to tell me not to invent problems," Margaret said, trying to smile, looking ill.

Dr. Bishop was watching them so closely Irene thought she might be able to hear. Irene smiled at her, nice and big, and gave her a little finger-tiddling wave, to say, *I'm afraid of you, yes, but remember that I can also make you afraid.*

"Irene," said Margaret.

"I can't say hello?"

Mrs. Conrad came to the door to call Pearl's name.

"Keep Joe away from the doctors so he can't say anything to them about the trap. Take him right upstairs. And don't talk to him any more about it than you have to, or he'll start seeing how none of what you told him adds up," Irene reminded Pearl as she rose.

"Oh, you don't think I should lead him over for a nice, long chat with the doctors about trapping? Really, Irene, you're not the only person who can figure anything out." Pearl turned and forded dining-room chairs, misjudging her own proportions and failing to slip through spaces.

When Irene was called next—when she sprang up and rushed forward—she found herself clumsy in the same way. She craned to ease herself past chairs but bumped them in her hurry. And outside the dining-room doors was George. His hair was longer than Irene had ever seen it, growing over his ears. His face lit her whole, no matter what she'd felt or expected to feel ahead of time.

Inside her, the creature gave a great full-body squirming that felt, suddenly, nothing like the wriggling of a snake: Irene could feel the motions of several distinct body parts of a new kind of bulkier, larger animal.

Little possum.

Something once thought couldn't be unthought.

Through her joy and dread, Irene watched George's face— what was happening to it? Why were its lines loosening that way, and slumping? Could he see the possum somehow? Could he see through her? She grew cold with the memory of him in her vision, how all at once he hadn't seemed to know her, or maybe knew her for the first time.

"What?" she asked.

"You can really tell now," said George. He put out his arms to Irene first and hugged her very close, then touched her stomach. "Anyone could tell it's a baby."

Was it? But Irene would worry later. For now she was here with George, her George. She didn't want to stay where Dr. Bishop could see and hear them, so she took his hand and pulled him through the foyer, bright again now for the husbands, then up the steps.

"Slow down!"

"Keep up!"

He gave a giant comical bound with her hand held in his.

"What a ridiculous man you are. How did I end up married to such a ridiculous man?"

Irene led him into her room. George made a circuit, lifting things from her dresser, cupping them, then setting them back down.

"George, you've been in here before." But that had been quick, right before he'd left on his last visit, after she'd taken him to the garden because she hadn't understood enough yet to know better. Now she had time and space to look across this room and really see him. She wanted some way of making him appear less distant.

"I'm trying to notice everything," he said. "Every single thing in here. It's stupid, but I worry when I'm not with you that maybe I made you up."

His fingers were searching out proof, then.

"Come here," Irene said.

On the bed, George shook a little against her, the way he had when they'd kissed the very first time, outside the high school gymnasium in the dark. It had been their first date, a school dance. Irene had never felt so powerful. Maybe all that had happened since was only nature trying to right the balance of the too-much she'd taken to begin with, just the eventual tax on that happiness.

She didn't have to pay it now, though. Now there was George, right beside her on her bed, warm and unchanged in his essentials by any of those interrupting events. That was a kind of miracle, wasn't it? To pass into so much and come through in the end. Irene kissed him hard and felt a falling sensation, a delicious swoop deep in the center of her, deeper even than where the little creature (*little possum*) lived, even more central to herself.

"Irene," George murmured. His hands were on her arms, on her neck, on her breasts, her throat, her cheeks, her hair, touching these as he'd touched her things, trying to drink her down through his fingertips. Her own hands she kept pressed flat to his back, and pressed them harder.

Then: "Irene." George pulled back. "Oh, Reny, we'd better stop or I won't be able to."

"Don't, then."

Inside her the little possum spun and kicked, tapped and nosed. It felt the quickening of her blood in its ears again. It knew what she was feeling, how much, in a way she didn't think George himself could.

Not now, she told it with a quick pat. *This is mine.*

"You know we can't, Reny. It's the one rule, isn't it? The only one they told us about, anyway."

"I wondered what they'd told you."

"Not much. She was the one who said it—I think that was on purpose, so we'd be too embarrassed to ask her anything. She said we had to remember it was a delicate system engaged in other pursuits."

Full of rage, Irene imagined the expression on Dr. Bishop's face as she told them this, its whole cast made to say, *You wouldn't ask me an actual question about such a thing, would you?* Dr. Bishop probably felt she had a right to use all aspects of being a woman that made anything easier, given how hard it must have made everything else. But she had no right to interfere with Irene and George, with the best thing Irene had.

The little possum squirmed.

Maybe including you, maybe not, we'll have to see.

"*A delicate system,*" she said. "How tactful, when really there isn't a tactful bone in her body. You didn't ask why?"

"That would take a far braver man than I am."

George never had been especially brave, it was true. They were still touching, but he kept the distance he'd imposed between their most central parts. Irene could tell he was monitoring the thickness of that space all the time. A little pocket of safety, like the one the chaperones at that first dance had insisted on (this was why Irene and George had ended up in back of the gym in the dark). Like the space Irene had kept between the dead possum and her own.

Irene laid her hands on George's face and pressed her fingers to the ridges of his cheekbones. "You wouldn't break me, I promise."

"It's not worth the risk, Reny."

An achy welling rose at the back of her throat and spilled forward until his image went wobbly in front of her.

George pulled her head to his chest. "We'll have our whole lives long, after. Let's just get this baby here first."

Just. That word had no business in the air in this house where Irene had been cloistered, shot through with drugs, made to talk, made to kill snakes and possums and wonder if she was actually losing her mind. But she smiled stoically for George, the way sometimes, while he was overseas, she would smile into the mirror and pretend he was seeing her pretend, for him, to be someone else. She kissed him now as that stoically smiling woman would. That woman didn't hunger for him except for the exact, correct amount. She never worried that her need had eaten them alive.

At her center, the possum gave one last lazy twitch, then stilled.

Her need had always stopped Irene from asking George why he'd first chosen her. If it had been anything more than her position in that row of desks that afternoon in April when they were fifteen, inside that dress, with its red bright as a strawberry. If he would have felt mostly the same if it had turned out to be some other girl in there. She could stand to hear only one answer. Dr. Bishop would never have to wonder in this way, though both of their husbands had spotted them first in classrooms—she, only girl, was so clear in that story that Dr. Hall could never have mistaken her for anything other than what she was.

Irene patted George's cheek the way a moment ago she'd patted the little possum. None of this was really his fault.

"I'll get us some tea. If you mean it, then we need something else to occupy us."

"Let me get it."

"You don't know where anything is here, dummy."

George grinned and lay back on her pillow. Irene made a note of the placement of his head—off-center, by the right bottom corner—so she could bury her nose in that place tonight. "I'd trade all the tea in the world, you know," he said. "If things were different."

"I know."

Why was Irene crying again, walking down the hall? There was nothing new to mourn. George wasn't mourning anything— George thought they had everything to be happy about. George was considering their *whole lives long*.

Because Irene was crying, she didn't hear the slight sounds that might otherwise have stopped her until she'd already turned the corner of the hall.

And saw, against the wall of the secret corner but still plain enough, Dr. Hall and Mrs. Conrad, the receptionist Mrs. Conrad and their very own Dr. Hall. Dr. Hall's whole self pushed up against her. Mrs. Conrad's eyes closed, her mouth loose, as his mouth moved on her neck.

Mrs. Conrad's eyes flew open. She looked at Irene with an incomprehension that made Irene wonder if she herself were haunting them.

(*We're the ghosts?* Pearl had said.)

Mrs. Conrad pushed Dr. Hall back, and he whirled to meet Irene with his face all flushed, the same flush George had worn a few minutes ago, George's now cooling.

"Mrs. Willard!"

"That's me."

"We were just . . ." Mrs. Conrad started, but her crisp receptionist voice lost its way.

It seemed she hadn't really been *keeping herself to herself* after all.

"I was just helping Mrs. Conrad with something," Dr. Hall said.

"Her burning passion for you?"

"Something she dropped. I was helping her look for it. Maybe it looked like something else, but that's what it was."

Dr. Hall met Irene's eyes. He was trying to regain his footing. She couldn't believe he thought he might.

"She dropped it down her shirt? Onto her neck?"

"I'm going to faint," Mrs. Conrad said, but she didn't, she just sat down, right on the floor.

"Laura," said Dr. Hall, reaching out a hand to try to catch her, much too late.

"Laura," Irene said.

Mrs. Conrad let out a pained sound, as if Irene had struck her. *Oh, you're fine,* Irene wanted to say. *I haven't done anything to you. You've done everything to yourself.* Though she knew that wasn't the whole truth.

Dr. Hall's mouth trembled, but his voice kept its self-possession. "All right. All right, Mrs. Willard, let's just think carefully."

"About what?"

"Let's just talk this through."

"Before I go telling anyone, you mean."

"No. Yes. Let's not start a big production over nothing."

So Dr. Bishop didn't already know, then. This wasn't part of some understanding between them.

"I'll start what I want," said Irene.

She walked right past the happy couple, then, toward the tea. Nobody behind her did a thing about it. Dr. Hall did call her name, but only once and only softly.

When Irene got back to her room she would tell George. Just let Dr. Hall try to stop her. She thought about what she might do if Dr. Hall tried, while she poured the water, while she balanced the teacups on their saucers out of the dining room. Dr. Hall and Mrs. Conrad had removed themselves from their corner. Where had they gone? Surely not to resume the activity Irene had interrupted; surely that was too brazen even for them.

"You'll never guess what I just saw," Irene told George, who was still on his back on her bed. She put the tea down on the desk and filled her face with the secret.

"What?"

Irene could tell George. She could. But she saw suddenly that her new knowledge was a valuable currency, and in telling—even George, maybe—she'd spend it. Otherwise, if she used it well, it might buy her anything, whatever she wanted: a pass to stay here as long as she liked, no matter what either doctor found in the garden, no matter what either doctor said.

Irene waggled her eyebrows at George. "A couple on the verge of actual coitus, right out in the hallway."

There, neither lie nor truth.

"They'd better watch themselves, those rule-breakers."

"They'd better."

George stood, reached for his tea, and touched Irene's shoulder to thank her, as if they were very good friends.

*

On her way back up to her room after showing George out, Irene rounded the stairs and saw Dr. Bishop ahead of her down the hall, facing away, roaming. The doctor had no idea what had been happening to her marriage and her life, and Irene wouldn't tell her, not yet, not until exactly the right time.

Ahead of Dr. Bishop, Pearl's husband emerged from her room and into the hall. He waited for the doctor. He put out his hand for her to shake when she reached him, the way he would have if she were a man.

How could Pearl have let Joe out here? All that work to get him upstairs without talking to the doctors, and now she was just letting a chance meeting happen. Panic hummed across Irene's shoulder blades. She hurried toward them.

"Good to see you, Doctor," Joe said. "I was just stepping out for the washroom—glad I ran into you. She's doing all right?"

"Oh yes. Nice, smooth progress, Mr. Porter, you should feel very hopeful."

"Hello there," Irene said loudly, when she was still too far away, so the greeting felt unnatural. They turned toward her in surprise.

Where was Pearl?

"Oh, hello," Joe said, and then to the doctor: "Great."

"It certainly is. Where's your husband gone to, Mrs. Willard?" Dr. Bishop asked.

"He had to get home."

"Hope it was a nice visit." Dr. Bishop smiled at Joe. "And I'll let you get on with yours now, Mr. Porter."

"Happy I could help out with the trap. Pearl tells me it got the job done."

The doctor's forehead creased.

"Nasty buggers."

Here was Pearl's face, too late, in the crack of the door. "Joe? Oh"—seeing Dr. Bishop and Irene too—"Joe, are you lost? The washroom is right at the end of the hall."

Irene could tell Joe thought of himself as a man who didn't get lost. "I'm going. Thanks again, Doctor."

Off he walked.

Dr. Bishop said to Pearl, "What's this about a trap?"

Pearl looked down the hall as if she'd have liked to fly away down it.

"Could you have said something about *feeling* trapped, maybe?" Irene said.

"Oh, oh yes, that must have been it. I *did* say something like that earlier. I guess he must have misunderstood."

"You feel trapped, Pearl?" the doctor said.

Pearl laughed and spun an arm that included her stomach and the room behind her and the hall and the house and the whole world.

Dr. Bishop's calculating eyes on Pearl, then Irene, then back to Pearl. "Well. We'll have to discuss those feelings some more at our next session."

Beatrice Loomis appeared at the top of the staircase, at the end of the hall. She saw them and rushed toward them very fast for a woman so far along. "Doctor!"

"Beatrice? Are you having contractions?"

Beatrice shook her head. "It's Willa Cobb, she needs you right away."

But Willa Cobb was only eighteen weeks along.

Dr. Bishop's face readied itself for what was coming. Irene knew she herself had never looked so ready for any difficult thing. The doctor followed Beatrice at a run.

*

(Willa was working to believe that what was happening was not happening at all. That was her last thought before she managed to stop herself from thinking and made herself a silence inside her head: *I won't believe this, it isn't real, it can't be, because this isn't what I was told would come next.*)

14

While they finished their wait to check if the dead possum was still dead, Irene and Margaret and Pearl didn't see the possum, not once, but they did see:

A beetle in the washroom, trundling along the baseboard, its shell faultlined like a smashed cup glued back together. (Margaret.)

A beetle in the dining room, approaching the place where the tablecloth brushed the floor, then touching it, then beneath—though when she lifted the tablecloth to check, discreetly, so no one would see and wonder what she was doing, there was no beetle there. (Margaret again. *The same beetle again?* she wondered. *Was it always the same one?*)

A tiny snake—or was it a worm?—in a water glass Irene had left beside her bed for the middle of the night when she often woke up thirsty. Twisting around at the bottom, pale, elegantly drowning, spinning its flattened head. When she got closer to look, no snake, no worm. She poured the water out in the washroom anyway.

A roly-poly curled in the nook of the stair as Pearl went to lie down after lunch. Just a tiny bit of lint, when she stooped to peer at it.

And the moth Irene saw, low down in the corner of her bedroom. Closer in she found only dust, and when she touched that dust and brought it up on her fingertips, close to her eyes, she couldn't tell if it was *dust* dust or wing dust, the kind moths left on your fingers when you touched them, when you pinched their wings between your fingers to lift and carry them somewhere.

Was there any difference? All just dust anyway. Weren't they all. Each of them just moving their personal bodily collections of dust around for a time—that moving was all a life was. Strange to think that really their entire work here, the whole of this elaborate project, was just to keep one collection of dust moving longer.

*

"I have to say, Pearl—I don't see how you could have let that happen, Joe and the doctor and the trap," Irene said to Pearl.

The third night was here, finally, and they were going to the garden. Irene would have thought nothing else could matter. But she'd been getting angrier and angrier that Pearl had been so careless, and avoiding Pearl as best she could, and now, walking beside her, that nervous profile, Irene's rage was too vast to hold in anymore.

"What was I supposed to do, go to the washroom with him? He went out in the hall and she happened to be there, it's not my fault."

"What?" Margaret said.

"Joe and Dr. Bishop had a nice chat," Irene told her.

"But she'll call our husbands." Margaret clutched Pearl's arm. "She'll tell them to take us home, and it'll be all over for me then. I *can't* go home."

"None of us can," Irene said.

"You know it's not the same. I'm not big enough, it doesn't move enough—it's different for me than for you two."

It was hard to know what to do with this truth, so Irene said, "Dr. Bishop would never want to send us home—she's worked too hard. She's done too much."

"You can't be sure of that."

"Margaret, really, I think Dr. Bishop forgot all about Joe, because right after they talked, Willa Cobb—" Pearl stopped. Her cheeks pinkened—Irene could tell Margaret's hand on her arm was tight enough to hurt. "Dr. Bishop went rushing off."

"A lot of good she was able to do for all that rushing," Irene said.

Willa Cobb was still upstairs, but everyone knew she wouldn't be rejoining their ranks.

"There's something else too, actually, something that might help us. I caught Dr. Hall with Mrs. Conrad while the husbands were visiting. He was all over her, right in the hallway, bold as you please." Telling Margaret and Pearl wasn't the same as telling anyone else; funny how they'd become extensions of herself in this place in a way not even George was.

Pearl whistled. "Dr. Hall."

"It shouldn't be surprising, he's an attractive enough man," Margaret said.

"Attractive? He makes my skin crawl," said Irene.

"Oh, but he's handsome, and that white coat—really, Irene?"

"To each her own, I suppose." But how could they not want to cringe away from Dr. Hall's touch? That he was handsome, that he knew he was, made it worse—the knowledge turned his movements too smooth. Hands moved differently when they expected to be well received where they landed, faster and with less hesitation. "Anyway, I've been thinking we could use it, if we had to. If one of the doctors—whichever—wanted to send us home, we could maybe get them to stop."

Everyone settled a little. It was nice to have something you could use, if you had to.

"You don't think, with Willa . . ." Pearl trailed off.

"We don't know enough yet. And anyway, she was much too early," Irene said.

There was also the question of how many of them the garden might serve, what might happen if they tried for Willa and the door closed somehow for the rest of them—when they were the ones who'd found it, they were the ones who were making it work.

Would it work?

Irene sped up, walking faster, fast as she could given the pain she had all the time now at the very midpoint of her pubic bone, which made her think of dried wishbones after turkey dinners: pull, pull, pull, *snap*. And given the way the little possum kept shoving some lumpish body part (back or rump or head) into the space under her ribs so she couldn't get a full breath. Her doctor back at home, the family doctor who'd stopped really being able to look her in the face after a while, he was the one who'd given her the idea to walk, the third time, which she'd done religiously. He'd said in an offhand way at one of her appointments that walking short distances, nice and slow, could help. *With what?* she'd asked, and he'd said, *To keep everything in condition*, looking as usual at the wall, at the clock, everywhere but at Irene, and she'd taken that to mean that if she took a walk every day and didn't miss one, not ever, she'd manage this time and this baby would be born. So that was what Irene did. Around the block, once and then twice, in all weathers for the autumn month she lasted after that appointment, noticing the small changes each day brought, which leaves were turning, which were falling, which were gone. The second lap let her check on the changes she'd noticed during the first. By the end she'd started to imagine herself pushing a pram around the same circuit.

Now she could see that the doctor had never meant the words the way she'd taken them. He'd been talking about the kind of pains that walking gave her now and how to minimize their effects, referencing a phase she'd never then experienced and needn't, then, have bothered preparing for.

The garden gate, was it ajar?

"She's found it," said Margaret.

"She can't have," Irene cried, but of course Dr. Bishop could— whose house and whose garden was this?

They hurried in. Nothing was there on the fountain lip.

"Okay, okay," Pearl said as they rushed toward that empty space, as they peered into the fountain's dry bowl. No crumpled possum lay at the bottom and no living one tried to scramble up the walls. The leaves they'd used to cover the thing were scattered at the fountain base, or at least some leaves were.

"What happened to it?" Margaret said.

Why were Pearl and Margaret both looking at Irene? Why did they keep expecting her to know?

Then: a rustling. The sound of movement through leaves.

They turned. The possum was nosing its way along the edge of the garden, the left edge where no bramble had been cleared. Its movements made a shuffling noise, like thick dragging feet. A fleshy scraping sound, under the leaves, that Irene couldn't tell if she was hearing or feeling as a series of shudderings up and down her spine.

Margaret clamped down hard on Irene's wrist, but Irene shushed her. They needed a good look at it, they needed not to startle it—above all else, they needed to know for sure if it was the same one. She stared as best she could as it shambled, but she couldn't see it when she looked straight on, had to turn her head a little because her vision would only let it in at the corners. She had to inspect it with her gaze fixed slightly to the side that way, as if she couldn't be caught looking. Even peripherally, though, she could see the mark of the trap on its back and belly, a place where the fur looked wet and dark and crushed down. The raw skin there bled.

The thing moved out of sight beneath the densest part of some bushes.

Irene shut her eyes.

Opened them.

Saw Dr. Hall and Dr. Bishop on the ground, in the same leaves. Both of them younger, naked, sprawled out as if floating. Her arms flung wide to the sides of her, trying to let in everything she felt, but also knowing already she had no hope of holding on to him, or to anyone. The look on her face was the look of a person about to weep, as if she always knew what this would cost her. Irene's own face had worn that expression.

Dr. Hall's face wasn't visible for reading.

Irene closed her eyes, opened them again.

Dr. Hall thrusted on top of another woman now, not Dr. Bishop and not Mrs. Conrad, no one Irene knew, a woman with dark hair, her face hidden in his shoulder. Dr. Hall looked abstracted and purposeful about the rhythms of the animal thing he was doing. Rutting, flesh in flesh.

Irene closed, opened, trying to get him to stop appearing, she didn't want to see him anymore, but here was Dr. Hall again with another woman, her face exposed, her nails painted pink and digging into Dr. Hall's skin.

And then Dr. Hall looked straight at Irene.

A plunge deep in Irene's belly—because he saw her, and because the skin of his face seemed to be hanging a little, graying a little.

If I say it, I do it, Irene, he told her. *This is what you are, all of you; this is what you're good for. Nothing else. George knows it too, no matter what he's always told you, what you've always told yourself. This, what you're seeing now, this is all it comes down to, and it doesn't matter much if it's you or someone different.*

But George would never. Irene knew this.

That's what you think.

Irene's possum kicked her.

When she opened her eyes this time she saw only Margaret and Pearl, staring at the place where the possum had been. They hadn't seen anything but the possum, she knew.

In a high, shrill voice Pearl said, "What's it doing out? Aren't they only out later at night?"

"Maybe dying changed its habits?" said Margaret.

Irene laughed a laugh that she knew she had to swallow quickly or it would go on forever.

"It could be . . . ," Pearl began.

"It *isn't,* there's no point saying that, it *was* the same one. We all saw," said Margaret.

"Now what?" Pearl said.

"Now we know—it works on bigger things."

Some things remained unknown about costs, about terms, but nobody said this. There was nothing to be gained by talking about it now.

*

The possum didn't take long to show its face. Its face, its snout, its whiskers. Its back with that terrible crimp in the flesh, like wet hair braided and then taken out of the braid. Its small peachy scrabbling paws, its toes like human toes. In the corner of the foyer as Irene was going up the stairs after lunch the next day, she saw it, and it turned its head, beady-eyed, in her direction. Too large to be there, impossible, yet there anyway. And inside her, her own possum gave a greeting kick.

It had gone, of course, when she looked full-on, but Irene knew better by now. It wasn't ever going to be gone again. The possum also knew its terms: that was why it had looked right at her.

Did you like the rest of what I showed you?

She didn't want to be shown anything else. She went straightaway to find Margaret and Pearl. She brought them with her into her bedroom, where they sat on her bed, and she tried not to think of kissing George there, George pulling away from her for the very first time in all their lives.

"Have you seen it yet?" Irene asked.

Pearl shook her head.

But Margaret nodded. "You will soon, Pearl. It's horrible."

"More horrible than the others?"

"There's more of it," said Irene.

"I don't ever want to see it."

"You knew what we were doing," Margaret told Pearl.

"But what *were* we doing, exactly?" Irene said. "We wanted to find out, we've found out. So if we need it—"

"There's still no reason to think we're going to," said Pearl.

"Pearl," Margaret said.

"*If* we do," Irene continued. "Now that we've had time to think. Now that we've seen what it's like with something bigger. Say we could figure out how to do it, some way of leaving . . . what would need to be left there, for enough time. Say we could. Would we, actually?"

Though each of them had, of course, been asking herself that question already, it was something different to hear it out loud.

"They might not really belong to us, if we did," said Pearl. "They might not really, fully be there, not in a way we can reach."

She was right. They might revive their babies, yes, but would anyone else be able to see them? Would even they be able to? What if the babies were like all the other creatures, with means of disappearing, maybe blending right into walls and floors and drapes, submerging, and as they grew, if they grew, crawling out of view, or toddling? They might grow lanky limbs and use them to run—to where, to whom, their left-behind mothers wouldn't know. They would only be able to try again and again to catch the image of these children, their children, whose faces they'd never once clearly seen.

Margaret shook her head. "I don't believe that. I won't. It wouldn't be like with animals and bugs, because these are *ours*. We just have to make them live. We can figure the rest out, I know we can."

They checked one another's faces, and of course the choice was clear and obvious and had been from the start—they were all here, after all, weren't they? Yes, of course they would do it. They would take their babies on any terms, because any terms had more hope in them than no babies at all. They could see only the decision that was right in front of them—dead or not dead—and there could be only one answer. After that, like any mothers, they would take what came, because the future was and had always been as dark and sealed as a womb. Wasn't that the terror, cling- ing always to the love, like a scent? All children went into those sealed futures. Even the woman at the lake had told Irene as much. All of them were made to disappear.

*

A few days after that, Irene lay awake during one afternoon rest time. She kept thinking about the mothers she had known. Her own mother, whose face was marked by the pain Irene routinely caused her. Elizabeth and her screaming baby. Irene's two closest friends, who had toddlers about the same age now: Evie had stayed pregnant-looking, and Barbara had thinned until her wrists turned knobby, while both of their children put their sticky hands all over everything. All the mothers Irene had seen all her life in grocery stores and clothes stores and shoe stores buying things upon things for their insatiable children, who were always crying or touching or pulling and making their mothers say *no*.

Which of these mothers' skins could Irene tug off and over herself? She wanted to fold herself inside and pull the skin closed, the way Dr. Bishop did with her white coat.

She emerged to go down the stairs for dinner and caught another glimpse of the possum creeping at the end of the hall. She was turning from it, so as not to look anymore at the choice she'd made, the wrongness of a large outdoor creature here crawling across carpet and wood, and so she didn't see Dr. Hall, not until he was already at her side and taking her by the elbow.

"Mrs. Willard. Irene. I'm so glad I've caught you," he said, and steered her back into her room.

He shut the door behind them.

"So you have, Doctor," Irene said.

To be in this part of the house, he had to have been lying in wait, and she didn't like that he'd used her first name. Irene took a step back, which he released his grip to allow. She thought of how he'd looked with his hands in Dr. Bishop's hair, and then the dark-haired woman's hair, and then the pink-nailed woman's hair, and Mrs. Conrad's too. She thought of the way his skin had begun to loosen.

She told herself, *Be careful.*

"I wanted to talk to you about the other day. That situation you saw, which, I do see how it could have been misleading"—he held up a finger before she could even begin to speak—"and I wanted to tell you that if someone had to see it, I'm glad it was you, out of all the patients. You have a good head on your shoulders, Irene. I've always thought so. I'm glad that a confusing thing like that was seen by a person who can see the way things really are."

She wished he'd stop saying *see*—it made her think of seeing creatures at the ends of long halls, and his hands on women, and what the vision of him had said to her in the garden. What was he thinking would happen next? Did he think Irene would smile back, and he could pat her on the head and go off down the hall, and afterward she'd remember mostly that he'd told her she was special? Or that she would close the distance between them to return his touch, even with the big globe of her belly between?

He narrowed his eyes to perfect his approving gaze, and Irene saw that, for him, either of those would be fine. He wouldn't have planned beyond this moment. He would take as his due whatever it would win him.

How exhausting, that he'd made Irene think through what he might have wanted to happen next, when he hadn't even thought it through himself.

"I *do* see, yes," Irene told him. She walked to the door and opened it. "You have a good evening, Doctor." She would wait to go downstairs for dinner until he was gone, long gone.

"Irene." He spread his hands with a rueful smile. *You and I both know how the world works.*

"Off you go now."

She watched the back of him move away down the hall, and the little possum gave her a quick pattering kick from inside.

*

Later that following week, Beatrice Loomis went into labor in between lunch and dinner. Irene could tell something was happening from the rhythm and increased quantity of footsteps on the floors overhead. She wondered what these other imported doctors were thinking of their hospital by now.

She found Pearl and Margaret out in the bedroom hallway. Margaret said, "We should go up there. In case."

"But—" Pearl started.

"I'm not saying we would; I don't even know if I'd want to. I just think we have to know what's going on."

Terrible words, too much in them, but of course she was right.

They weren't as lucky as the last time, though. As soon as they arrived at the end of the hall, they were halted by the wailing that came from somewhere along it, and then Dr. Bishop came out of a room—the wailing louder, then quieter again as she closed the door—and saw them straightaway.

"What on earth," she said. She bustled toward them. "You can't be up here."

"Why would you leave her sounding like that?" Irene said.

"Dr. Bradshaw and Dr. Sterrit are both in there, and Tom."

Dr. Bishop never called him Tom in front of them—her full possession of herself had slipped. Irene imagined what would happen to Dr. Bishop's face if she were to say what she knew about her Tom.

"So why aren't they helping her?" Margaret said, because the wailing went on and on. Irene cast a glance in Margaret's direction and saw that her lips trembled.

"She doesn't need much in the way of help right now. The intensity of the labor is actually a good sign. Everything is progressing and nothing is wrong."

"She's all right? She can't be all right—listen to her," Irene said. Pearl had taken a couple of steps back.

"She's declined pain relief so far."

"What kind of pain relief?"

"Morphine. It's been used safely in childbirth for many years, but she says she doesn't want it. There's also scopolamine, should she wish to be aware of nothing at all."

Imagine, Irene thought, feeling the way Beatrice sounded and turning down something that could save you from the feeling.

"Please don't concern yourselves. Really, there's no point worrying about labor ahead of time. And the three of you must know better than to come up here," Dr. Bishop said.

"You're afraid of letting us see," said Irene.

"Birth, even when everything is going well, can be upsetting," Dr. Bishop said. Then she watched while they left, with nothing to do but hope that Beatrice's baby wouldn't need them.

*

(Beatrice looked up and the doctor, where was the doctor? She felt as if she were burning alive from the inside out, the doctor should be here, not these men in white coats she didn't know.

The door opened. There she was.)

CHILD

15

Irene paused warily on the therapy-room threshold. Dr. Bishop gave her a tamped-down smile from her chair.

"No more walks?" Irene said.

"No more walks." The doctor rose. "Let's do your injections, get them out of the way."

"Out of the way of what?"

For an answer, Dr. Bishop gave only her strong fingers on Irene's arm and the small habituated sting of the needle. Irene's possum rolled and seemed, within, to use its teeth on her. A little tug, a small sharp pulling, then release.

"Are you all right?"

"Just a twinge." Irene would have let the possum chew on the flesh of her heart if it wanted.

"It can be uncomfortable during this phase."

"What phase?"

"The last."

Irene asked, "How's Beatrice? And her baby?"

"Surely you've heard already."

"Not from you."

"They're both well. They'll be going home in a few more days."

The world brightened, despite everything, in a way that made Irene frustrated with herself and her own easiness.

"You seem both happy and not happy about that," Dr. Bishop said. "I wish I understood."

"Understood?"

"Don't you see that you're working against yourself? I can't understand why you won't just let me help you. Why you keep fighting my helping you, when all I've ever wanted is for you to be Beatrice in a few weeks' time." The doctor leaned toward her.

Because I've seen too much of what's behind your face and too much of what you've managed not to see.

"I'm still here—isn't that enough?" Irene said.

"You seem to have developed some theory about me, some idea that makes you resistant. All of you need to be calm, and you're making that difficult, Irene, for everyone. I thought eventually you'd stop spending so much energy on defiance, but that doesn't seem to have happened. Why are you so angry? You're still pregnant, aren't you?"

"What would you do if I weren't?"

"What do you mean?"

"What would you do with me, you and Dr. Hall?" She leaned on his name with more contempt than she'd intended, and Dr. Bishop flinched a little. "What would happen if I lost it?"

"Well, you would leave," the doctor said, her brow furrowing.

"You'd just be done with me."

"You couldn't very well stay. Our program is for pregnant women. At that point there'd be nothing more we could do for you."

Nothing, nothing, nothing, the same thing the father and the professors and Dr. Hall had said to Dr. Bishop, over the years, all in their own ways. Had said the grandfather in every current of air in this house. Dr. Bishop had created the thing she was giving the women here, but she'd created it to spite the men, and that meant she sometimes forgot about the women almost as completely as the men did.

"But don't you see? That's exactly what everyone else has always been telling us, for all the years before we came here. I don't see why I should trust you any more than I trust all those others. You aren't so different. It's just a question of when you say the exact same words. I'm angry because you're acting as if you're something new, when really you aren't."

Dr. Bishop shook her head furiously. "What am I if not new? That's the one thing I've always been sure of."

Again the possum used its teeth.

Dr. Bishop stood and opened the door. "You can go now, Irene."

Irene felt the doctor's eyes on her back as she walked from the room. Someday soon she would teach this doctor to really see them all. She would use everything she knew about her, all the things Dr. Bishop had managed not to know about herself, and she would make Dr. Bishop know every woman who was here.

*

A few gardening times had been spent in the innocuous side patch, but then, one morning in late June, the walled garden was open again and waiting for them.

Only Phillips stood inside by the fountain. "Thinning out the new plants today," he said.

Irene, Margaret, and Pearl didn't even have to angle for their spots around the back this time—every woman positioned herself where she'd been before. Irene found her gaze wandering toward the place where the possum had shambled. Pearl's and Margaret's too, she saw.

She pulled a few sprouts. Were tomato buds supposed to look like this, so swollen? She nipped one off between her fingers and opened it up with her thumbnail, and warmish wetness flooded the gap between skin and nail. The meat inside was bloodiest red.

She elbowed Margaret. "Is it supposed to be this way?"

Margaret's eyebrows shot up. "They're supposed to start green. Green even once the flower's fallen off, until they're much bigger, then yellow. *Then* red."

The buds of the marigolds in front of her also looked swollen, Irene thought. And the ones in Pearl's and Margaret's patches.

Everything all down the lines in front of every woman.

In this space where the grandfather had tried to control growth itself, train it into a display of his ownership, growth had, maybe, done its own designing. It might have made itself beyond controlling, slipped the reins, seeded itself with strangeness—that might be what they'd been seeing here all along, growth making its own wild shapes.

Swiftly, Irene began pinching the buds off, with crisp little squeezes of index finger and thumb, and flicking them to the ground.

"What are you doing?" Pearl whispered.

"We can't let them bloom—everyone will see how strange they are. If people see, they'll start to wonder about this place. We can't have people wondering."

Margaret cast a glance at Phillips, whose back was turned. She set to work too, and after a minute, so did Pearl. "It's freakish," Pearl whispered. "Should we stop?"

"Stop taking these off?" said Irene.

"Stop everything. Stop even thinking about this garden, stop worrying about trouble that might never happen to us. Just let everyone else see what they see."

Margaret shook her head. "We knew already. We didn't think it was *normal*, Pearl." She kept pinching.

"I don't like looking at it," Pearl said querulously.

"Pearl, *please*," Irene said.

Pearl set to work again.

They would wait until the others had left, until Phillips had shown them all out. They would sneak back in to finish snipping. Though how could they help but miss one? Somewhere hidden amongst the leaves, one would go on budding, expanding, enlarging to bursting, and then it would burst and make everything visible, no taking it back. They would lose their best hope.

But they had to try. Pearl's mouth set itself, and Margaret put all her skill to work with this anti-gardening. Her expert fingers flew.

*

"I really can't let this go any longer, I'm afraid," Dr. Hall said, during Irene's checkup that afternoon. "I can't keep turning a blind eye and hoping it will resolve itself. Your weight gain isn't behaving the way it should, and neither are your hormone levels."

Dr. Hall seemed to catch himself and paused. Unbelievably, he smiled. "I don't want you to worry, Mrs. Willard. You aren't the only patient this is happening to. But that means it's time for me to confer with Dr. Bishop and make a plan about how best to proceed."

This was professional, unruffled concern he was showing. He seemed to have forgotten his more personal worries about Irene, maybe because he thought he'd taken care of them with that little scene in her room. Or because she hadn't said anything and he figured she would have by now.

Dr. Bishop would never want to send them home, Irene still believed that. But if Dr. Hall made her. If he raised this point about what he was seeing and it was unanswerable, he might be able to make her shut the hospital down. He could probably make Dr. Bishop do things, he probably had his own methods for making her, that was the way marriage worked.

The strange pattern he thought he was seeing, Irene was desperate to know what it was, but not as desperate as she was to stop him from thinking about it, so that she could stay. Because Irene still knew what home meant and what could so easily happen to her there, away from the garden she might need.

Time to do what she could, then.

"I wouldn't, Dr. Hall," she said.

"I'm sorry?" He was flipping the pages of her chart so he could gather numbers into his palm for carrying to Dr. Bishop: slight individually, but together like a whole amassed bulky colony. Irene had read that all the ants on Earth when measured that way outweighed by many multiples all the humans.

A mouse and a moth and a roly-poly and a beetle and a snake and a possum too, what did they weigh, what could Irene make them weigh?

"It would be better, I think, to forget all about it," Irene said.

That got his attention. "What?"

"Whatever it is you feel you're seeing, just look at something else. Worry about something else. You don't need to talk to Dr. Bishop; you don't need to say a thing. You've already made plenty of choices about what you and Dr. Bishop do and don't need to talk about, haven't you, Doctor. Think of this as one more."

"Mrs. Willard—"

"Because if you start thinking you need to talk to Dr. Bishop, I might too. I might have to tell her what I saw."

He winced. "That would be foolish, since you're wrong, Mrs. Willard."

"I could be wrong. That's true. We both could be."

"Really, it would be very foolish."

"Lucky it doesn't need to happen, then."

Irene felt more like herself than she had for weeks. These moments belonged to her most: moments when she held the reins, the rod, the stick; when she was the one who set the terms; when she and the other person, whoever the other person was, were both waiting to see what she'd do next. She loved George and she loved every minute she got to spend with him, but the self required of her in those minutes had always been a little beyond her, in reach, maybe, but requiring extension. This, what she was doing now, required none.

"So if I don't say anything," Dr. Hall said, "if I don't, you won't either. That's what you're telling me."

"That's right."

Dr. Hall stared down at his numbers again. Then he shook his head. "It doesn't make sense. For the life of me, it doesn't. Why would you want it this way? Why wouldn't you want us to talk this over and make the best decision about what we should do?"

Dr. Bishop would have understood. Dr. Bishop knew what it was like to want something desperately enough not to care about its cost. But Dr. Hall, look at him, his smoothly self-sufficient face—even whatever he felt for Mrs. Conrad could only be the faintest taste of need. A muffled hint of the feeling, like touching something hot through a glove.

"Don't worry about why. It doesn't matter."

When Irene found Pearl and Margaret that night to tell them that Dr. Hall had started to have qualms, when they tensed, she said, "It's all right. I told him not to tell Dr. Bishop or I'd tell her what I know too. It worked, it really worked, and we can stay."

Irene pressed her bare palms to her stomach: *This, little possum—this is who your mother is.*

*

Beatrice left on a sunny day, a little later than she should have, according to precedent—maybe the doctors were being extra careful now with even the properly delivered fruits of labors. The women gathered to watch her being brought down the stairs.

No one had seen Willa leave. It seemed possible she never had and was still up there on the third floor, stealing into corners, hiding behind doors, and it seemed possible too that she'd vanished into thin air.

"You see," Pearl hissed to Irene and Margaret as they watched Beatrice beam, "it's going to be fine. We've been silly."

"Fine for who?" Margaret whispered.

"Careful with him," Beatrice said to her husband as she handed him the baby, with all the awkwardness of handing over a limbed thing.

"Oh, he isn't too fragile," said Dr. Bishop. "He's a nice, healthy full-term infant. You don't need to worry."

"He's a good boy," Beatrice said with utter seriousness, though she was talking about a baby so new she couldn't know a thing. "I *told* you he was a boy," Beatrice said.

"A fifty-fifty chance," said Dr. Bishop, smiling.

Beatrice looked wan in the bright morning light—the curtains were open again for this ceremony—but so did Dr. Bishop, as if producing this baby had bled them both of something. Dr. Bishop also seemed to move with caution. Dr. Hall, on the other hand, looked and moved just fine. Irene was sure he considered himself racked with guilt and fear, but those were feelings through gloves again. Irene caught his eye and he turned his head fast, as if she might decide to deliver on her threat right there, in the middle of the foyer: *Excuse me, everyone, I have an announcement.* Where was Mrs. Conrad? She'd been making herself scarce lately, maybe fearing the same thing.

Dr. Hall took his wife's elbow and stood with her, to smile too at Beatrice and her husband.

"Shameless," Margaret whispered.

Pearl shrugged. "Nobody teaches them shame."

"Who?" said Irene.

"Husbands. They get to feel anger instead, that's what I've always thought."

But George had almost no anger in him that Irene had spotted. Irene supplied that. She tried to imagine how George would behave in Dr. Hall's position, what approach he might take to his own crimes, but the effort caved something in near her middle. She'd had this kind of thought sometimes while he was away, and after he was back—*were there women? . . . did he in all that time . . . ?*—but blinked the thought off there, always. Until Dr. Hall in the vision, with his gray loosening face, had said it out loud.

Irene herself had come close only the once. When George's letters were never coming, never coming, and there was all that aloneness in their house, she'd been furious with him, and with herself for doing nothing but waiting. Her dreams about George had been the warmest part of her life, and it had occurred to her that her marriage existed at that moment only in those dreams. So one morning she'd put on a new dress and gone out to meet the man who delivered their ice, whom she'd been watching, because there weren't many men home then; he was home. "I *was* over there," he said when she asked. "They shot me in the ankle." He pulled his pant leg up and showed her the scar. It shone like a blind eye atop his tendons. He met her gaze. He brushed his hair aside, and she saw the muscles of his arms move and push up against the insides of his sleeves. He saw her see them.

"Everything else still works," he said.

She laughed.

Irene had drawn near enough to feel the warmth of it, like coming close to a pan on the stove with her palm—no glove, not for her. But she hadn't put her palm down. She said, "I'm sure it does" and turned, went back into the house, shut the door behind. What counted was that she'd shut it, that was what she afterward decided. She'd pulled back instead of touching. It was possible that wasn't enough and she'd still poisoned everything enough to lose all their babies in the years since—but still, she had pulled back. She thought she'd have forgiven George for almost touching and retreating in the end.

Irene didn't know what shame looked like in George, unless, as the vision Dr. Hall had said, she'd seen it for years without knowing.

Beatrice's husband held the baby awkwardly, shifting it around so he could grip it in one arm and open the door for Beatrice with the other hand.

"Careful!" Beatrice said again, sharper.

The movement tipped the baby toward the women, uncovering it from its blanket enough to reveal its face, scrunched, with eyes open but not seeming to see, made into two dark, wet holes by the shine on them. A mouth that worked repetitively, as if eating or desiring to eat. A chin that puckered and released, wrinkling like a thumbprint. Its tongue protruded. Its feet kicked within its bundling, the way they must have kicked from inside.

Inside Irene her little possum kicked too.

Is that what you look like in there?

"Look at him watching!" Beatrice said in a sugary voice. She reached out a hand and stroked the baby's head. The dark holes of eyes followed her hand; the mouth opened wider as if to fasten on and suck and take her flesh in.

With a wave to them all, Beatrice walked through the door.

16

A couple of weeks passed. It was July now, and Irene was thirty weeks along, then thirty-one. While she dressed for breakfast one morning, a knock came at the door, light and soft, fast as a rabbit's heartbeat when you've caught the rabbit and pinned it between your hands.

Margaret and Pearl stood outside, Pearl's hand on Margaret's elbow.

"She's bleeding," Pearl said.

Irene looked to Margaret's whole hands, her unscathed arms, and her pale, bloodless face. Margaret's eyes were too wide. She held up her underclothes. "I took them off, I don't know why. I couldn't think what to do, but I knew I didn't want the blood on me."

"It's not much," Irene said. And it wasn't, a single reddish-brown streak, only just soaked through. From the underside of the cloth you would barely know anything had happened. "It might be nothing." Irene was surprising herself with this impulse to tell Margaret there were still ways for the disaster not to be a disaster at all, when it was the last thing she believed. When they'd all felt, hadn't they, that this was coming.

"*Irene,*" said Margaret.

"All right, come sit down."

"What if sitting makes it worse?"

"Don't sit, then," Irene said. She wanted those underclothes out of view, having seen underclothes that looked just like them before and knowing where they led. She understood why Margaret had taken them off. It was like her dream of the ink all over her bedroom, the horrible prospect of touching the shame that had come from inside. "Now we have to figure this out."

"Figure what out?" said Pearl, who should have understood— but her whole body was oriented toward Margaret, helping her sit down on the bed, tending to Margaret in the present, not yet considering the future they'd talked about, which was now here.

"What we want to do," Irene said. "Margaret, listen, we don't have to go to the garden. I know we always said we would, but it's different now that it's real. It's up to you. We can go straight to the doctors instead." The gamble of it, the mad, hopeful clutching at this one last chance, when they didn't know what its terms would be—Margaret had to be the one to decide.

"Yes, Margaret, I'm sure there's something the doctors can do," Pearl said quickly, because Pearl would have loved to back away long ago from what they'd found. "Or maybe they don't even have to do anything. You're very far along—maybe this kind of thing means nothing now."

Or maybe, all of them were thinking, Margaret was becoming Dorothy, the way she herself had said she would.

Margaret raised her eyes from her lap. "The garden. That's what I want."

"You're sure?" Irene asked.

"I'm sure. But then, what, do I have to stay there?" At the prospect of this, Margaret went still and pale.

"No, of course not," Irene said. "For three days? You can't. They'll look for you and find you and send you home for being crazy, Pearl and me too probably."

"What, then?"

In her anticipation of this moment, Irene had always pictured the tiny red curled things that had come out of her, with their dots of maybe eyes. But whatever was happening to Margaret's creature, it was still inside. It had only sent them this sign.

"Well, what if we left this?" Irene touched Margaret's wrist on the hand that held the underclothes.

"Could that work?" Margaret asked.

"It might," Pearl said slowly. "Why should the garden need all of it? It could still fix it, right where it is. It always fixes the things."

Irene thought of the crimped back of the possum, the ragged wings of the moth. "It makes them alive again, anyway. Margaret, I think it's all we can do."

"It's not all *I* can do," Margaret said, louder. "I can stay there. I can. It doesn't matter if they find me—what do I care about that?" Her fingers raked her hair.

"They'll find you long before it's had time to work, though, and make you leave too early," said Pearl.

"Leaving this is better," Irene said, gesturing to the underclothes.

"For *you* two it's better."

"There's just no way you could stay. They'd miss you so many times tomorrow alone—at breakfast and calisthenics and lunch and therapy and your examination. They'd stop you. But they won't find this, if we leave it there."

Margaret considered, then, after a minute, nodded.

They hurried from the house. Once they'd made it outside, though, they walked slower than before, in case walking too quickly would be bad for Margaret. Irene and Pearl each held her by an elbow. From a distance they'd have appeared friendly, like they only wanted to walk touching one another. If you couldn't see their faces.

"How do you feel?" Pearl asked Margaret.

"Like I'm losing my whole life," Margaret said. "It's going to hurt so much, it's going to be so awful—you both know how it feels, and this late? It will be as bad as having a baby, probably, but with no baby at the end. I know all of that and I don't even care, because I keep picturing Victor's face when I have to tell him.

That's how I feel." She stood like any aching woman—hunched and hugging herself—but the way she spoke was only hers. The same voice she'd have used for speaking from the head of her Ladies' Auxiliary table while she partitioned out the caretaking of a person she loved: *Yes, it's really that bad, so what do we gain by pretending otherwise?*

"Maybe none of that will happen. This could work," said Irene.

"Or maybe the doctors . . . ," Pearl began hopefully, but trailed off when she saw Margaret's expression.

"The *doctors*," said Margaret with hatred. "Dr. Bishop promised me, she promised she was fixing whatever was wrong."

Irene thought of her own extra shots and cold washed down her back. What if in trying to help Margaret, Dr. Bishop had hurt? Dr. Bishop would never hurt on purpose, Irene knew that—she had never doubted the doctor was trying to help, even if she was trying to help herself too. But she might act and act until helping and hurting were the same. How could Dr. Bishop ever know whether she'd done too much or not enough? She couldn't know, so she kept doing.

And all of that, she'd been doing to Irene too, and to all of them.

"I'll have to call Victor, or they'll bring him to me and I'll have to tell him, or they'll tell him for me, and he won't even be surprised. That's almost the worst part." Margaret clutched her middle and crumpled while they held her, but Irene couldn't tell whether the pain was from some disaster inside her or from her own words. "I know he's been expecting it for months now."

Irene raised her gently up again. "Margaret, we're doing what we can."

Time for them to act and act for themselves.

Pearl opened the garden gate for Margaret. They led her straight to the fountain, and Margaret laid her offering down. She stood for a minute with her head bowed. The cherub loomed above, his legs frozen forever at that one still point of a kick, his blank eyes aimed at something above Margaret's head. Irene wanted to take a stone and smash the smile from his face.

Margaret turned to go, but she'd forgotten the leaves—she and Pearl both had and were walking away with the final step undone. Irene scooped up a handful. She looked down into what she'd gathered and some new fruit dangled from a stemmed cluster, a spiky green ball that looked like a horse chestnut but shinier. What was its meaning? Was it better or worse to make it part of the pile? She didn't know, but she put it down with the rest.

Margaret turned and saw what Irene had done. "Thank you," she said.

*

They learned back at the house that Nancy Montgomery was in labor. While they'd been in Irene's bedroom, or walking to the garden, or performing their ritual inside, Nancy had been hunting down the doctors to deliver her life's most momentous announcement: *I think it's time.*

Hours passed (hours in which Nancy kept asking the doctors what to do next, then trying to do it, the pushing, the waiting, the stretching, as wholeheartedly as she could, pretending her older sister, who always knew what to do without being told, was holding her hand).

These hours Irene, Margaret, and Pearl spent in Pearl's bedroom. Labor days were always looser in structure, and no one seemed to have noticed they'd separated themselves off in this way, or at least no one came looking for them. "Shouldn't you go find the doctors now, Margaret?" Pearl asked.

"No, this is good for me, that Nancy's happening today," Margaret said. "We won't have our regular examinations. If there's no heartbeat for now, only for now"—this part she said in a private-sounding voice—"then Dr. Hall won't have to find out yet. I'll get closer to my three days before anyone even knows anything's wrong."

This made sense to Irene. Of course it would be better never to have to exchange a baby that wasn't alive for a baby that was somehow alive again in anybody's understanding. "We don't know it's a full three days either—we never tried shorter," she said. The chances had always been too hard to come by to waste one by checking early.

"We don't even know anything really *is* wrong," said Pearl. "I still say you should just go tell them. It might just be spotting. You aren't cramping, are you? You aren't having pains?"

Margaret shook her head.

"So it might be something very small that they can fix."

"If it's very small, they don't need to fix it," Margaret said, "and if it's big, they can't. I want to do this the way we're doing it."

At dinner that night they learned Nancy had delivered a healthy girl. Matilda Lawrence, one of the newest arrivals, came running into the room with the news, on the verge of tears, as if speaking about something to do with herself.

Irene and Pearl turned to Margaret in the tentative way you might look at a rickety table you'd piled a weight on.

"Oh, good," said Margaret, with a bright, false smile.

*

While Margaret was in with Dr. Hall for her regular examination the next day, Irene and Pearl waited at the end of the hall together. They stood by the window so it wouldn't look like they were standing right outside the door.

"It sounds all right, don't you think?" said Pearl.

"I don't hear anything."

"Exactly, we'd hear something."

Irene wondered. The disaster itself would consist of quiet. When Dr. Hall pressed the metal tube of the fetoscope to Margaret's belly, instead of a sound, a nothing. *Nothing, nothing, nothing* again, and why should nothing sound like something?

Irene had called George this morning and there'd been quiet on the line with him too. "How are you feeling?" he'd asked. How could she answer? What had been happening to her here was a wide body of water between them. No way to call across it loudly enough for him to hear about the shape that had been weight and mouse and moth and snake and possum and would be, she presumed, other things too.

Please let it arrive in a form they both could see even when they looked at it head-on, a form they could touch, a form that occupied the same kind of space they did, please, please. "Please."

"What?" George sounded amused—he'd thought Irene was witticizing.

"Well, how would you expect me to feel? I'm huger than huge, it's amazing I can walk at all. Wait till you see."

Please see, Irene had thought.

"She should be almost done, shouldn't she?" Pearl said now.

But the next door that opened was to the side, not the one they'd been waiting for. From its threshold, Dr. Bishop narrowed her eyes. "Did I startle you?"

"That's all right. We were just . . . ," Pearl started, waving a hand.

Irene could have hit that hand from the air. You never explained. You rejected their right to an explanation unless it was demanded outright, and even then, if you could.

"Just waiting for Margaret," Pearl finished, after too long a pause.

"Why?"

Irene said, "Aren't we allowed?"

"I wondered if there was some particular reason. Margaret seemed a little preoccupied in her session earlier."

So this was how the quiet disaster revealed itself. Margaret had tried to keep what was happening from Dr. Bishop, because what could she have said? *Yes, I'm spotting, yes, there's a good chance I've lost this one too, but don't send me home, we've taken some steps, you see, and I might be able to get it back again.* Margaret would have talked about anything else: her favorite childhood doll or her last fight with Victor, while her terrified eyes roamed. But Dr. Bishop had seen what was happening inside Margaret anyway, through her walls.

"I don't know anything about that," Irene said. Pearl shook her head.

Dr. Bishop left them, and there, by the examination room doorway, a shadow broke away into movement and took on a brownish shade. Not big enough for the possum, but with too much mass for the insects. The mouse again, probably.

What had they set in motion here?

When Irene turned back, Pearl had gone to the far end of the hall, facing out the window with her hands on the sill. "Do you think you'll be able to go back to your own house after this and act like nothing ever happened?" she said. She looked out at the world as if she didn't recognize it.

Then Pearl's hands tightened on the ledge. So tight Irene could see the whitening of her knuckles. They released again and color flooded them.

"Are you all right, Pearl?"

"I've been having pains since this morning. Coming and going for a while, but now just coming. It's early still for me, though, so it's maybe a false alarm, that's what I'm thinking."

"You haven't told them?"

"Not until we find out about Margaret."

Pearl looked out the window, and Irene looked at Pearl's hands. Those hands that had plucked at licorice like seeds, that had smoothed Joe's sleeves in nervous tending. Were they hers still, making this motion? After a while they tightened again and went white. Released, pinkened.

At last the door opened. Margaret came toward them. Her face shone with tears. "There's a heartbeat," she said.

"A heartbeat." Irene took her hands.

So it had worked then, what they'd done. The garden was working.

Pearl put her hands over theirs too. Then tightened, tightened.

*

The doctors said Pearl was a little early but nearly full term, there was nothing to worry about, it was time, and she might gather a few things to bring up with her to the third floor. Margaret held the bag while Irene walked around picking up and dropping inside the things Pearl, from her seat on the bed, requested: the hairbrush, the tiny ceramic dog, the pair of woolen socks. "How should I know what to bring? Like packing for a trip to the moon," Pearl said giddily. "Things that will make me comfortable, that's what they told me."

Pearl had no space inside her for thinking much about Margaret anymore, Irene knew, now that she was being moved ritually to this different floor of their lives. Margaret met Irene's eyes and smiled in a resigned way to show she understood. And anyway, she had that heartbeat to cling to.

Margaret and Irene walked Pearl up. "Do we knock?" Pearl said, laughing, outside the delivery room. The laughter stopped, and she stooped again under another of the pains.

Dr. Bishop opened the door. She spun an arm to display the room she'd made ready: the bed with its gleaming rails and foot-rails, the stainless-steel trays to its side. One held instruments— a bulb, something like an enormous pair of tweezers, gauze, and scissors—and one bottles and needles. The bed, with its head tilted up, had a white sheet on it. At its precise midpoint had been laid a square white towel.

"Please come in, Pearl, and make yourself comfortable."

Pearl started to do as she'd been told but paused.

"Could they come in with me? Can they be here for this?" She gestured to Irene and Margaret, wanting to pull them over that frightening threshold for herself.

"Oh no, I'm afraid not," said Dr. Bishop.

"Why?" Pearl balanced between out and in. They all waited. Irene knew why the doctor would never allow them to be present, but she wanted to hear her say it: that it was a shock every time to see the body stretch and strain to do its impossible job of bringing the inside out, forth. That she didn't know what it would do to Margaret and Irene in their current circumstances to watch such a thing.

"It's a sanitary concern, first of all," Dr. Bishop said.

"You could give them gowns and make them wash their hands, couldn't you?" said Pearl.

"What looks clean isn't really, most of the time—no need to introduce new sources of contamination. And when it comes down to it, you wouldn't end up wanting them, Pearl. There's a reason we do things the way we do them. This is something that's best left private."

Dr. Hall was coming down the hall now, eyes on the chart he held.

"I just wanted them with me," Pearl said in a wobbly voice.

"What is it?" Dr. Hall said, looking up and registering her tears, Irene and Margaret's presence.

"It's best this way," said Dr. Bishop.

"What is?" Dr. Hall said again.

"Nothing," said Pearl. She turned toward Irene and Margaret. Irene stepped forward to embrace her, and then Margaret did too.

"It's going to be all right," Irene whispered into her hair, because of course Pearl had no choice, really, about whether to enter, and none of them had any idea what would happen to her inside.

"It will be, for all of us," Pearl said in a high pleading voice.

What would Pearl's next hours be like? Irene wouldn't have known even if they'd never done what they'd done in the garden, even if Dr. Bishop had never done what she'd done with the injections, even if Pearl's pregnancy had been easy and typical and conducted somewhere far from this house. There was nothing about the little possum's occupation that suggested an endpoint: Irene's body felt as sealed as ever, as if what was happening to her would carry forward indefinitely in the same direction, in a straight line. Forward, forward—but eventually into that room where Pearl would go now.

Where Dr. Bishop was pulling her by the elbow.

Dr. Hall followed. He closed the door behind them. In the narrowing space as it swung shut, Irene watched Pearl settle herself against the pillows.

Irene and Margaret moved away from the door. They knew they wouldn't be allowed to stay in the hall, so they descended to the landing between the third floor and the second, partway up the stairs. Floating between the layers of this house, where they might not be noticed, or at least not made to move. There were two chairs in place as if waiting for them, so they sat and watched two white-coated doctors, the foreign recruits, climb the stairs. Everyone smiled politely as they passed.

"They don't seem to be in much of a hurry this time," Margaret said once they'd gone. "That's a good sign."

For a while, they couldn't hear anything happening at all.

*

A few hours in, a moan drifted down to them.

"What was that?" Margaret said.

"*I* don't know, why would I?"

They watched the turn to the third floor as if with enough time and attention they might see straight to Pearl. "We're like husbands in the waiting room," said Margaret.

But Irene didn't like this invocation of the normal version they would never get of this scene. Their husbands would never get to be this close to the befalling miracle or disaster.

It was befalling Pearl now. Why had she gone so quiet? You couldn't want to moan like that only once, could you? Whatever had made you feel that way surely wouldn't stop making you feel that way so quickly. Maybe something had cost Pearl the ability to make any sound. The only people in a position to know were the doctors, and Pearl, and the baby. If the baby lived. If it was in fact an actual baby. If any of theirs was.

A black-rot version of the tree-falls-in-the-forest question: *If a woman has a baby, and there's no one there to see it, and the baby is dead, or something not quite a baby, did she have a baby at all?*

Is she a mother at all?

Irene put a hand on her little possum, which kicked. Alive in there for now, if what happened in there could be called life.

"When it's getting close to my turn I'm going to call George no matter what they say. I'll just have him come, and he can wait where we are now, like he would have if I'd never had to be here."

Margaret shrugged. "What's the point, though? A door's as good as all those miles, that's what I think."

Irene cupped her kneecaps and imagined what might be happening upstairs. Maybe Dr. Bishop had already lifted and applied a shining instrument somewhere deep inside, and that was what had caused the noise. Now she might stand with it posed in the air, waiting to decide if she would use it again, while Pearl's feet pushed and hands clutched at the rails.

While past Pearl's feet the grandfather from the portrait watched, leaning in the way he'd leaned to watch other kinds of progress, that terrible sloughing skin stretching and starting to give. Dr. Bishop wouldn't see him, not unless she thought to look behind her.

Next Irene and Margaret heard the sound a person might make if she were trying to tear the whole world in half. They rose and rushed up the stairs: you couldn't hear a sound like that without moving to do what you could to help the person who'd made it.

*

(Pearl felt her body choose to jitter and jag itself apart, rend and scatter itself, and she shut her eyes and waited for this to happen— as deep down she'd known all her life it must, sometime.)

*

Outside the door, Margaret and Irene heard a thin, ragged crying.

The baby, the baby was crying. The baby had been born and was crying. The baby had been born and was crying and was *alive*.

Irene and Margaret took each other's hands.

Time passed. They waited through it. Whatever was happening now, a line had been drawn at the threshold of Pearl's room, and Irene and Margaret were on the other side.

The nurse opened the door with her arms full of bedding smeared with red. She stopped at the sight of them on the floor.

"You can't be here now," she said.

"Is Pearl all right?" Irene said.

The nurse pressed her lips together and cast her eyes behind her into the room.

"We won't go until we hear if she's all right."

"And the baby. How is the baby?" Margaret's voice climbed.

"Shh."

Dr. Bishop came through the door to lay a hand on the nurse's shoulder. "It's all right, Mary, you go on."

The nurse turned and walked down the hallway. Dr. Bishop waited a moment before speaking. "She's fine. Pearl and the baby are both fine. The baby is on the small side but nothing out of the ordinary."

Being small might help you out of the trap's teeth, Irene thought—you could wriggle and slip right through.

"We want to see them," Margaret said.

"You have to let us, she isn't a prisoner," Irene added.

Dr. Bishop paused to consider. "I suppose I don't see why not. At this juncture it can't do much harm." Now that she'd been successful, she meant; now that she counted Pearl a win. "If she's feeling up to it, you can come in and say hello, once we've put everything to rights."

Maybe all the furniture inside the room had been pushed to crazy angles. Maybe Pearl had gone roving and shoving at all of it, and streaking it with everything that had come out of her.

"A few minutes," Dr. Bishop said. She handled the door so carefully they didn't get even a peek around it. Inside, the grandfather from the portrait might even now be drawing close to the baby, crouching over the bed, ready to do—what? *Oh, hurry,* Irene thought at Dr. Bishop.

After a minute, Dr. Bishop opened the door and let them in. There was a smell in this room, Irene thought, the kind of smell that makes an animal lick something, a sore spot, a raw spot. It made part of her want to open a window and another part want to lie down and roll.

They moved toward Pearl, Pearl with something in her arms.

Margaret was cooing already, closing in not on Pearl but on the bundle she held. Pearl smiled, and her arms and chest opened to show this something that had made her irrelevant. Nothing on earth, from the look of things, could have pleased her more.

Margaret perched on the bed. Irene leaned in too, for a better look at this baby. It stayed put in Irene's field of sight, and Irene let out a breath. Just the head visible, but only skin there. No fur no wings no shining carapace no blood, no visible blood.

"Here it is," Margaret said.

"Here *she* is," Pearl corrected.

"She." Margaret put her hand out toward her.

"Don't touch, please."

Margaret drew back, and Irene too. They'd forgotten Dr. Bishop was still there, against the wall with Dr. Hall, watching. None of the other doctors—they must have gone home, job done—but yes, Irene had been right, for a moment there was the grandfather, in the dark corner of the room, bent and shadowy, planning and rotting. There was something important about his presence here in this place of newness, Irene thought, something worth figuring out, but she couldn't now, not with Pearl looking at her.

Irene looked into the face of her friend. Pearl's pupils were very wide and still and shining. What had the doctors given her? One of those drugs, certainly: Pearl didn't look quite like herself.

"Remember, you haven't washed your hands," Dr. Bishop said.

So they could not unwrap this baby and inspect it as they would have wanted to.

Pearl was smiling at them, but the smile was somehow hard. Though the angle of her chest might be open for display, though her eyes were glassy, her arms were tight on the bundle. They couldn't have touched the baby even if Dr. Bishop had left them, Irene saw: Pearl never would have allowed it.

"How do you feel?" Irene asked.

"Me?" said Pearl. "Oh, I'm fine."

"It wasn't too bad?"

Pearl raised her unfocused eyes to the ceiling. "It was awful, but that doesn't matter now."

"But what did it *feel* like?" Irene said. "You might as well tell us. We'll know soon enough."

"Let me think how to say it."

Dr. Bishop said, "You don't need to talk about this, Pearl. There's no need for you to upset yourself."

"Why would I be upset? I've done it, haven't I? I'm all done," said Pearl. "It's just a hard thing to put into words."

"I know," said Dr. Bishop soothingly.

"*None* of you know," Pearl said with relish. "I'm the only one here who actually knows, aren't I? It felt like splitting open, that's what it felt like. I was dying and dying and dying, and surely the next time I'd really truly die. And then there she was instead."

Margaret looked stricken.

"Well, that doesn't sound too bad!" Irene said wildly. Pearl laughed.

They were still laughing when the sound of the door stopped them. In the opened space stood Pearl's husband. He hadn't felt the need to knock and wait for anybody to open the door for him.

"Joe!" said Pearl.

But Joe didn't look at Pearl either. Like everyone else, he looked at the bundle, the baby.

"Come and see her," said Pearl unnecessarily.

Then Irene and Margaret had to cede their places; it didn't matter at all what they knew about Pearl, about the baby, about what they'd all done and what they'd all been willing to do to bring this baby here, because here was Joe, who didn't seem to notice how his wife didn't want to let the baby out of her arms. He simply took her.

"He hasn't washed his hands either, has he?" Irene muttered, eyes on Joe's big ham-hands, on his daughter.

"*Look* at her," Joe Porter was saying, to Pearl, to the room in general, or to himself. "What a thing. Thank you." This he directed to Dr. Hall.

MOTHER

17

The doctors lodged Joe up on the third floor in an adjoining room to Pearl's. Irene realized for the first time that they must have put the other husbands there too. The husbands had always seemed so irrelevant to everything, before, that she'd never thought to wonder. Now there was no stealing a moment alone with Pearl, because Joe was in constant occupation, reading a newspaper over in the corner of the room and flapping the pages like a large, irate bird. Pearl looked up tiredly whenever the door opened. "Come see BabyGinny," she said, seeming barely aware of what she was saying or whom she was saying it to, her mouth all blurry. She never called the baby Ginny alone. "Isn't she precious?"

Irene found that the more time she spent with Pearl, Pearl *after*, the more she wanted to pinch her to wake her up. Was she sounding like this because Joe was always watching and listening? Or was there something that happened at the tail end to do this to a person? As if the baby left behind a vacuousness that couldn't be filled except with meaningless words.

BabyGinny was pretty, with that little flourish of dark reddish hair. Irene didn't want to hold her, though, which seemed to hurt Pearl. Margaret always reached for her first thing.

Joe became agitated very quickly by BabyGinny's crying. "What does she need?" he asked every time, as if Pearl was supposed to have this information.

"Oh, she's just fussing," Pearl would say vaguely.

Joe would sigh and shift, resisting, Irene could tell, the impulse to plug his ears, but he never budged from his chair.

So in the end Margaret and Irene had to steal their goodbye in the midst of everyone else's, during Pearl's ritual send-off, just a few days after Nancy's. For her own great occasion, at least, Pearl did seem to wake up a little. She smiled at them self-consciously as she came down the stairs, then succumbed to the general worship and smiled wider and more impersonally, there in her spotlight. Irene thought she might get so caught up she'd just let Joe steer her out the door, but she did remember to pull back and reach toward Margaret and Irene. She clasped their hands.

"It'll be you *soon*," she said.

BabyGinny made a fussy squawk in Joe's arms. Joe winced at Pearl.

"Call me after, both of you, promise," Pearl said.

Then she was gone.

*

Irene had a dream that the possum chewed its way out of her stomach with hot, sharp teeth. She woke and her middle was clenched tight. It held itself that way for the space of two breaths, long enough for Irene to start wondering what she would do if it didn't release, before it did.

"Braxton Hicks contractions," Dr. Hall told her at her examination the next morning.

"Contractions? So it's starting?"

"Oh no, not yet, these contractions aren't dilating you. Trust me, you'll know when it's the real thing. These are only warning shots."

He loved telling her this, Irene could see. He loved that she didn't know it until he explained it to her. "What are *you* so pleased about?"

He turned wary. "We should all be pleased, Mrs. Willard. You're very nearly there."

Irene breathed in and caught a whiff of the antiseptic smell of this room, which she was rarely aware of now because she was practically pickled in it. They had taken her body here and given her a new one, and even that was a placeholder for the real change, still coming. She wondered how her self in its final shape would feel when she tried to move it around in the broader world. She wondered if she would still know how to inhabit that self.

How she hated these doctors, both of them in different ways, for all of that.

"How is Mrs. Conrad these days, Dr. Hall?" Irene said.

"Fine, I assume," Dr. Hall said stiffly.

"You assume?"

He met Irene's eyes. "Really, I only ever saw Mrs. Conrad in passing."

"Is that what you call it, *in passing.*" She thought of him with woman after woman in the garden vision. They did pass, she supposed, to make room for the next.

If I say it, I do it.

"It isn't a lie," he said, flushing. "It isn't, at its heart, a lie. It was nothing, or it might as well have been nothing, for all it meant." There was that word again, *nothing.* "The tiniest of moments in my life. In my feelings."

"Why do it, then?"

He lowered his face into his palms. The gesture invited a hand to the nape of the neck, so Irene sat on her hands.

"I don't see why I shouldn't tell Dr. Bishop," she said. "Surely she has a right to know. Why should I hide this for you?"

Dr. Hall raised his eyes again. "I *will* say . . ." He held up a finger. "I *will* say that you have no idea what it's like to be married to my wife."

Dr. Bishop with her arms spread wide beneath him in the grass, never even trying to hold on.

"Does she make you feel small?" Irene asked.

He looked at her in surprise. "Yes. Smaller than I am, I think."

Everyone around this man his whole life long would have been impressed with him until Dr. Bishop, which was why he'd wanted her, to win her over. It was why he loved her and why he hated her too. Not that he knew any of that. He just knew he'd been wounded. Look at him, that hurt, hanging head.

"You can't imagine the way it wears on a person," he said.

Irene thought of George and the enormity of his goodness. Had she felt small beside it? Of course. Sometime in their earliest weeks together, Irene had decided that the interior of George was like a wide green field. She knew from the way his face turned, so open, on each new person he talked to—he held a whole world, warm and sunnied, inside himself, and while he offered that view to everyone, it was the great gift of her life to be the special one allowed to walk around in there.

If only George could have grown their children.

"A person gets tired of it," said Dr. Hall.

"So it's all Dr. Bishop's fault, then."

"Lou can't change for the life of her." Dr. Hall smiled wearily. "Really, I don't know why I'm saying all these things to you— I've needed somebody to listen, I suppose."

Those words too, delivered smoothly enough to be beautiful in their way. Meant to charm her right out of remembering what he'd done.

"You're very good at this," Irene told him. "She can't say you're not the best at something."

He closed his face to her then. He put the fetoscope to her belly and held it there, and pressed.

*

In the days that followed, Irene watched Margaret expectantly. Every morning when they first saw each other, she asked, "Anything?" Meaning labor pains or bleeding, either one. Margaret always shrugged. Irene would say, "What does that mean?" and Margaret would say, "Nothing. There's nothing," again that word. But all day when she shifted in her chair, when she let out a sound of discomfort, every time, Irene asked, "What?" Margaret wasn't even quite at her due date yet, but her timing had been so like Pearl's all along that, one way or another, everything must change for her soon.

Irene waited for the arrival of the change, for the end of the question. Margaret's baby still had a heartbeat at every examination—she came and found Irene to report this each time—but they'd really know anything for sure only when they looked at it. If they could look at it.

"Should we go to the garden just to see?" Irene asked over one lunch, when she wasn't sure if she could stand it anymore, because she'd been waiting for Margaret to tell her she was ready to check, and Margaret kept not saying it.

Margaret thought for a moment. "I don't want to really."

"We can't just leave the underclothes there. Somebody might find them."

"They won't be able to tell it has anything to do with us."

"But don't you want to know?"

"*Want?*" Margaret said. She laughed. Her eyes widened and in them, for an instant, Irene glimpsed Margaret's huge and howling fear. "I just can't."

Irene wasn't sure what they'd be expecting to find in the garden anyway, or what anything they would or wouldn't find would tell them, because of the way Margaret's crisis had actually occurred. The blood would be gone or not gone, but the creature their act had served or not served was hidden inside Margaret either way, buried in her flesh, saved or not saved by what they'd done, transformed or not transformed, in any case inaccessible.

It would emerge soon enough, she supposed, and then they'd see, they'd have to see.

She glanced at Margaret, chewing. Margaret's worries too were, once again, buried and invisible, for now.

But as it turned out, Irene didn't see the start of things for Margaret after all. It came overnight, and Margaret didn't wake her. Irene slept through the whole thing.

*

(Margaret, remembering singularities. Remembering Victor explaining singularities, out in the dark fields behind her parents' house, pointing to stars to name them for her—Arcturus, Canopus, Vega, Rigel—but more interested in naming what couldn't be seen. Singularities were his favorite, he talked about them for a long time, the way space and matter could squeeze itself down until it broke every rule. That was what Margaret felt now: her body compressing itself with so much force that it was turning itself into something else.

So it made a kind of sense to her when she stopped being able to move, when her new body started moving itself instead.

The doctors' rhythms shifted into urgency around her. If she had breath enough she'd have told them.

Stop, stop, there's no helping it, I'm something else now.)

*

Irene rose, put on her most expansive dress, and went downstairs. Her feet were swollen today, which was new. Their flesh felt like slippers she'd put on. She had a terrible taste in her mouth even though she'd brushed her teeth.

Margaret was usually sitting in the dining room already when she arrived for breakfast, so it surprised Irene when, at the foot of the stairs, out of the corner of her eye, she caught a glimpse of her. Margaret with her hair curled, with rosy cheeks, with an attitude of distraction—Margaret moving away.

"Where are you going?" Irene said, turning toward her.

And Margaret wasn't there.

Irene's body held very still for a moment, as if hoping her mind would stop moving too and she wouldn't ever have to understand.

Then she slapped her meaty slipper-feet as fast as she could up the stairs, cramps pulling both her sides, to the third floor.

Dr. Bishop stood in the hall as if she'd been waiting for her.

"Where is she, where is Margaret?"

"Shh." Dr. Bishop pulled Irene smoothly into the bedroom Joe had occupied, shut the door, sat her down on the bed.

"Where is she?" Irene said again. "Let me see her."

"I'm sorry, Irene." Dr. Bishop's voice was sad, slow, calm, but underneath Irene could hear a blunt horror.

This horror struck Irene, and her whole body seemed to reverberate. She would ring with it forever.

She said, because she had to, "She died, didn't she?"

Dr. Bishop's eyes shone like a trapped animal's. "I'm so sorry."

"How did it happen?"

"I'm going to explain to the whole group this afternoon."

"No, I want to hear it now."

Irene watched Dr. Bishop take a breath and try to gather herself.

"Dr. Bishop, what happened to her?"

"There were complications. There was absolutely nothing we could do. We tried *everything*." Dr. Bishop's voice broke itself on the word. "I did every last thing it's possible to do. You have to believe me, I did."

Those blue eyes met Irene's. Now when Irene looked in the mirror her own eyes seemed to be the wrong color, because she spent so much more time looking at Dr. Bishop than at herself. The doctor's were red-rimmed, but if she thought Irene was going to take pity on her, she hadn't understood Irene.

This doctor had lost Margaret.

"What are you hoping I'll tell you? That I believe you? That you did well? She's dead. Margaret is dead. How well can you have done, really?"

Dr. Bishop drew back, and Irene saw the hurt on her face before it sealed. That was fine, that was good; Irene hoped she'd hurt the doctor grievously. Yes, she and this doctor had lost themselves somewhere in the mirrors they'd pointed toward each other, and yes, Irene knew this doctor, had seen what she'd endured and what she'd fled from, and she knew what it felt like to her, watching these women's bodies fail them and her both, watching everything drain out of them no matter how much of the drug she'd pumped in. But this loss was unforgivable. It was beyond Irene's capacity to forgive.

Her mind spun for solutions. "Where is she now, Margaret?"

"What? The body has been taken away, if that's what you mean."

"To where? I have to know where, Dr. Bishop," Irene said. "I have to, you have to tell me."

"I don't. I can't, in fact. Because Margaret is nothing much to you, Irene, remember? Isn't that what you said?"

Irene had, of course.

"I was wrong," Irene said. "You know that. Please, this will help. You have to tell me where she is."

For a moment Irene thought she might reach the doctor. Through the glass between them they might finally touch each other. But Dr. Bishop straightened up, then stood. "What I know doesn't change anything," she said. "I'll have more to say this afternoon."

So the grandfather ran too deep in her veins for her to give anyone something simply because they'd asked for it. All the ways he'd hurt her, and still, in that way she was his.

All right, all right, then Irene would just find out for herself. She would break into the doctors' desks and find Margaret's chart with its answers, with its address, drive there, find Victor, and make him tell her where they'd taken Margaret's body so she could bring it back and let the garden have it. Irene was partway through imagining the physical logistics of this—the stiffening weight of Margaret, how she might manage—when she understood.

They'd done it already, hadn't they?

There was nothing more to do. Because the garden had already done its work, of course. It had given what it had to give. That was why she'd seen Margaret downstairs—seeing her was the proof. Putting the body in the garden could only bring the kind of vision Irene had already seen, could make nothing further happen. They'd been thinking only about babies, dying babies, and they'd made assumptions without even realizing they were making them.

They hadn't stopped to think, somehow, that they had no way of knowing whose blood was whose.

And so Margaret was gone—Margaret of the Ladies' Auxiliary and summer camp, Margaret of facing every truth, of laying every plan, of diligence and bone-deep devotion. Margaret of spending all of what she had, every time. Margaret of humor and skillful pruning hands. Margaret of the cleanest line, the fiercest will, the clearest, quickest grasp. Margaret of catching every falling thing someone else had let slip, her whole life long. And they had not caught her.

Irene looked into Dr. Bishop's eyes, searching out the panicked animal the doctor had shoved down deep.

"Oh, what have we done, Dr. Bishop?" she said.

*

Later that day, Dr. Bishop summoned them all to the blue sitting room, a new ritual for this new catastrophe. She gathered and spread them on sofas and chairs, steering them by the shoulders to make room, as if they were bulky, rude equipment. She sat too, in an armchair at the center of the circle, and Dr. Hall stood behind in a portrait pose, with his hand on the back of the chair. Once they were quiet, Dr. Bishop gave a performative sigh. All of them looked at her and waited.

Irene watched in fury. Dr. Bishop was going to attempt to smooth this, even this, over. But Irene knew the doctor's panic was still there, stowed away beneath her carefully calibrated face.

"I have something very difficult to tell all of you," Dr. Bishop said softly, clasping her hands.

"Is it true Margaret's dead?" said Annie Sellers.

Annie was months away from her due date still. She'd barely known Margaret. What right did she have to sound so devastated? Irene had been desperate to hear whatever Dr. Bishop was going to tell them next, and yet what she wanted now was to cram that question back down Annie's throat.

But it was too late, it couldn't be undone, it had set new events in motion. Annie seemed to have called Margaret somehow, pulled her from who knew what shadowy space to join them, in her way. She took her place in a chair in the room's dim corner, a chair they'd left for her without meaning to, and curled over, folding into herself. Waiting with all the rest to hear about her own death. When Irene looked head-on she wasn't there, of course, but she lingered at the side of Irene's vision.

Irene tried to catch Margaret's eye and shake her head, despite everything she knew by now about these visions and what was and wasn't possible. No one should have to hear about themselves what Dr. Bishop was going to say.

Dr. Bishop tucked a straying lock of hair back. Irene could see her hands shaking. "Yes, I'm afraid Mrs. Crowe experienced something called eclampsia, a sudden and uncontrolled increase in blood pressure. It's one of the most common causes of maternal mortality. Despite our every effort to regain control of her hypertension with magnesium sulfate, Mrs. Crowe succumbed to her convulsions."

Mrs. Crowe, as if Margaret were any patient, someone she'd barely known or had known in only one way. The doctor's face was still soft, and her shoulders too, soft and rounded—but these words the women didn't know, coming at them so fast, were meant to make them quiet, while Margaret in the corner let herself sink, folding further at the middle until her forehead rested on her knees. Was she trying to understand, trying to remember the feeling of shaking herself apart? Or trying to defend herself against remembering?

"What's the connection to our treatment here?" Irene said loudly.

Dr. Bishop raised her head warily.

"How did all these drugs you're giving us contribute to what happened?"

Now Dr. Bishop squared herself like some soldier, like she would have in that long-ago classroom where Dr. Hall had met her—though now, Irene saw, the change made him withdraw his hand from the back of her chair. Dr. Bishop was disavowing her womanness, shrugging it off herself like a too-soft cape.

While Margaret in the corner crumpled beneath the weight of hers.

"I know Mrs. Crowe was your friend, Mrs. Willard, and you're upset. I promise you, though, that this particular pregnancy complication existed long, long before our treatment."

"Pumping her full of extra hormones didn't make it more likely?"

"There's absolutely no evidence of that."

"We've all been getting a lot of shots lately."

The women buzzed a little. They were almost all newer than Irene was, now, and most of them had probably never thought to question why they got some shots from Dr. Hall and some from Dr. Bishop, because it had been that way since their arrival. Dr. Hall tilted his head slightly to the side, watching Irene, then Dr. Bishop. His face took on an understanding, and the first tint of rage.

"You've been getting the shots you need, no more, no less," said Dr. Bishop. Her voice shook now too.

"What about the baby?" somebody asked.

Irene felt startled: she'd almost forgotten about the baby. How could she have forgotten about the baby?

"The baby is alive," Dr. Bishop said.

There was a face in the words; there were two hands and two feet, ten fingers and ten toes; there was a cry. As if she heard it, Margaret sat up in her chair. Her whole body bloomed.

A collective breath ran through the room like wind. And Irene had the feeling that if she'd only been able to get closer, to listen closer, she might have heard Margaret breathe it too.

*

When Victor arrived the next day, they all knew he was there instantly. Irene would never be able to remember, after, whether this was because she'd heard his car crunching the gravel of the drive herself, or whether she'd heard one of the other women saying he'd come, or whether she'd only felt a tensing of the air inside this house as it let a father in.

He went straight up to the third floor, so fast most of them didn't see him. The women milled about by the bottom of the staircase to wait. It was a heartlessly sunny day. The doctors had opened the blinds for Victor, because he was still a husband, even now, and the women were all too warm, so they tried to avoid the places where the light hit the insides of the house. But they would stand watch here, right here, where he'd have to pass them to leave. He'd have to let them get a look at the baby.

It wasn't his, not really, and they wouldn't allow him out without letting them see. They'd tear him to pieces with their teeth first.

Soft murmurs. They turned their faces upward like people reading the sky for signs. And yes, there he was, Victor, holding a bundle, the doctors to either side. He looked more disheveled than when Irene had seen him at the husbands' last visit. His hair had been parted in an uneven and moist-looking way, as if his drenching grief had caught him unawares. He blinked in surprise at the sight of so many gathered women, but didn't nod or acknowledge them or stop moving—he wanted out of here, that was apparent.

He held the baby like it was an inconvenient parcel he wished he didn't have to carry.

"All right, all of you," Dr. Bishop said, fanning an arm at the air, as if that could part the sea of them.

In the back corner, Irene caught a glimpse of Margaret again, lingering in the shadows to watch her sunlit baby borne out of this house alive. What was the expression on her face? What wouldn't Irene have given to be able to look directly at it, so she could read what Margaret was feeling? The movements of Margaret's arms were discernible even in the periphery, though, reaching toward the baby. Irene watched Margaret take a step, one step, before she had to pay for her effort at approach by disappearing.

Irene made her eyes follow the line of the vanished Margaret's motion toward the bundle Victor held. The blanket was pulled up so high it was hiding the baby's face, so she couldn't see to judge its wholeness, its solidity, but the baby was moving, she could tell that much, at least.

"What's its name?" Irene called out, clear and loud, for Margaret, because Margaret might be able to hear even wherever she'd gone.

Victor paused. His face crumpled, then smoothed itself out again. "She doesn't have one yet."

She.

He resumed walking. Dr. Hall had a hand at his shoulder, to comfort or to hasten.

"We're so sorry, Mr. Crowe," somebody called out.

Here it was, Irene's last chance to get a look at the baby. With Victor's back to her, Irene felt pulled and pushed at once. She wanted to chase him and move the blanket and see everything, and she wanted to turn her back and run.

She stood there, gripped, tugged, and didn't move—the bitterest betrayal of Margaret, who'd tried to move even when she must have known moving was impossible.

So the door closed behind them, father and child.

*

Irene went to her room and unearthed Pearl's phone number from the bedside table drawer. In the corner of the room stood Margaret again, like a disobedient student dunced there, as Margaret wouldn't have been, not a single time her whole life long. Margaret leaned her forehead against the wall.

Was Margaret in pain, and would she be in pain forever, and what would her particular kind of forever mean? Would she stay here even after Irene left and there was no one anymore to see her? Or would she go too whenever Irene left this place, so she could keep haunting Irene for failing to reach out and touch her baby on her behalf? How could Irene have just let Victor walk through the door?

"Margaret, wait," Irene said to the corner, which was already empty because she'd turned her head toward it.

Irene dialed and asked to be connected. The line rang a moment before Pearl picked up. BabyGinny was crying loudly in the background, and Pearl said Irene's name as if she were angry at her for causing the telephone to make noise.

"Who's with you? Are you by yourself? It's happened, Pearl, the worst thing's happened, with Margaret."

"What? Irene, what? Oh no."

BabyGinny's wails were shrill enough to hurt Irene's ear.

"Hold on, I can't hear you, I can't even think, let me feed her," Pearl said, and the receiver clunked against some hard surface. Irene heard rustlings, as if a small creature were trying to make a nest for itself inside the earpiece. Irene wiped at her eyes.

"There. All right," Pearl said. "The baby . . ." She couldn't even say it.

"No, not the baby. Margaret."

Pearl gave a sob that sounded like a stifled indecipherable word.

"Dr. Bishop's saying it was something to do with blood pressure and wasn't related to anything that's going on here, but I don't believe her, and Margaret doesn't either."

"What?"

"Margaret isn't gone. She's still here, Pearl. You know, the way it happens. Twice so far I've seen her, just halfway, just barely, and then she disappears. Margaret's own blood, that's what we must have put on the fountain. I don't know why we didn't think . . . But it's awful—she wants her baby."

Pearl sniffed a couple of times, then let out a long crackling breath over the line.

"What do we do?"

BabyGinny gurgled. Irene could see Pearl stroking her head as if she were in the room with them.

"Irene, listen," Pearl said slowly. "Ever since I got home, even before I knew about this, I've been thinking maybe it's better if we just let this whole thing go. Now I feel sure. I know how that will sound to you—I know you can't see it yet, there's no way you can, you're still there, you're still waiting. But you will. You're going to see that I'm right, once you're home with your baby. There's no room. I can't give it room, Irene, I just can't."

Irene drew her fist across her eyes to clear them. "Pearl, Margaret doesn't get to go home."

"It would be different, of course, if there were something we could do. But there's nothing, you know that. So what good does it do to keep talking about it?"

"We have to figure out some way of helping her. We can't leave her like this."

"There's nothing, Irene. We knew the whole time it might turn out this way—that they might not be fully there."

"We didn't know *this*. And there must be something, we just haven't thought of it yet. Maybe we could go back to the garden, try making some sort of offering, I don't know, or try calling her somehow to see if we can make her stay, or—"

"I don't *have* anything else to offer," Pearl said harshly. "If I have to keep thinking about this I'll die. I have to keep it far away from us."

Pearl was trying to make a world for her baby that wouldn't ever touch this one, then.

"I can't believe you," Irene said.

"I know. But you will."

"You're just going to forget about Margaret? You can't just pretend it all didn't happen. *Isn't* happening."

Because after all Irene was still here, wasn't she, still lagging behind the other two, as she always had been, so everything still hung in the balance for her, anything might still happen to her and to her little possum.

"I'm not *pretending*."

"Pearl, what's going to happen to me? What do I do now?" Irene heard her voice climb imploringly. She was too afraid, she needed someone to tell her—whatever they said she would do.

BabyGinny gave a coo that reminded Irene of a sound in a barnyard.

"You do this," Pearl said. "You eat a lot, and sleep a lot, and keep your eyes straight ahead, and have your baby, and take it home."

Irene knew, hanging up, that she could never love Pearl in the same way again, not after what she'd just refused. But Pearl had at least told her what to do next. What if, for the sake of her little possum, little unknown, little unknowable place at the center of things, Irene tried to listen? Maybe she should assume Pearl knew better and try what Pearl had said she should try, just until the little possum was born, which would be only a couple of weeks from now. If Margaret was both alive and not alive, so in its way was Irene's own baby. This baby she'd waited years for.

Surely she owed her baby as much as she owed Margaret. Even Margaret could never have argued with that.

Then, once what was coming came for her, once she made it

through in whatever way she could, Irene would tell George. Not everything, but enough. He would help her find Victor and Margaret's baby, and she would touch the baby's cheek so she could remember its feel the next time she saw Margaret, and pass the feeling to her somehow, like a gift, and she would tell Victor as much of the truth as they both could stand.

She would handle all of that, later, once she got her own creature here. She would know how to think again. She'd figure out how to satisfy the Margaret shadow. She would.

*

Two women left the next day. A woman named Jane something, who'd been at the house only a week, was gone before the rest of them were even downstairs, and then Annie Sellers's husband arrived to take her home after breakfast. "We don't want to risk it," Annie said. "He can't let *me* risk it, that's what Sam says— he'd never really understood the risk to me before."

Irene wanted to ask her what risk she thought leaving would help her avoid, exactly, since Annie had already been here for a month, awash in the doctors' drugs and breathing in the air of this house. But maybe there was still hope, maybe Annie hadn't been here too long yet.

One or two women stood to hug Annie goodbye. Matilda Lawrence spoke from Irene's table. "Annie, you heard Dr. Bishop. What happened to Margaret could have happened anywhere."

"It happened here, though," Annie said. She turned to leave.

At their tables, the women muttered.

Matilda said quietly, "Honestly, I thought about it too. I thought about calling Bobby last night and having him come get me. But the thing is, Margaret's baby lived, didn't she?" Her hands were tight on her belly, her fingers clinging to its curve. "I think somehow I've already decided."

Down the table, two of the women, who'd overheard, looked uneasily at Matilda's treasuring hands.

Matilda caught sight of Irene's face. "I'm sorry. I know she was your friend."

After that, the other women in the house might have been talking about Margaret when they whispered, but Irene wasn't listening. She sat as far as she could from everyone else at every table. She said nothing unless directly addressed. The doctors resumed business mostly as usual, no matter what Dr. Hall had guessed about his wife and her drugs—when had he ever stopped anything in his life? There was a new stiffness in his manner with her, that was all.

One more woman went home two days later, but everyone else seemed, in the end, to have made the same calculation Matilda had, not so different from the calculation they'd all made already before coming here in the first place.

Had Irene? She was trying her best to make no calculations at all.

A little extra feeling did hang in the air of the house. It wasn't easy to contemplate your own erasure, to stand still and wait willingly for its possibility. Small arguments became tearful. There was a concerted, defiant effort to dress in brighter, cheerful colors. Somebody dropped a plate at dinner one night and three women shrieked.

That might have been Margaret in the corner of the dining room at lunchtime, holding out her arms as if hoping someone would put her baby into them. Irene couldn't say. But then no one was asking her to.

*

Two weeks passed for Irene in this deliberate not-thinking. The air around her felt thick and liquid and she let herself sink. Let George ask her how she was doing over the phone, let him believe she was *fine*, that was what she told him, *it just keeps kicking me and I'm so tired*. She let Dr. Bishop inject her—because yes, she was afraid, yes, Margaret had been given these injections, but so had Pearl and Beatrice and the others. Irene walked only in the opposite direction from the garden and let herself, made herself, stop considering what it held or what she'd done.

And she let Margaret appear. She let the force of Margaret's wanting break over her, that posture full of desperation, the pose for begging for a glass of water or a sip of air. It was her baby she wanted, but what could Irene do about that? She kept turning away, letting Margaret stay behind her, thinking at her *I'm sorry.*

She woke one morning too early for getting up, fell back asleep, and had a fitful dream about Margaret. In the dream, Margaret leaned close. "Come and see her," she said, and Irene was so relieved Margaret had her baby in her arms that she did, even though she still didn't want to see.

The baby looked pink and strange in the same way they all looked. Solid, present, for now at least. Eyes pressed shut, feet and hands stirring a little. Less than other babies had stirred?

Margaret leaned close to Irene. Her breath was sour. "She looks all right, don't you think?" she whispered. "I think she looks perfectly all right."

Irene looked again so she could pretend to be considering. There was only one answer to that question. Even Irene with her impossible answers knew that. She smiled at Margaret.

"She's perfect," she said.

"You have to go back and check," Margaret said. "Go check on what we left there."

"Your underclothes? You wouldn't let me before, and it's all done now."

"Go and check, Irene."

Irene shook her head—in the dream, but also she must have been waking up, she could feel her hair on the pillow in the real world too, crisping beneath her shaking head. "I don't want to go back there ever again."

"But you have to," Margaret said.

Irene was awake. She would obey Margaret's instructions— she could do that, at least. So she sat up, stuffed her feet into shoes, and lumbered down the stairs and outside without seeing anyone. It was early still, no one else was moving yet, and the grass was wet with dew. She found the garden gate stiff, the growth of the grass choking its motion below and the ivy from the sides and above, but she got it open in the end.

Inside, the leafy smell enveloped her. Margaret's underclothes were no longer on the fountain rim, were nowhere visible. Maybe the green had grown right over them.

Irene breathed in once, closed and opened her eyes.

And there was Dr. Bishop, vision Dr. Bishop.

She was probably fourteen or so, a little older than the version of her that had seen her father and the woman in this space, with a body so new she occupied it tentatively. She crouched in the thick summer growth, poking at something on the ground. What was the thing? Irene looked closer.

A bird. Sad, brown, and drab, limp and dead, with folded wings.

Dr. Bishop used a stick at first, poking. Then she dropped the stick and used her hands. She moved the wings in a clearly experimental way, with the same expression that Irene had seen trained on herself, her own face and middle. The wings gave and moved. Only newly dead, then.

Fearful understanding grew in Irene's throat as she watched Dr. Bishop's probing fingers, as Dr. Bishop pulled the wings back and exposed the bird's tiny breast, where a red spot glistened, a wound so small that if it were on a person that person would barely have noticed. Dr. Bishop touched a finger to it, then held the finger up close to her face. She wiped the blood off in small circles between the forefinger and thumb. Then she reached down to her feet, plucked a green leaf, and tore off a strip. Irene watched her fold it into a small square.

Dr. Bishop lifted the bird to the fountain rim, where she could work more easily, and prodded the leaf square, so gently, into the tiny divot on the bird's little chest.

Irene shut her eyes in dread. She knew already what she would see when she looked again, but what could she do, not open her eyes?

So she did, and yes, there was Dr. Bishop, still the same age, at the same time of year, but wearing a different dress now, so it must be a different day. She approached the fountain to see what her mending had accomplished. Irene looked with her at the fountain lip, where she knew already no bird body waited. The girl Dr. Bishop hurried over, brushed her fingers over the empty place, and then whirled.

Her eye had been caught by the plain brown bird flapping over by the garden wall, up and then over.

The girl Dr. Bishop put her hands to her chest like an overcome little bride.

She extended her hands before her, palms up, and looked at them.

"No!" Irene shouted. "No, it wasn't *you,* you didn't do that, you didn't make that happen!"

But how could this girl from three decades earlier possibly hear her?

*

Dr. Bishop was in the study with the door open. She looked up from her writing when Irene came in and sat in the chair before the desk.

Irene hadn't been in this room since her arrival interview on the first day. Here they were, she and the doctor, in their positions from that morning, as if they occupied a picture torn in two and the George and Dr. Hall half had fluttered irrelevantly to the ground. Everything that had happened here since, everything Irene had allowed to happen—all of it was because she'd thought this doctor could see and do things no one else could, because that was what the doctor had told them. But what if all of it was based on a mistake? A wrong impression Dr. Bishop had taken up long ago as an origin story, blocking out so many parts of the view?

Irene said, "I want you to tell me again how you decided you could do what you're promising us here."

"Good morning to you too, Irene."

Irene waited. Early sun came through the windows with their open drapes—no patients in this room usually, no need to cut out the light—and warmed her.

The doctor set down her pen. "I've never *promised*—"

Irene waved a hand to swat the words away. "Tell me."

Dr. Bishop looked startled. "All right. We had an idea about a way we might solve a particular medical problem. We undertook various experiments to test it. When the experiments bore our idea out, we decided to act on it. And now here we are."

"That first idea, though, where did it come from?"

"From our observations in our practice—from long study and a great deal of careful thought."

"I mean before that. There was something before that."

Dr. Bishop narrowed her eyes.

"A long time ago, something happened that made you think you were better at this than anyone else. Isn't that right? Something that made you think you were special, and everyone was wrong about you, and there was more to you than anyone saw or would have believed. You decided you were going to be the best doctor that had ever been and fix every last thing, and nobody could stop you."

"*Nobody.*"

It was the grandfather's voice, slipping on a current of bad air into this room that had, like all the rooms, been his. Irene turned and he was sitting, terribly, in the chair George had occupied when they'd sat in this room all those months before. Slumped and twitching, like a pile of live wet rags.

"Poor Louey, she was going to say it and then do it, wasn't she?"

Watching his eyes on Dr. Bishop, Irene felt an impulse to try to shield the doctor from his view. But she reminded herself what she was doing here, what she had to find out for sure.

"I think it was meant to be your way out," she said. "Your way of making your own life. You thought you had proof you could do it, didn't you? Things other people thought were impossible, *you* could do them. But what if you were wrong about your proof, Dr. Bishop? The bird, what if there was something else that explained it?"

"What?" Dr. Bishop whispered. Her face pursed with disbelief, and the color drained from it as if she were bleeding from somewhere.

"Without that one moment, would there still be enough to make you sure, really sure, about everything you've done since?"

"How could you know about the bird?" Her skin was the color of old fruit.

"Did you think you'd brought it back to life?"

"Of course not," Dr. Bishop said. "I mean, I was a child, who knows what I thought then. But with time, it just came to seem, I don't know . . . a kind of sign, maybe. Whatever the real explanation was. A kind of waking dream my subconscious gave me so I couldn't miss it. I still don't see how I—how it seemed—"

"How could *any* of this happen? But it all did, it all has. The trouble is, it wasn't what you thought. It wasn't *you*, Doctor, with the bird. You thought it was, even if you didn't understand how it was possible; you thought it was you because you were so ready for it to be. And ever since, you've never let anyone stop you from pressing forward, have you, because you've always believed *you* can fix anything, with enough work, enough of yourself, isn't that right?"

"I *can*," Dr. Bishop said defiantly. "It's a matter of refusing to accept that something *can't* be done, that's all. Refusing to give up, trying harder than anyone else. Especially if you're a woman and what you want to do is more than what they want to let you. So that's what I did, that's all I've done, just worked harder, always, than anyone else. I'm not claiming to be so unusual."

"Of course you are," Irene said.

The grandfather laughed wetly. "That's all she ever wanted." Mocking her, as if it hadn't been all he ever wanted too—to be the one with the most, the very most, at the end.

So Irene was talking to them both when she said, "Did you ever think about what you might be doing, pushing all the time to make it all yours?"

Because a damage might be done when you tried to hold an unholdable thing, when you tried to contain it with your own walls. You couldn't succeed in giving it the shape you planned, but that didn't mean you hadn't reshaped it. It grew wildly to get away, to get far beyond you. It grew sometimes past bearing.

Dr. Bishop shook her head. "You must see I've done substantial *good*. I *have* solved problems others thought weren't solvable. I *have* done that."

"Did you solve the problem of Margaret?"

At the sound of her name, Margaret came and stood over by the window, crouching down again to clutch that middle that held nothing anymore. She straightened and took a step toward Dr. Bishop with confusion on her face. This shape should never have been hers. It wasn't a shape she'd ever been meant for.

Irene turned to look at the doctor, and Margaret vanished.

"Margaret," Dr. Bishop said softly, and closed her eyes.

Had she seen too? Had she felt?

But then Dr. Bishop took a deep breath and said, "I gave Margaret the best chance she had. Margaret herself knew it."

So the doctor had found the protection of her reasoned and official voice. Again she was measuring wins against losses, balancing numbers in two columns, when one of the numbers was Margaret.

Irene had to be sure, really sure, that Dr. Bishop saw and felt and paid somehow, for Margaret, Margaret whom she'd loved.

She had to hurt this woman. What would hurt her most? She needed something that could never be numbers to her.

She thought again of Dr. Bishop's arms flung wide on a bed of leaves, too full of feeling to close.

Irene said, "I wonder if you understand how much you *haven't* ever fixed. Dr. Hall, for example."

"What are you talking about?"

"I saw them."

"Who?"

"Dr. Hall and Mrs. Conrad."

Dr. Bishop opened her mouth. "What?" she said again, and Irene knew she'd guessed right about degrees of injury. Dr. Bishop's faith in her origin story was rooted too deep, maybe, for weeding out, after all these years and all this tending—but her certainty of being beloved in exactly the desired ways was more vulnerable, had shallower roots.

The doctor stood quickly, walked to the window, and turned her back. Looked outside at the shorn, green, mannerly manor lawn—how static it was in all weathers, under snow in the winter and under the heavy sun on a hot, still day like the one this day was fast becoming. Everything as stationary through the window as if trapped under terrarium glass.

But that wasn't right, was it? The glass was closed over them in here: over Irene and all the women; over the doctor too.

The grandfather, drawn to her suffering, left his chair to hover behind Dr. Bishop, inside this space he'd closed over her.

"He promised me never ever again," Dr. Bishop said quietly. "We took this on together and we decided it was a new start, and he promised. There was only one—a single, solitary woman under the age of sixty who wasn't pregnant in this whole place— only one, and he . . ." She stopped.

"I knew which stops on my railroad were worth making," the grandfather said. "Susan in North Carolina, May in New York,

Helen in Boston, Viola in Delaware." The grandfather turned to Irene, inviting her to look at him full-on, to watch him fail to disappear when she did. The skin of his face was a terrible wet purple gray. It hung loose around his shoulders now, having lost all connection to the anchoring structure beneath, and Irene understood: it was rotting, yes, but that was fine by him, he was going to shed it. He was entering into all the newness here. Dr. Bishop was feeding him with all the newness she made, and he would go on and on.

Dr. Bishop had always carried him. She'd never meant to, but that didn't mean she hadn't done it—with all her grasping, her relentless hands; all the pain she'd felt and all the pain she'd inflicted.

They were all carrying him with them now. All the carrying women.

The knowledge surged through Irene's whole body: she had to do her best to get her little possum away from here. No matter the cost. Even if she didn't know whether getting away would be possible.

"He told me it had been nothing the other time," Dr. Bishop said.

"*Nothing*—he loves that word. I'm sure it's true, in a way, but if it was nothing, then how do you know you aren't nothing too?"

Dr. Bishop shuddered, and the grandfather shivered with pleasure. Her face was blotchy in the same patterns Irene's own became when she cried: reddest around the eyes and on the apples of the cheeks.

"As if *you* know," she said to Irene. "As if you have any idea what your George is up to out there without you."

Irene nodded. She'd wanted to hurt and she had, and now she felt purged of her anger, terrified but ready to leave last truths behind her before she ran as far and as fast as she could. "I think I'd have staked everything once, but then you took me away. How should I know anymore what he's doing?"

"You couldn't know even if you were right there with him. Nobody's ever completely with anybody else."

"Except with me," the grandfather said, and again the words were almost a smell, Irene almost seemed to breathe them in.

Not for long, I swear it, Irene thought.

"You're right," she said, and put her hand on her stomach. "I don't have any idea who's in here." What its parts were, what its thoughts were, what it would love and hate.

"Somebody is, though, you do know that. You said I've taken you from George, but that's not what I've done—I've *given* you something. I've made you a whole new life and given it to you."

And hadn't Irene made the same mistake as Dr. Bishop, worked as hard, in ways the doctor would never even know about, to keep that life, no matter what it was? Hadn't she been trying to hold an unholdable thing too?

"Just like God, Dr. Bishop," she said.

"You *let* me, Irene. You wanted me to do what I did."

Past her shoulder, her unseen grandfather smiled, making skin hang from each corner of his mouth.

"I'm not going to let you anymore," Irene told her, and her voice surprised her, because it was gentler than she would have believed her own voice could sound. It was a mother's voice, almost.

*

George answered on the first ring. "Is it time?" he said, speaking so fast it took Irene a minute to decipher what he'd said, to move backward in understanding to where he still was.

"You have to come get me," she said.

"Are you—is the baby coming?" She heard rustling, movement, a crash as he knocked something over, and she could picture what he was doing exactly, sweeping everything he thought he needed into his arms to come to her.

As if you have any idea what your George is up to out there without you.

"It's not that. The baby and I are both fine, but you have to come. I'll explain when you get here."

"Explain what?"

She could tell he was only partly listening. He'd drive all the way here thinking she must be in labor no matter what she told him. But that didn't matter, she didn't care as long as he came, because once he was here she could hold his face in her hands and make him see well enough to drive them both—them all—away from here. This was her George, and he loved her.

"George, just come."

"On my way," he said.

Irene hung up and sat for a moment. Soon she would sit in her own house, look out her own open window, and when the time came George would take her to the kind of hospital where other women had their babies, with its rows of white-sheeted beds. She would have this baby the way other women did, and it would all be fine, she would will it to be fine, and in any case she would be far away, far beyond the reach of grandfathers, gardens, drugs, if not beyond the reach of herself. She couldn't undo what she'd already done here, but she would stop now.

To her room, then, to pack. It didn't even have to be packing, not really, only getting things into bags. She emptied her stockings drawer. She pulled her blouses from their hangers. She had just put her rose silk maternity dress from her very first day into the suitcase—draped over the top of the stack, like, yes, an emptied skin—when she turned and reached and felt a dull, painless popping inside her, not especially strong, as if something very tired of holding had given out.

A hot flood ran down to her feet. The water was clear but with a pink tint on her white socks. She sprang away instinctively to try to escape the splash but brought it with her, more gushing out of her as she moved.

Dr. Hall had told Irene at one of her examinations months before that labor rarely started with the water breaking, despite the frequency with which this happened in mothers' and grandmothers' tales of childbirth. "It makes for a good story, so those stories get told more. Far more common for the first sign of labor to be contractions that gradually intensify." So all this time Irene had been monitoring and waiting for the tightenings of her belly to take on a pattern, but it seemed this was what she'd gotten instead.

Of course, because something here was trying now to tighten its hold.

Irene pulled a blouse from her suitcase, wadded it up, and stuffed it into her underclothes. She crept down the stairs and hurried across the grass back to the garden.

Inside, she caught sight of something she hadn't seen this morning, in the women's tended garden patch: she'd been right, she and Margaret and Pearl had missed a bud, and it had bloomed. The flower was meant to be a marigold. It was red, as she'd guessed something grown here might be, but she couldn't have predicted the shape, this bulbous, irregular scarlet orb, too large for its stalk to hold up, brushing the ground. Like a bleeding cast-out eye, peering down into the dirt. It looked as if, were she to touch it, it would be wet. As if, were she to step on it, it would roll beneath her foot, solid as a ball.

Well, let it watch.

Irene went to the fountain. Sweating, doubled over around the bunching cloth she was still spilling into, she felt like a faulty seal. The boundary between inside and outside had gone.

"You can't have it," Irene said. She looked at the cherub statue, because she wanted to make eye contact with something. "Do you understand? It's mine, no matter what else it is, and you can't. I don't care what goes on here, I don't care what it is, you can't have it, it's not yours."

The cherub held still, just kept drooling dryly, blackly, over its chin while Irene filled her cloth. The garden around her was a welter of green so saturated it was also a smell and a taste of rich growing, and a sound, the buzzing of all the busy things living amidst and within and underneath it. The green made a thick blanket now, covering up everything in here so that a person could never hope to see it clearly.

Something gripped Irene and clenched. She bent more, her whole body becoming a fist, and there was another hot gush as all the fluid in her found the rupture that had been made for it. As soon as the clenching eased she straightened and turned to go. Beneath her and behind her she left a trail of water, as if she'd emerged dripping from a pond, or from this fountain. As if she'd swum here so long she'd taken all its water into herself to expel as she went.

Another clenching took hold partway up the stairs to the front door of the house. She hated this feeling of suddenly being unable to keep herself inside herself.

Dr. Bishop was standing there at the top, waiting for her.

Irene stopped short. She stood as straight as she could. "I'm leaving," she said. "George is on his way to get me."

Dr. Bishop's eyes went to Irene's belly, to the wetness she'd left behind herself, shining like a slug trail in the sun. Her brow knit, her mouth gathered.

"Of course we can't let you leave, Irene."

"*Let* me?"

"Your labor's started."

"I'll go to another hospital."

"That would take too long."

"Labor takes a long time, doesn't it?"

Dr. Bishop closed the distance between them and put a hand on Irene's elbow. "It wouldn't be safe. Now that your water has broken there's a risk of infection."

Irene shook her arm off. "I want to leave," she said, very clearly and slowly.

This time when Dr. Bishop reached out, she did it with both

hands. She clamped down right before Irene's next clenching, so that Irene's body seemed to echo and mirror and deepen her grip.

"I'm afraid it doesn't matter what you want just now, Irene," Dr. Bishop said.

Then Irene kicked, she screamed. Her contractions worked against her, but it still took Drs. Bishop and Hall both to get her up the stairs. No matter the effects of what Irene had told Dr. Bishop this morning, what Dr. Bishop now knew about her husband, they united to handle the disaster of her. So many stairs. The doctors pulled, and Irene's feet bounced at points like a doll's.

Once they'd gotten her onto the bed, the doctors held her down together. "Scopolamine. The patient is noncompliant," Dr. Bishop said breathlessly.

"I'm not," Irene said. She stopped moving and tried to summon the most reasonable voice she could. "I'm not, I'm complying. I don't want that, don't give it to me."

But Dr. Hall already had it in his hands, the syringe raised like a long finger making a strange sign.

"You'll feel so much better soon," he said.

"No!"

Irene barely felt the needle going in. A clenching gripped her, and more water gushed.

"George is coming," she said urgently. She clasped Dr. Bishop's hand.

"You can see him just as soon as you're all finished and ready for him," the doctor said.

Already Irene felt herself beginning to drift. The doctor spread her legs and reached up inside. Would she be able to see or feel the possum-snake-moth-mouse? Would Irene be able to tell what it was as she birthed it?

"A ways to go still."

"If my water broke, why am I still leaking?"

"It replenishes itself up to delivery. You'll keep leaking with each new contraction."

"Aren't there folktales like that?" Irene gasped—another clenching. "Bowls that fill up on their own?"

"There you are, then, you're a miracle," Dr. Bishop said.

Then the drug stilled her while the clenchings bludgeoned. Dr. Bishop had been wrong about this drug—it didn't take awareness or feeling away, only the ability to act on them. It laid Irene out, all alone, before the clenchings, which were a striking and then a wringing—of water from her body, of pictures from her mind.

All these pictures were green. Her childhood bedroom with its mint green and pink. The olive square of the army van that had carried George to boot camp. A summer Saturday, coming down the stairs, her father shouting something at her brothers across the room; knowing from the bounce of her chest in her new green dress that she no longer looked like a child. Looking at George across the table at their wedding reception through the white roses' green stems, how she'd crouched down to pretend to peek through a screen or a magical forest. How he'd laughed. Green grass snagged around her toes in fields as a girl before she was old enough for anyone to make her put her shoes on. The dark chill frightening wondrous green of the pine forest around the little cabin where they'd stayed for their honeymoon, how it made a moat between them and the world.

The green lawn of the house-hospital—the green garden—the green of the leaves they'd used to hide the changings—spring's unrelenting green—

Was this what dying felt like?

"You're not dying," Dr. Bishop said, and put another pillow behind Irene's back. "I imagine right about now you just wish you were."

At the tip of Dr. Bishop's long, lengthening face was one enormous red eye. The clearest-sighted eye in the world. And Irene wanted it to see her—look how well she was doing, inviting all this green in so it could be wrung out of her, over and over. Look at Irene bending her whole precious world toward what she wanted. Offering that whole world up, again and again and again.

For minutes or hours or days, then, the feeling of being in a boat by herself on a swaying sea of pain, far from shore, then farther. Irene tried to move her hand and found she couldn't, her foot and found she couldn't—but the clenchings, those could move. They started to feel different. They were directional now. Forward, forward, making demands.

The doctors were there suddenly, tying her down with heavy straps that pulled at and pinned her wrists and ankles, spreading her to four corners. Irene wanted to tell them she couldn't move her limbs anyway, but she couldn't speak to say it.

"Time to push."

The voice seemed to come from the walls of this house.

Margaret against the curtain over the window, there, then stepping back into the fabric, then gone. But she'd looked at Irene, and there'd been hope in her face, Irene had seen it. Irene cleaved to that hope and let it cleave her.

She only had to make it through whatever this was to the other side.

Pushing, was that what Irene was doing? She was clenching herself around the clench, a fist around a fist, bearing down as if her life depended on squeezing all the life out of herself. She'd thought her seals had given, but the last one was still in place, still holding, even as everything inside her strained against it. She strained harder. The straps pulled at her. She would have to break it, break herself, to go on living. Her vision greened over, a green curtain dimming all the light, green she saw green she saw green.

"The head," the house's voice said, announcing this arrival, out of Irene's body, into itself.

Irene felt that last seal give, give, stretch, stretch, tear, and then a slippery emptying. Every part of the feeling wettest wet, the slipperiness of a thing you could never hope to hold.

Someone caught it.

"Here she is!"

She.

Irene lost some time then. She blinked and sank, blinked and sank.

Blinked and, finally, rose.

They'd untied her. They'd sat her up a little.

There was a bloody, wet baby on her chest.

This baby wasn't a possum, or a snake, or a moth, or a mouse. She was a baby, and also her very own thing. First of her kind. She was making sounds and strange shapes with her mouth and looking right at Irene with her big eyes. These eyes that would look at Irene for the rest of her life.

Irene's mind, fixed by them, stopped drifting. The baby was drifting from her now. Because Irene had made this creature, but now she'd slipped out and away. She was separate. From now on, that was the way things would always be.

How was a person supposed to bear it? This beautiful, bloody child.

She was wriggling. Her mouth worked. Irene shook her head to clear it. "What does she want?" she asked.

"You could try feeding her," Dr. Bishop said.

"George. Where's George?"

"Not yet. I need to finish stitching you up first, so you're all ready for him."

The doctor went off for something in a drawer while Irene looked at her baby and touched her cheek.

"How do I feed her?" Irene said, but no one was listening, the doctor was doing something stinging with a needle now between her legs. Before Irene could ask again, the baby was scooting up on her chest, finding her breast, clamping down.

The pain of the mouth and the pain of the needle. Two sharp voices answering each other through Irene's body.

The baby's eyes were still open. Her mouth all puckered around Irene's nipple, her hands pinched shut in fists. Irene stroked the bloody skin. Marked like the animals had been marked, except this blood was Irene's, not the baby's own.

She'd been right about what she'd said. This baby didn't belong to gardens or grandfathers. They could never have had any kind of claim on her. Wrong, though, about the rest: she didn't belong to Irene, and she never would. She'd grown wildly beyond Irene, though she'd come from the grasping center of her—already she was beyond her utterly. She was Irene's to fear for, but Irene saw, looking at this small face, suddenly outside of her, that no amount of fear would give her knowledge or a claim. The baby was a mystery, with a newness no one could own. Not even herself, probably. Irene held to her as she waited for George, pressing as close as she could, which would never again be close enough, as she waited for the doctor to finish doing what she could to repair the seal.

They let George into the room, finally.

"George!" Irene sang. Her arms tipped the baby toward him.

"Ah," he said, he breathed. He stood above her, and his shadow fell across the baby.

From beneath like this, was that a bit of looseness in the skin below his jaw?

The baby's mouth twitched in the shadow he had made on her.

"We did it. We really did it, Irene," George said. He kissed her forehead. He put a finger to the baby's cheek too, with worship, but not tentatively. She remembered how Joe had taken Pearl's baby first thing on coming into the room.

But this was George, her George.

"We said it, and then we did it," George murmured. His eyes were still on the baby.

"What?" Irene said. "What did you say?"

He looked at her. Was that a shadow in his eyes too? "Well, we didn't let anything stop us, did we? We said we wanted a baby, Reny, and now we have her."

Dr. Bishop knocked on the open door and came back in. "How are we doing?"

George smiled and looked more like himself again. Irene reached for his hand, clutched it.

"She's all right?" George asked the doctor, gesturing to Irene, and this was different from Joe, different.

The baby made a small stirring against the skin of Irene's stomach, from the outside this time, which she recognized, like looking at the impression of a pencil drawing from underneath the paper. She would have known those movements anywhere. Irene's heart swelled, and broke, and swelled.

"Good as new," the doctor said.

This was a lie, Irene understood. It didn't matter how much work the doctor had done to repair her. She would never be able to hold out fully against the world again.

The world that now held this slippery, shadowy child. Hers and not hers.

The

Berkshires

*

1959

On an August Sunday afternoon, two women drove to Settlers Lake.

In the back seat of the car were three children.

The children were: a girl, a girl, a girl.

They parked the car in the lot. Released, the three girls ran for the water.

"I should have made her put on her bathing suit," one of the women said.

"I hear there's a precedent for swimming in your clothes here anyway," said the other.

They thought about laughing and didn't, quite.

The two women moved more slowly than the children had. They climbed with some care out of the car and into the day. One in a blue dress, one in a yellow. Now that they were free of the structure of seats, they drew toward each other as if they couldn't resist, but also with wariness, as if one of them might turn out to be hungry.

They moved to the white Adirondack chairs that were still there on the green lawn and sat.

"You're looking well."

"You too."

"It's nice to see you. We let so much time go by."

They'd done this on purpose, but they didn't mention that. They looked over each other's new shapes, which bore witness to the passage of all this time, then out again to the daughters, who were the fruits of it, along with everything else they were.

Though both women spent every minute they could watching their daughters, this, today, was the first time they were watching the third girl.

They inspected. They were each finding, separately, that they somehow didn't like the look of her. Of course she made them tearful with the echoes in her face, but they'd been expecting that. It was something else, something about the translucency of her skin, about the way she looked not quite fully present. As if you couldn't imagine her continuing to grow beyond the shape she held now, at least not in the usual ways.

Separately, each of them was trying to find herself silly for having these feelings. They'd never seen this girl before, that was all. Yes, she wasn't as tall as the other two, but then Margaret hadn't been a tall woman. Many girls were slight at this age. And whatever they thought of her, there was no reason to assume she suggested anything about their own.

Their own certainly weren't troubled by her: the three girls had never met before, but they were all splashing in the water together like friends. "Do they recognize each other somehow, do you think?" the woman in yellow said.

"I wouldn't read too much into it—mine's mostly just like this."

"Mine too."

Silence then under the futility of trying to put into words what their respective daughters were like.

"Margaret's seems like a nice girl," the woman in blue said.

"He just let you take her?"

"He seemed happy to have me do it. He said something about how she'd enjoy a trip and it'd be good for her to meet her mother's old friends. He doesn't seem to have wondered all that much about anything—too busy remarrying, maybe."

"They have children?"

"Two. Boys." She paused. "We'd have been luckier to get boys, maybe."

This was the closest they'd yet come to discussing what they'd come here to discuss, and once they said it aloud there would be no unsaying it.

The woman in blue continued: "Because it sounds like it's mostly the girls, what they've been saying about the babies."

"Still, I would never change mine, would you?" said the one in yellow.

Unanswerable question, so the woman in blue said nothing.

"What have you heard, exactly?" the woman in yellow asked, in a softer voice.

"That their organs, their feminine organs—that there are things wrong sometimes. From the drugs, that's what they're saying. It's the result of having given us all those drugs, it affected their organs as they developed, and sometimes it seems to mean things in there won't ever mature in the right way. They won't ever work how they're supposed to."

As they spoke, they didn't take their eyes off the girls in the water. That seemed especially important just now.

"It's almost like we passed on to them whatever was wrong with us," said the woman in blue.

"*We* didn't pass it on," said the woman in yellow.

They remembered the doctor so clearly they could almost see her. In their memories she loomed with the dimensions of a fairy tale, much taller and much larger than she'd really been.

"Well, but we did things too."

The woman in yellow nodded. They would have done anything. "It can't possibly be *all* of them, that's what I think," she said.

"Nobody knows yet—all the girls are just now getting to be the age where we'll be able to tell."

Margaret's daughter drew back for a moment and stood with her hands on her hips to say something to the others. The movement made her look so much like her mother that the woman in yellow gasped and put her hand on the other's arm. Neither of them had visions of Margaret these days, but what else could they call this daughter-haunting?

"Margaret would be so proud of her," she said after a minute.

"She would," said the woman in blue.

The woman in yellow sighed and leaned back in her chair. "I still say it might turn out fine. Anyway, we have a couple of years. She isn't—she's still a child. Why worry yet?"

"They're eleven. Can't you remember being eleven? It won't be long."

"So what do we do?"

A space into which one of the daughters yelled, a high, silvery sound.

"We could go back to the garden, I guess. Or tell someone about it. Maybe from there somebody can figure out a way to fix things."

The woman in yellow laughed. "What on earth could we say, though? Can you imagine? And it was probably the drug, anyway, not the garden, and not anything we did."

The woman in blue wasn't sure. She never had been sure, not in all the years since. Pictures flickered into and out of her mind, as they often did; she could make them go but not stop them coming. An outstretched gray hand, fruit red as blood, the pinkness of her own birth water like an invasion. The looseness of the underside of George's jaw, a square of skin her eyes had ever since avoided. She'd also avoided his questions, always, about *another,* by gesturing to the one they had and saying, *Isn't she enough?*

Every time, his eyes flooded, and he said, *Of course she is.*

See? she would say.

Because their sweeping, theatrical girl was a whole world, even if it was a world she was making for herself, one that didn't quite have space to hold them.

"Is the garden even there anymore?" she asked.

"The doctors aren't."

"I heard the house was sold."

"I heard they separated."

"I heard she went away."

"I heard no one knows where she is, she just disappeared, she isn't well, she doesn't treat patients anymore."

"I don't believe *that*. She's doing something somewhere," the woman in blue said. "She wouldn't know how not to."

"Well, then we could find her. We could track her down, make her figure out some way to help, make her fix what she did."

"Or we could find somebody else, even, some other expert."

"Yes, that's what we'd do."

"All of that."

They looked at each other. As always, they would do everything.

Then they gazed back out to the daughters. The doctor had stood just there, where the daughters stood now, at that same edge where the water and land met, watching her patients. She'd been in the midst of taking everything solid from them, dissolving every certainty—she'd safeguarded them only because they were the means to her end.

But her end had been theirs too.

Look at them, their ends, those daughters. Those shifting shapes at the line between the darker land and the lighter water. Laughing and constantly moving, to kick, to reach down and lift a rock, to throw that rock and then another one, to push each other. No shadows inside them were visible.

But then even the girls themselves weren't, not really. They were never still for a second, and the sunlight fell on and picked out different parts of them to paint with each movement: now a hand, now an arm, now a knee, now a foot. All of it dappled and shining, parts coming together again and again into wholes, all of it too bright to see.

ACKNOWLEDGMENTS

The earliest whisper of *The Garden* came to me in the history of diethylstilbestrol, a synthetic estrogen pioneered for treating repeated miscarriage by the husband-and-wife researcher/physician team of Dr. Olive Watkins Smith and Dr. George Van Siclen Smith and prescribed in this country from the 1940s through the 1970s, which has since been found to cause severe health complications and birth defects. *The Garden* is not the story of that drug, but that drug's story—along with my ongoing fascination with Frances Hodgson Burnett's *The Secret Garden* and all its willed health and secret spaces, and my abiding love for Shirley Jackson's *The Haunting of Hill House* and its mingling of inward and outward terrors—set mine in motion. Of the other books that informed these pages, some of the most crucial were *Lying-In: A History of Childbirth in America*, by Richard W. and Dorothy C. Wertz; *Brought to Bed: Childbearing in America, 1750–1950*, by Judith Walzer Leavitt; *Eternal Eve: The History of Gynecology and Obstetrics*, by Harvey Graham; *Iconographia Gyniatrica: A Pictorial History of Gynecology and Obstetrics*, by Harold Speert, MD, and *Freud*, by Jonathan Lear.

This novel and I have many other debts:

To my extraordinary publishing team: the visionary and indefatigable Michelle Brower, for steering me once again into and then through the wilds; Lee Boudreaux, my work's perfect editor, whose preternaturally keen eye saw straight to this book's truest self and made sure it lived up to its own terms (neither of which

I could have done without her); and to all the other wonderful people at Doubleday, where I am so lucky to have found a home, including Cara Reilly, Maya Pasic, Rita Madrigal, Jillian Briglia, Milena Brown, Jess Deitcher, and Emily Mahon (with many thanks for another beautiful cover! and many thanks, as well, to Catharina Suleiman for the use of this gorgeous art). Much gratitude too to Beth Parker. Working with you all has been the most shimmering of dreams.

To the doctors in my own family, who are exacting and compassionate caretakers and, thankfully, very different from the doctors in this novel: my maternal grandfather, Dr. Robert Muenzer, OB-GYN, whom I never met but who has lived in my memory as long as I can remember; and to my amazing brother and sister-in-law, Drs. Owen and Eden Beams. (And of course to their daughters, my wonderful nieces, Madelyn and Cadence Beams, for all of the joy!)

To the brilliant writer-friends who read full drafts of this novel at various points: Ruth Galm, Alexis Schaitkin, Rufi Thorpe, Annie Hartnett, and Tessa Fontaine. I am more grateful than I can say for your insight. And I was fortunate to have the invaluable eyes and minds of Kate McQuade, Keija Parssinen, Eva Hagberg, Dina Nayeri, and Amanda Dennis on an early section at a key moment: thank you all. I am so lucky that each one of you is part of my writing community.

To Jessamine Chan, Julia Phillips, Rufi Thorpe, Kelly Link, Dan Chaon, Rachel Yoder, Megha Majumdar, and Paul Tremblay for the early gift of your beautiful words in support of this novel.

To MacDowell, for giving me a glorious two-week residency that spanned at least ten times as long in productivity-time, during which I completed a full revision of *The Garden,* and to the many inspiring writers and artists I met during that magical stretch. To the Randolph MFA program and to my brilliant colleagues and students there, who have enriched both my writing and my life.

To Bard College and the support of its Fiction Prize, which came at an important time in the writing of this book.

To the many Pittsburgh neighbors and friends who sustained me during the writing of this novel, which took place mostly during a pandemic and with small children at home, especially Irina Reyn, Anjali Sachdeva, Michelle Gil-Montero, Lauren Shapiro, Meg Goehrig, Mary and Jonathan Auxier, John Fried, Elizabeth and Rob Felter, Alex and Megan Poplawsky, Caroline Carlson, Adlai and Jill Yeomans, Becky Cole, Lauren Burdette, Renee Prymus, Lisa Collier, and Christine Van Kirk. And to farther-flung, beloved sustainers, in particular Lydia Lanzetta, Amy Wu Silverman, Anna Mirabile, Keri Bertino, Michelle Adelman, and Kate Schlesinger.

To my family, whose support and caretaking of my children has, enough times, made the difference between writing and not writing that the novel you hold in your hands would not exist without them. Special thanks to my in-laws, Christine Graham and Mike Rosen. And to my parents, Mark and Ann Beams, on this front and also for the love and belief that have made my whole life possible.

To Finnegan Calabro, whose love and faith in me have been my greatest gifts. For building with me a life that has room for every last thing I ever wanted.

And to Tess and Joanna Calabro, my life's great wonders. For raising every feeling's ceiling, and most of all, for being your miraculous selves.

Clare Beams is the author of the novel *The Illness Lesson*, which was a *New York Times* Editors' Choice and was long-listed for the Center for Fiction First Novel Prize, and the story collection *We Show What We Have Learned*, which won the Bard Fiction Prize and was a finalist for the PEN/Robert W. Bingham Prize, the New York Public Library's Young Lions Fiction Award, and the Shirley Jackson Award. She was a finalist for the 2023 Joyce Carol Oates Prize and has received fellowships from the National Endowment for the Arts, the Bread Loaf and Sewanee Writers' Conferences, MacDowell, and the Sustainable Arts Foundation. She lives with her husband and two daughters in Pittsburgh and teaches in the Randolph College MFA program.